Wounding of the Beast

By M. Ward Leon

Beacon Publishing Group

ISBN (Paperback): 9781961504127

Wounding of the Beast

Cover Design by Jerry Parsons
Exterior Design by Lori Pace
Edited by Gerard Hernandez

Beacon Publishing Group, New York, NY 10001
www.beaconpublishinggroup.com

Manufactured in the United States of America

For my Joanie and Meghan

Part One

The greatness of a nation can be judged
by the way it treats its animals.

Rodin

The Story of an Eco-Assassin

"Attack! Attack! Everybody down!" The poacher called Dinesh shouted just before a bullet ripped his left arm clean out of its socket.

Rodin and his partner Isala had been after this particularly heinous Sri Lankan group of elephant poachers, who use what is called a "*Hakka patas*" to kill their prey. It's gunpowder mixed with poison and vegetables that the poachers leave for the elephants to eat. It literally explodes inside the elephant's mouth, and almost always, the victims will die an agonizingly painful slow death.

They had followed the poachers for over a week, and every time they thought they were closing in on them, they would give them the slip.

Lunugamvehera National Park was to serve as a sanctuary for elephants and other wildlife. But, because the park is ninety-two square miles, tracking the small, agile group of poachers proved difficult. But Rodin and Isala finally came across them when they heard them using chainsaws to extricate the tusks of three elephants, one of which wasn't dead. Of course, that didn't stop the poachers. The dying pachyderm was calling out in pain when they caught up with the butchers.

There were six poachers; all were heavily armed with AK-47s, machetes, and side arms. Rodin took the first shot, hitting the poacher, who was using the chainsaw, striking him in the arm, and blowing the arm away along with the chainsaw. In a panic, the poachers started shooting blindly in every direction. Isala and Rodin were hidden within the heavy brush and were well camouflaged in their ghillie suits. They were both using M40A5 Sniper Rifles and were comfortable hitting their targets at 1000 yards.

Isala shot next, hitting her mark with deadly accuracy. Within minutes of the encounter, the five poachers lay dead next to the elephants they murdered. Dinesh was leaning against the dead body of the elephant that he was chainsawing and slowly bleeding to death.

As Rodin and Isala approached the dying man, Dinesh looked up and said, "Help me."

Rodin knelt beside the man and said, "Le Gang de la Clé de Singe. "

The man nodded acknowledgment that no help was coming; he closed his eyes and died.

Rodin and Isala lined up the poachers' bodies next to each other, placing the traditional yellow flags with the black skull and crossed monkey wrenches emblazoned on their bodies. This symbolizes the name of Le Gang de la Clé de Singe, the Monkey Wrench Gang.

They then placed a letter describing their crimes in each poacher's pockets.

Le Gang de la Clé de Singe has declared a proclamation of war against all Poachers, Big Game Hunters, all Big Game Safari Outfits, as well as anybody anywhere in the world that targets, kills, profits, and/or supports the killing of any animals that are endangered or any animals that are hunted for sport. Be forewarned: do so at your peril. You will be hunted down and pay with your lives. Be it man or woman, there will be no exceptions and no mercy; we will show no quarter. You have been warned.

These men were found guilty of the poaching of elephants and have been sentenced to death.

After the bodies had been laid out, Rodin made a call to the Lunugamvehera Park Rangers to alert them to the attack and its location. They then had to make their way to the tiny hamlet of Okanda on the southeastern coast to meet up with and be extricated by Captain Suranga Rodrigo, captain of the Marlu 2, a 49 Ft Longline fishing trawler.

Captain Rodrigo served as a crewmember with Sea Shepherd Conservation Society for over fifteen years. He was involved in some of the organization's noblest operations, Operations Galapagos, Jairo, and Milagro V.

Rodrigo worked his way up the ranks to serve as Captain on the 195-foot Island class patrol vessel, the Ansell Adams. The vessel engaged in dozens of successful Antarctic Whale Defense Campaigns against the Japanese whaling fleet.

He eventually was recruited to Le Gang de la Clé de Singe and has been in various campaigns worldwide. Today, he is tasked with retrieving Rodin and his partner from the fishing village of Okanda, Sri Lanka, and transporting them to the seaport of Port Muhammad Bin Qasim, Pakistan.

It took the two of them most of the day to reach the fishing village, as they were constantly altering their route to avoid tourists and Park Rangers. Once there, they radioed Captain Rodrigo to let him know they were in position.

His instructions were to sit tight until zero two-thirty when he would send a Zodiac raft powered by a 55 horsepower two-stroke engine equipped with a shrouded impeller for maximum stealth capabilities to pick them up.

At precisely zero two-thirty, the Zodiac landed on the beach, and in less than a minute, they and all traces of them ever being there were gone.

Once Rodin and Isala were safely on board, Captain Rodrigo and his crew began the forty-eight-hour trip to the southeast tip of Pakistan.

"Where are you two off to?" Rodrigo asked.

"We're headed up north to the Kalash Valley; gotta date with some rich American asshole who likes to hunt goats," Rodin said.

"Goats? An American comes all the way to Pakistan to hunt goats?"

"Yeah, These goats are extremely rare; they're mountain goats called Astor Markhor, commonly known as the screw horn goat; it's the national animal of Pakistan.

They are a threatened species, and it's estimated that there are only 2500 left in Pakistan, so naturally, this dickhead wants to come over and kill one. He spent a whopping one hundred and ten thousand dollars to shoot it. Apparently, the goat was so close to the "hunter" that he probably could have bashed its brains in with the butt of his rifle, but where's the fun in that. Besides, he might mess up his designer hunting outfit."

"This guy's got way too much disposable income," Rodrigo said.

"And they always claim that the money he paid for the privilege of slaughtering this magnificent creature will make its way to the impoverished people that live in the goats' habitat area. In reality, the majority of the fees usually make their way to some official's bank account.

So, that's what we got planned; how about you, Captain?" Rodin asked.

"Well, the boys and I have our eye on a group of turtle poachers and the illegal egg harvesting trade."

"That sounds like it could be a fun outing."

Le Gang de la Clé de Singe, the French eco-terrorist group, took its name from the American writer Edward Abbey's novel *The Monkey Wrench Gang*. The story is a fictional account of four environmental warriors who liberate parts of Utah and Arizona from evil road-builders, miners, and rednecks. Le Gang de la Clé de Singe was formed in Paris by two brothers whose father was the CEO of the French oil giant Elf, which was involved in the Great Oil Sniffer Hoax of 1979.

Jean-Paul and Philippe Renault were two spoiled rich kids who wanted to shake up the establishment and piss off their father all at the same time. They started out with some college friends organizing protest marches, which became more violent over time. As the oil scandal grew more prominent, so did the movement. Eventually, there were clashes with riot police, who would fire off tear gas and rubber bullets and then start making arrests as the protesters fought back. Some protesters began throwing rocks and bottles, and sometimes with Molotov Cocktails. Soon, the police escalated to live ammunition, killing dozens of protesters, some as young as fourteen. The Renault brothers never dreamed that what started as a way to piss off their father would evolve into a movement of international outrage. Over time, they extricated themselves from the group as Le Gang de la Clé de Singe became increasingly militant and violent. They unwittingly achieved their goals beyond their wildest dreams.

☠☠☠☠☠☠☠☠☠☠☠

Port Muhammad Bin Qasim was like most ports: dozens of container ships were unloaded, hundreds of semi-trucks were loaded, and thousands of people were running around.

The Marlu 2 was able to squeeze in between two container ships flying flags from Russia alongside Berthside Road. The Marlu 2 flew the flag of the UAE so as not to draw any attention. Although ships from the West were welcome, they usually received much more scrutiny.

Rodin and Isala were traveling on Argentinean passports under the names Mr. and Mrs. Jose Cabrera. Unlike several American tourists entering customs and immigration, they encountered no problems passing through.

Once they made their way outside the port entry, they hailed a cab to the Karachi Mövenpick Hotel in the heart of Karachi. When they arrived at the hotel, it was seven in the evening.

After checking into their suite and freshening up, they went down to Kabab-Ji, the hotel's Lebanese restaurant, where they met Mihaal Taimoor, their local contact and guide.

Mihaal was tall, with a dark complexion, a short cropped black beard with matching long black hair worn in a ponytail, a good looking man with a hint of Omar Sharif.

Taimoor has been at the forefront of Pakistani animal conservancy since he graduated from the National University of Sciences and Technology. He is on the board of both the World Society for the Protection of Animals and the Snow Leopard Conservancy. He has been a Le Gang de la Clé de Singe member for eleven years and participated in over a dozen offensives against poachers of tigers, snow leopards, and markhors. This will be the first time he meets and works with Rodin, the legend.

When they arrived at the Kalash Valley, he had arranged for a rental car, lodgings, and a mountain guide/tracker. Their guide, Ibrahim, comes from Arandu, a small town in the Chitral District on the banks of the Landai River, which borders Afghanistan. They're primarily farmers and sheepherders but also excellent trackers and hunters.

Mihaal greets them in the hostess area of the restaurant, "As-Salam-u-Alaikum."

"As-Salam-u-Alaikum." Rodin bows slightly and holds out his hand. "Mihaal, I am Rodin, and this is my partner, Isala. We are very pleased to meet you and grateful for your help."

"Please, the pleasure is all mine. I am honored to finally be able to work with you."

The hostess appeared and asked if they would like to be seated. They requested a secluded table away from several large parties celebrating birthdays and weddings.

The room was very elegant, with cherry wood ceiling beams, red-upholstered cherry wood Morgan chairs, and white tablecloths. The centerpiece fireplace gave the whole environment a warm golden tone.

Rodin and Isala deferred to Mikaal to order their meals. For a salad, they had the Fattoush, mixed greens, tomato, cucumber, radish, parsley, and green onion tossed with seasoned pita chips, pomegranate molasses, fresh lemon juice, and olive oil.

For their appetizer, Mihaal ordered one cold and one warm; for the cold, they had Moutabel, a hearty dip of roasted and chopped eggplant with sesame paste and lemon juice. For the warm Mezzeh, he ordered the Kibbdeh Dajaj, sautéed chicken livers drizzled with pomegranate sauce.

He insisted the main course be the Themar Al Bahr, the grilled half lobster, fillet of hamour and jumbo prawns served with lemon garlic mint sauce. Finally, an order of assorted traditional Arabic sweets with a cup of Turkish coffee to top off the meal.

The dinner conversation was light and spent learning about each other; they would have plenty of time on their journey north to discuss the mission.

☠ ☠ ☠ ☠ ☠ ☠ ☠ ☠ ☠ ☠ ☠

Mihaal stood in the hotel driveway next to a Toyota Land Cruiser Prado, waiting for Rodin and Isala.

"Good morning. I trust you had a restful night?" Mihaal asked.

"Yes, thank you, and you?" Isala inquired.

"Yes, very restful. Would you care to drive?"

Both Rodin and Isala declined. "Maybe later, after we get out of the city," Rodin said.

Mihaal worked his way through typical big city traffic jams and highway congestions until he jumped on the Faqir M. Dura Khan Road, where he then switched to the Mirza Adam Khan Road. He headed north for ten miles before merging onto the Lyrai Expressway that runs parallel with the Lyrai River and finally settling in on the M-9 to the N-5 that would take them to Khairpur, where they'd stop for the night.

Khairpur is one of the industrial centers in Pakistan, known for textiles, silk, and carpets, as well as its handicrafts and jewelry. Rodin and Isala found Khairpur to be very monochromatic, without many colors, mostly browns and earth tones, as were the people's dresses. Rodin always found that the more colorful the clothes the people wore, the more vibrant the culture.

They stayed the night at the Sajjad Hotel, a small, secluded hotel with its own restaurant just off the N-5, which intersects the N-55, which will take them to Arandu.

They traveled on the N-55, built as the national highway that threads the needle in the natural Greenbelt valley. This runs between two great arid mountainous areas on either side when they arrive in the city of Dera Ismail Khan, where they will start to ascend into the Toba Kakar mountain range to Arandu.

It's a twelve-hour drive from Dera Ismail Khan to Arandu, where they connect with their guide, Ibrahim. The journey crisscrosses Afghanistan and Pakistan several times before reaching Arandu, which sits on the border.

Having left Dera before sunrise, they finally arrived at the village of Arandu at five in the evening. Ibrahim's house was located north of town on a small goat farm at the edge of the Kunar River across from Afghanistan.

The three of them were graciously greeted by Ibrahim and his wife Fahmida and invited into their home. The house was a typical blocked mud house with a wooden door and cloudy panes of glass for windows. Rodin and Isala could tell their hosts were ashamed of their humble home.

Rodin smiled and gave a slight bow, "As-Salam-u-Alaikum. Isala and I thank you for inviting us into your home; we are most grateful."

"As-Salam-u-Alaikum. It is our honor to have you and your lovely wife stay with us," Ibrahim said.

Neither Rodin, Isala, nor Mihaal corrected him on the fact that Rodin and Isala were not married.

"Mihaal, my brother, it is good to see you again," Ibrahim said.

"And you, my friend."

Ibrahim gestured for everyone to enter their house, "Please, everyone, come in, come in."

Once inside, Ibrahim asked Fahmida to bring their guests some refreshments, green tea and badaam phirni.

"Please have a seat and make yourself at home." Ibrahim offered.

The dirt floor was covered with a wall-to-wall woven straw mat rug. There were beautiful woven covered floor cushions that ran the length of both sides of the living room and large woven covered pillows resting against the wall to rest your back against. In between the two rows of cushions facing each other were two wooden tables, approximately four feet long and twelve inches high, where Fahmida placed the green tea and badaam phirni.

Mihaal took a sip of his tea and then asked, "Ibrahim, were you successful in obtaining the equipment that we requested?"

Ibrahim smiled and said, "Yes, although it was tricky. But I did manage to get everything you asked for. Forgive me, but it was more than I thought it would be."

"Don't worry; you will be reimbursed and compensated for all your help and troubles," Rodin said.

"I have some unfortunate news. The man Howard Van Slake has already left the country after killing his Markhor, but there is another American who is here and has yet to collect his trophy, a Doctor Joseph Rowe."

"We have a temporary reprieve for Mister Van Slake and an appointment with the good doctor." Rodin quipped.

"Would you like to see the weapons I procured for you?" Ibrahim asked.

"Yes, please," Mihaal replied.

Because the Pakistani government has been allowing Americans to pay hundreds of thousands of dollars to kill their national animal, the Markhor, the people of this region, are used to seeing foreigners walking around with guns.

Ibrahim left the living room and returned with three Glock G17 pistols with shoulder holsters, two M40A5 Sniper Rifles, and three CamoSystems Jackal ghillie suits.

"Gentlemen, pardon my asking, but will the Misses accompany us on our mission?" Ibrahim asked.

"Yes, she will. Is there a problem, Ibrahim?" Rodin asked.

"No sir, not with me, but the villagers aren't accustomed to seeing a woman in such a powerful position."

"Well, not to worry. The three of us will be wearing balaclavas, and with our ghillie suits on, no one will be able to tell."

"Very good, sir, no offense, ma'am."

"None taken, Ibrahim. We appreciate your concern." Isala said.

Ibrahim bowed and said, "It is getting late, and we must leave early. Let me show you to your rooms."

* * *

When Ibrahim walked into the living room the following day, he found what looked to be three mountain bushes holding weapons sitting on his futons.

"I see that you all are ready. Can I offer you anything to eat or drink before we depart?"

"No, thank you. We like to stay hungry; it keeps us sharp," Rodin said.

"Very good, then let us begin."

It was still dark as they walked through the village, and the village dogs started to bark. This started to awaken the villagers. Lights began to appear in many of the windows and there was the occasional opening of the doors and occupants peering out as they walked by.

Ibrahim would wave and say, "Subah bhair."

The higher they walked, the colder it got; they would stay cold until the sun rose high into the sky. As they climbed, they saw a group of Markhors off in the distance. They heard a rifle shot and saw a large male Markhor fall and tumble down the side of the hill and land at a group of men's feet.

Rodin and the team were a good thousand yards away. Rodin told the others to proceed while he took a shot. He loaded a single RIP bullet into the chamber and waited until the American hunter had positioned his trophy just so for his photograph. The man was sitting on the back of the Markhor, holding up the set of twisted horns that measured four feet tall with both hands.

Rodin made his shot, hitting the base of Markhor's left horn, shattering it to pieces. In effect, he ruined not only the trophy for exhibition but the man's selfie for social media, which, after all, was one reason the man killed the poor creature was to show the world what a great hunter he is.

By the time Rodin met up with Mihaal, Isala, and Ibrahim, they had disarmed the hunter, Doctor Joseph Rowe, and his two guides.

"God Damnit, you just cost me 100,000 dollars! What the Hell is going on here, and who the Hell are you?" Doctor Rowe demanded.

Rodin said nothing. He reached inside his ghillie suit, pulled out a yellow canvas flag with a black skull with crossed monkey wrenches, and held it up.

Doctor Rowe turned white, "Listen, I paid the government a hunting fee. I'm not a poacher; the money I paid will go to help build a hospital."

"So, you kill this Markhor to help build a hospital?" Rodin asked.

"That's right, I just wanted to help."

"If you wanted to help, why didn't you just donate the money for the hospital? Why did you have to kill something?"

"Look, you have it all wrong. I'm not a poacher. This is legal; here, I have a license." Rowe was starting to panic as he waved the document in the air. He backed away from Rodin and towards the dead Markhor as he spoke. He wasn't paying attention to where he was backing up. The heel of his boot touched the Markhor's front hoof. That spooked the poor Doctor; he turned too quickly, tripped, and lost his balance. As a result, he fell forward onto the Markhors corkscrew horn and impaled himself through the abdomen. The more he struggled, the more he slid down onto the head of the beast where he lay dying.

Doctor Joseph Rowe did achieve the two things he set out to do: one was to kill a Markhor, and the second was to get a lot of views on social media. The picture Mihaal took of him skewered by the Markhor that he killed was posted. The doctor recorded a world record of views and over two million likes and still counting.

☠☠☠☠☠☠☠☠☠☠☠

"Good evening, I'm Nigel Williams, and this is the BBC World Headline News. Our top story this hour comes from the Kalash Valley, Pakistan, where the bodies of American Doctor Joseph Rowe of Austin, Texas, and his two Pakistani guides were found murdered.

"It seems that Doctor Rowe had been hunting the rare Markhor, a screw horn goat that lives in the northern Afghanistan and Pakistan. Hunters have been known to pay over eighty-two thousand Pounds to hunt.

"The men were found with yellow flags bearing the skull and crossed wrenches around each of their necks, along with a letter of declaration of war. Le Gang de la Clé de Singe, the French eco-terrorist group, has claimed responsibility for the killings. Worldwide commendation is pouring in as many..."

☠☠☠☠☠☠☠☠☠☠☠

The organization Worldwide Affiliates of Safari Partners, better known as *W.A.S.P.,* holds one of the largest conventions every year in Las Vegas. It's the ultimate hunters' market, featuring everything a hunter could dream of. It has the world's largest display of guns, hunting equipment, seminars, auctions for guided hunts, taxidermy, outdoor art, and firearms.

Among the exhibitors at the convention, tucked in amongst the mega exhibitions, is a small, plain 10' X 10' booth without the large color photo panels, scantily dressed women posing with whatever product they're hawking, or with flashing lights and music; just a table covered with a black table cloth. There sitting all alone taking orders is fifty-seven year old Enzo Morricone, the world's most sought after taxidermist from a little town outside of Florence, Italy.

Enzo can not only mount a single animal head or a stationary zebra, but he can also create everything from a stampeding elephant to a tree full of baboons to a pack of lions hunting a pair of water buffalo. Mr. Morricone is *the* master taxidermist to the hunting elite, so Rodin and Isala had no doubt who would be preparing Howard Van Slake's Markhor.

Enzo Morricone, the owner of Zampe e Zoccoli, has over forty years of experience as a full-time taxidermist's well-being. He is an avid hunter, trapper, and fisherman. His talents have earned him dozens of awards worldwide, but his most treasured award is Taxidermist of the Year, voted on by the members of W.A.S.P. for eight years running.

Morricone's workshop is atop Monte Ceceri at 18 Via Peramonda, in a stone building built in the 1500s. It overlooks several olive groves and the city of Florence, which is off in the distance.

He employs four craftsmen and two apprentices who are constantly busy with a six-month backorder. His prices are the highest of any of the world's leading taxidermists, ranging from $2500 for a life-size crocodile to $150,000 for a life-size elephant.

The Ristorante La Reggia Degli Etruschi is located on one of the most panoramic terraces in Fiesole. Once a monastery, it's now the most exclusive restaurant in the city, with a breathtaking view over Florence and its monuments. Where better to meet the world's greatest taxidermist?

Isala and Rodin sat across from each other on the terrace under a cream-colored umbrella. They were enjoying a glass of Chianti Classico Castello di Ama with zucchini rolls with ham and robiola cheese when Enzo walked by.

"Scusa, Signore Morricone, ti piacerebbe unirti a noi?" Rodin asked.

"American?"

"Yes, my wife and I are huge admirers of your work; please join us."

"Grazie, that's very kind of you, but only for a short time. I am to meet a client soon."

"Let me introduce ourselves. I'm Roger Williams, and this is my wife, Linda."

"It is a pleasure."

"Please sit down. Can we offer you something to drink, some wine?"

"Si grazie," Enzo bowed slightly and sat next to Isala.

"Cameriere!" Rodin called for the waiter.

The waiter came and asked, "Yes, sir?"

"A glass of?" Rodin looked at Enzo for the answer.

Enzo looked at the waiter and replied, "Ornellaia per favore."

Once the waiter left, Enzo turned to Isala and said, "Are you and your husband hunters?"

Isala smiled, "Yes, we are on our way to Botswana."

"Ah, Botswana, what are you looking for?"

"I want a giraffe, and Roger is looking for an elephant."

"Magnificent. I have always wanted to hunt the mighty elephant; it would be such a thrill. I envy you, signore e signora."

"Grazie, signore," Isala said.

Enzo's wine came, and Rodin raised his glass for a toast, "Cento di questi giorni."

"Molte grazie e a te," Enzo said as he touched glasses with his hosts.

"It was a pleasure meeting both of you, but unfortunately, like I said, I am to meet a customer here at this time. I would like to invite you both to see my studio."

"That would be wonderful," Rodin said.

"Shall we say tomorrow, Friday, at four in the afternoon?"

"Four o'clock would be great."

"Addio," Enzo said as he left the table and went inside.

☠☠☠☠☠☠☠☠☠☠☠

"Saluti, my friends, welcome to Zampe e Zoccoli. Inserisci per favore, enter please."

"Oh, thank you. What a fantastic studio," Isala exclaimed as she looked around at all the finished taxidermied animals surrounding her. There were lions, bears, giraffes, water buffalos, warthogs, tigers, and even elephants. The mounted heads, skins, rugs, pillows, and life-size specimens brought tears to Isla's eyes.

After the tour, the workday was over, and his employees were heading home for the weekend. Rodin and Isala stayed behind, talking to Enzo.

"Say Enzo, a friend of mine, Howard Van Slice, recently shot a Markhor in Pakistan and said he was having you, and only you work on it."

"Yes, of course, the Markhor. Mr. Van Slice decided he just wants a head mount for his office."

Rodin smiled, "Perfect."

☠☠☠☠☠☠☠☠☠☠☠

The black Lincoln Town Car would sit in front of 912 5th Avenue every weekday at seven am sharp, waiting patiently for its rider, who always got into the backseat at exactly seven twenty-eight am, rain or shine.

The rider had instructed the building's doorman explicitly that the black Lincoln Town Car must be able to park precisely at the end of the green awning that extended from the edge of the building to the street curb, or there would be Hell to pay. Howard Van Slake was not the kind of man who should be expected to deal with any impediments, barriers, or encumbrances within his perfect world.

Howard Van Slake grew up in one of the oldest and wealthiest families in Manhattan society. At the age of five, Howard started his perfect life at New York's exclusive preschool, Riverside Country School, where he spent his days speaking Spanish, French, and Latin. He would learn to play the violin, the culinary arts, and mathematics and, of course, have spa days at the reasonable tuition of forty thousand dollars a year.

Next, Howard attended the best prep school New York had to offer, the Triad School, where, in addition to classrooms, science and computer laboratories, art and photography studios, music rooms, and administrative offices. The school included a rooftop garden and polo practice field (known as the "sward"), a skeet shooting range, two dining rooms, one theater for dramas, one theater for musicals, three libraries, four swimming pools, six playgrounds, two weight rooms, and four gymnasiums.

It was then off to the New York University Stern School of Business, where he graduated at the top of his class. After a two-month trip through Europe as a graduation gift from Mater and Pater, he landed a prestigious position as a stockbroker at the Wall Street firm of Johnson, Williams, and Van Slake with a starting salary of a quarter of a million dollars.

Howard got the shooting bug while at Triad Prep School, where he was a top shot on the skeet shooting team. When he was twenty-six, he took his first African safari, killing two lions, a jaguar, and a wildebeest. Since then, he has gone on a hunting expedition every year, and every year, he has continued to hunt more and more of the rarest animals in the world.

Today, Howard is a multi-millionaire. He keeps all his big game trophies in the Hamptons' house. The most exotic of his trophies is in his condo in Manhattan, and he has a special place all picked out for his Markhor trophy: over the fireplace in his den/library that looks out over Central Park.

Rodin had Enzo make a few modifications to Van Slake's Markhor trophy; he had Enzo place a miniature AREBI HD wireless spy camera behind the right eye of the Markhor, as well as leaving the mouth slightly agape with a small remote control feeder roller placed inside the muzzle of the Markhor.

Enzo was able to send out the Markhor to Howard Van Slake late Saturday night with an arrival date of the following Tuesday via DHL Delivery.

On Monday, when the employees of Zampe e Zoccoli returned to work, they found the body of Enzo Morricone sitting at his workshop bench with his head stuffed into a Mountain Reedbuck's head. Around his neck was a yellow flag with a black skull and crossed monkey wrenches. Enzo had been shot once in the back of the head; inside his pants pocket, the Polizia found a note.

"Let it be known that Enzo Morricone, having been found guilty of profiting from the deaths of animals that had been killed for sport, is hereby sentenced to death by Le Gang de la Clé de Singe.

"Having declared a proclamation of war against all Poachers, Big Game Hunters, all Big Game Safari Outfits, as well as anybody anywhere in the world that targets, kills, profits, and/or supports the killing of any animals that are endangered or any animals that are hunted for sport. Be forewarned: do so at your peril. You will be hunted down and

pay with your lives. Be it man or woman, there will be no exceptions and no mercy; we will show no quarter."

The Polizia di Firenze did a thorough search for any form of evidence, DNA, ballistics, fibers, etc. They did find one clear fingerprint that didn't belong to any of the workers; it was that of Benito Mussolini on a plate skiving knife.

When Chief Investigator Giuseppe Esposito heard the news he said, "Ok, chi é il ragazzo saggio?"

☠ ☠ ☠ ☠ ☠ ☠ ☠ ☠ ☠ ☠ ☠

Interpol's Inspector Morris and Inspector Volker arrived at the Polizia di Stato at 27 Via Giovanni Sercambi in Florence the day after they found Enzo's body. They walked into the foyer and spoke to the officer sitting behind the sliding glass window.

"I'm Inspector Morris, and this is Inspector Volker; we're from Interpol."

"Non capisco."

Inspector Morris flashed his badge, "We're here to see Chief Investigator Giuseppe Esposito."

"Ah si, Capo Investigatore Giuseppe Esposito, un momento."

The officer pointed to the door, rang the buzzer, and said, "Terza porta alla tua sinistra."

As they entered the station, Volker said, "Now where?"

"He said it was the third door, but to the left or right? You go left, and I'll go right."

Morris looked into the third door down to the right and knew it must be to the left; the third door on the right was labeled "Bagno Femmimile."

He turned around quickly, caught up to Volker, and quipped, "The ladies' loo."

When they reached the third door, they knocked and walked in.

"Chief Investigator Esposito. I am Inspector Morris, and this is Inspector Volker. We're from Interpol and are here regarding the death of Enzo Morricone."

"Si, it was the work of those bastardi Le Gang de la Clé de Singe; they kill poor Signore Morricone, and for what? Nothing."

"Would it be possible to visit the crime scene, Chief Investigator?" Volker asked.

"Si, si, naturalmente."

Chief Investigator Esposito drove the two Interpol Inspectors on the Via Francesco Caraccilo, which runs along the Mugnone River. They then crossed the river onto Via Madonna della Querce, weaving their way through the easternmost part of Florence and finally working their way up the hillside towards Fiesole.

Zampe e Zoccoli still had crime scene tape on the door when they arrived. A police officer in uniform was standing guard at the front door. As they approached, the officer snapped to attention and opened the door.

Morris whispered to Volker, "I wish our officers would do that for us."

"Fat chance."

When the three men entered the studio, they found discarded blue latex gloves that the CSI units had used and just thrown on the ground. Fingerprint dust was everywhere, papers were strewn all around, drawers and cabinets were opened, and their contents were scattered about. The whole place was a mess.

"Cosa diavolo é successo!" Morris exclaimed.

"What did you say?" Volker asked.

"I said, what the Hell happened?"

"Mi dispiace per il casino. I'm a so sorry."

Inspector Morris and Volker did a quick look-see and then gestured that they had seen enough. Esposito drove them back to the station to review the photos and ME's report.

After reviewing all the reports and photographs for four hours, Morris asked, "Chief Investigator Esposito, we would like a copy of everything if it wouldn't be too much trouble."

"Certo, not a problem."

The two Interpol Inspectors got up, shook the Chief Investigator's hand, and gave him each of their cards.

"Grazie, Capo Investigatore per tutto il vosteo aiuto," Morris said.

"Sei il benvenuto e grazie."

As they were driving away in the cab, Volker asked him what was said as they were leaving.

"I thanked him for his help, and he thanked us. You know Volker, you really should try and learn another language."

"Vaffanculo."

"Oh, that you know. Well, fuck you, too."

When Howard Van Slake returned home at 4 pm after a hard day of wheeling, dealing, and scamming, Jose, the doorman, greeted him as he opened the front door and informed him that a rather large crate had been delivered from Italy. Inwardly, Howard was ecstatic; outwardly, he said, "Excellent, Jose, have the maintenance people bring it up." Howard learned early on from his father that one never allows others to see your emotions; it's a sign of weakness.

By six o'clock that evening, Howard's latest prized trophy, the Markhor, was hanging in its rightful place of honor, perfectly positioned over his fifty-thousand-dollar Aqueon fireplace in his den overlooking Central Park.

Howard felt this was indeed an occasion to celebrate, so he invited his girlfriend, Betty Bixler, his best friend, Skip Taylor, and his wife, Muffy, over for champagne and caviar.

As he waited for his guests to arrive, Howard stood admiring the magnificent job that Enzo had done for him once again; the little Italian man was a true genius. But now he was dead, how inconvenient. Now, Howard would have to find someone else to mount his kills. It was really annoying and tiresome that he would now have to be forced to use the number two taxidermist; it was simply pestiferous.

Three blocks away, sitting in Bemelmans Bar in the Carlyle Hotel on 76th and Madison Avenue, Rodin and Isala were tucked away in a corner booth having cocktails and watching Isala's iPad.

They had activated the mini spy camera placed inside Howard Van Sykle's prized trophy, Markhor's eye, and had a clear view of Howard's den. They watched him set out the champagne and caviar, beaming with pride over his latest souvenir; they heard him call his friends to invite them over to celebrate via the miniature microphone placed inside Markhor's ear.

Isala nuzzled up to Rodin and asked, "Now?"

"Now," Rodin said as he kissed her cheek.

Isala tapped the screen and waited with anticipation.

Howard had his back to the Markhor when he heard a slight, high-pitched whirling sound. He turned around, wondering what and where the noise had come from.

He quizzically took a couple of steps towards the mounted head, then saw something odd that he hadn't noticed before. A small piece of yellow cloth or canvas protruding from the Markhor's mouth. Due to his carelessness, that stupid, incompetent little Italian grease ball ruined his trophy; how dare he. It's a good thing he was already dead, he thought.

Howard reached up to pull on the fabric, and when he did, the yellow textile started to roll out from Markhor's mouth. Howard grabbed it and unwrapped it, revealing, much to his horror, it to be the yellow flag of Le Gang de la Clé de Singe. Just as he realized what he was holding, a small dart coated with kambo, the poison found on the skin of the black-legged dart frog, was ejected from the Markhor's nostril, striking Howard in the thigh, killing him almost instantly.

As he lay on the floor dying, looking up at the beast, it seemed to him from that angle that the beast was smiling down on him.

When he didn't answer the door, his girlfriend called 911; moments later, they found poor Howard's body on the floor with the yellow flag in his right hand and the small dart in his right leg. It would be several days later when they discovered that the Markhor's head had been rigged with a camera, microphone, and killer dart mechanism incorporated inside.

The NYPD went through Mr. Van Sykle's house with a fine-tooth comb, and all they came up with was a single fingerprint on the left antler of the Markhor belonging to Enron's CEO and Chairman, Ken Lay, who had been dead for over ten years.

Back in Bemelmans Bar, in celebration of the Markhor's revenge, Rodin had the bartender whip up two ounces of Bacardi Limón, 7 Up, and a splash of cranberry juice, or as they call it in Chicago's Billy Goat Tavern, two Horny Goats.

The next day, the New York Post's headline read, *"Pakistani Markhor Gets Wall Street's Goat."*

☠☠☠☠☠☠☠☠☠☠☠

"The Ivory Queen," Zang Jiao, has lived on Zanzibar, an island off the coast of Tanzania, for forty-four years. Originally from Shanghai, Zang Jiao went to Zanzibar in the 1980s as a translator for the Chinese government's attaché for the Ministry of Livestock and Fisheries.

In 1999, she decided to establish a private business on the island; in fact, she opened two. One was a Chinese seafood restaurant in Stone Town on the ground floor of a two-story building on Shangani Street next to the Park Hyatt Zanzibar.

On the second floor above the restaurant, she started a travel agency.

The Island Tea House restaurant was very successful, but her travel agency was where the real potential was. Especially when a man asked if she could help him bring in some illegally gotten ivory from Tanzania, he paid her five thousand U.S. Dollars for her troubles.

Over the years, she developed an underground railroad to transport tens of millions of dollars worth of illegal ivory into China. Because of her operation, poachers and ivory traffickers were threatening the very existence of elephants in Central and East Africa. Tanzania lost more than 60% of its elephants between 2009 and 2014.

Rodin and Isala caught the 11:50 am Emirates flight from JFK to Abied Amani Marume International Airport, Zanzibar. After passing through customs, they caught a taxi to the Park Hyatt Zanzibar, where Jacob Al-Qassmy, their local man, guide, and purveyor of anything they might require, would meet them at their hotel later that afternoon.

Jacob Al-Qassmy was sitting at a dining table on the hotel's veranda, which overlooks the Dhow harbor and the Indian Ocean, enjoying a Vodka Martini.

Jacob is a Zanzibar police officer who works out of the homicide unit. He resembles a young Sidney Poitier. He wears suits and ties as opposed to the military uniforms that regular police officers wear.

Rodin recognized Jacob from his dossier, "Jacob, good afternoon. I am Norman Leary, and this is my wife, Suanne."

"Mr. and Mrs. Leary, welcome to Zanzibar; it is my pleasure to meet you."

Rodin and Isala sat down at the table as the waiter approached; they ordered two Vodka Martinis and an order of Mix Bhajia, battered vegetables with coconut chutney, for the three of them.

As the waiter was out of earshot, Jacob asked, "I've been informed about the nature of your business. How may I assist you?"

"Would you be able to obtain two pistols?" Isala enquired.

"I can get my hands on two Sig Sauer 9mm's."

"I think that could work nicely," She said.

The waiter brought the drinks and appetizers, set them on the table, and asked, "Would you like to charge this to your room?"

Rodin said, "Yes, please, room 420."

Rodin held up his glass, "Death to tyrants."

Sources tell Le Gang de la Clé de Singe that Zang Jiao has been the critical link between poachers in East Africa and buyers in China for over twelve years. Le Gang de la Clé de Singe has been tracking her for more than a year.

The International Serious Crimes Investigation Unit, on charges of ivory smuggling, arrested Zang Jiao six weeks ago, but she escaped when her gang attacked the police van transporting her to the jail. The police gave chase but lost her in a high-speed pursuit. She is believed to be hiding somewhere on the island of Zanzibar, waiting to escape. The Zanzibar and Tanzania police, along with Interpol, are all looking for her, and unbeknownst to all parties, so is Le Gang de la Clé de Singe.

If the police or Interpol capture Zang Jiao, she will face 40 years in prison, but a more severe penalty awaits her if Rodin and Isala find her first.

Jacob told Rodin and Isala that the police and Interpol were concentrating on the airport and the seaports in and around Zanzibar City, the capital.

But he felt that she was much too clever; Jacob thought she would be hiding out on the island's east side, possibly in one of the shacks off the beaten path between the Zawadi Hotel and the Rock Restaurant off Michamvi Road. There are a dozen or so dwellings back off on the dirt roads, hidden from sight.

☠☠☠☠☠☠☠☠☠☠☠

Luck was on their side. That night, there was to be a new moon, so the countryside would be pitch black. The three of them, equipped with ATN PS15 Night Vision Goggles and wearing black SEAL sniper uniforms with balaclavas, were practically invisible. Rodin requested an additional weapon from Jacob that had to be specially sent via Le Gang de la Clé de Singe. It was his favorite M40A5 Sniper rifle with a special FLIR AN/PVS-27 MUNS high-resolution night vision sight that enhances the existing M8541 scope.

At midnight, they parked off Michamvi Road behind a grove of Soapberry trees and walked down the edge of the dirt road, knowing that no one could see them; Hell, they could barely see each other.

They peered into fourteen different structures before finding the right cottage; there was one sentry at the front door. There appeared to be four men, and Zang Jiao crammed into the tiny shack. They looked to be playing a spirited game of mahjong.

Rodin took aim at the man standing guard and fired one round, hitting the man in his right eye, forcing him backward, and collapsing onto the ground without much commotion. The occupants inside never noticed.

They quickly advanced, breached the premises, and had the drop on them before they knew what had happened. One of the men reached for his weapon, and instinctively, Isala fired her weapon, killing the man. That set off the others sitting at the table to react by going for their guns. In a matter of seconds, the four men were lying dead, and Zang Jiao, holding her hands high in the air, shouted, "Bùyào kāi qiāng! Bùyào kāi qiāng!"

Isala aimed her pistol at Zang Jiao while pulling out the yellow flag of Le Gang de la Clé de Singe to show her, and she said, "Hóuzi bānshǒu tuánhuǒ."

Zang Jiao, now pleading, "Do not kill me, Monkey Gang."

Isala softly said, "Bàoqiàn, sorry." and fired one shot to the heart.

Zang Jiao fell backward, collapsing onto a pile of elephant tusks that they had stacked in the corner. They were for the payment for passage or a bride if needed. Isala, Rodin, and Jacob quickly laid the six of them side by side in the hut, placed the traditional yellow signature flags around their necks, and put a communiqué of guilt in each of their pockets.

The Marlu 2, commanded by Captain Suranga Rodrigo, sent a zodiac to Dongwe Beach to pick up Rodin and Isala within minutes of their call. To signal their position, Rodin held out a blue strobe signal light alerting the rescue vessels to their whereabouts but not drawing too much attention to them.

They said their goodbyes and thanked Jacob for his invaluable assistance. Once out in international waters, Isala would call authorities and give the location of the "Ivory Queen" and her henchmen.

Interpol's Inspectors Morris and Volker would again be brought in to examine the crime scene and the evidence or, better yet, the lack of evidence.

As in all the murders and killings, Le Gang de la Clé de Singe left their trademark fingerprint; this time, it would be that of native-born, world-famous Queen frontman Freddie Mercury.

At the official gathering of local and national police forces to review the case of the "Ivory Queen," when Inspector

Morris heard that the fingerprint was that of Freddie Mercury, he said to the Tanzanian's Chief of Defense Forces, General L. T. Barongo, "Is this the real life? Is this just fantasy? Caught in a landslide, no escape from reality."

General Barongo asked, "Shakespeare?"

"No man, Queen!"

☠☠☠☠☠☠☠☠☠☠☠

"Captain Rodrigo, what a pleasure to see you again," Rodin said, seeing his old friend.

"And it is good to see you and your fine lady, Miss Isala," Rodrigo said as he kissed Isala's hand.

"Captain." Rodin asked, "How was your encounter with that group of turtle poachers you were off to confront?"

"Let's just say they got caught up in the moment as well as their fishing net traps. Unfortunately for them, like the turtles they trap, they also found breathing hard when snared in fishing nets underwater."

"Sounds a bit ironic," Isala said.

"Very ironic, but very satisfying."

"It's good to find satisfaction in one's work."

"True, you are very wise, Isala. Tell me, whatever happened to your rich American goat hunter?"

"In the end, the goat got its revenge."

"Excellent. And how was your meeting with the Ivory Queen?"

"We are the champions, my friends. And we'll keep on fighting 'til the end."

"Or you could say, another one bites the dust."

"Good one! Very apropos."

☠☠☠☠☠☠☠☠☠☠☠

Rutherford Remington Murdochski the third, a.k.a. Buzz Murdoch, was at one time the executive producer at one of the preeminent recording studios in the world of rock and roll, Bitchin Studios, located in Montego Bay, Jamaica.

Buzz was born into a very well-to-do family. The Philadelphia Murdochskis were among Philadelphia's nouveau riche, making scads of money in the post-war banking boom of the forties and fifties.

Buzz was born with a silver spoon in his mouth in 1945. He attended the finest prep schools and was accepted to Harvard but decided to attend the University of California, Berkeley.

He was a prominent activist against the Vietnam War and a member of the SDS and multiple other anti-establishment organizations; during that time, he met Todd Styles and became best friends. Buzz was arrested numerous times, primarily for petty infractions like disturbing the peace, with the odd misdemeanors for destroying public property and unlawful gathering.

At one point, his friend Todd was being sought after by the police and the FBI for allegedly setting fire to a government building. He had an Uncle in Canada but didn't have the funds to leave the country, so Buzz gave him several thousand dollars, not as a loan, but to avoid arrest. They had occasionally kept in sporadic touch over the years; Buzz is the only person Todd has ever confided in regarding his new identity, Rodin.

After the Vietnam War was over and his activist days ancient history, Buzz did a stint as a roadie for several big rock bands: The Rolling Stones, The Grateful Dead, and even Jimi Hendrix when he appeared at Woodstock. Then, in 1976, he took the advice of one Timothy Leary by "tuning in, turning on, and dropping out." He hitchhiked around the world. On his way back to the United States, he stopped off in Montego Bay, where he got a gig in a recording studio as a gofer. Over the years, he worked his way up the food chain to become the executive producer.

Buzz bought and lived on a 43½-foot Spindrift Sunrise sailboat he named The Sweet Mary Jane. In his spare time, he sails all around Jamaica, and over time, he got to know every inch of the coastline of Jamaica, from Montego Bay to Alligator Pond, from Port Royale to Salt Spring Junction, and all points in between. Not only had he become an accomplished sailor, but he was also an avid SCUBA diver.

Years ago, while diving in Luminous Lagoon, Buzz encountered Bumbley Bee, an *Epinephelus Lanceolatus*, also known as a Bumble Bee Grouper. The fish gets its name from the Bumble Bee-like markings they have as juveniles. As they mature, the yellow patches turn to more ornate patches, and their body eventually becomes green and grey or grayish brown.

Buzz met the 1600-pound monster when it got entangled in a large fishing net. The behemoth would have died had Buzz not come along and set it free.

The giant grouper and Buzz soon became fast friends. Buzz would bring Bumbley fish that he had speared and, on occasion, delicacies like pork roasts, baby back ribs, and a whole rack of lamb. He named his colossus friend Bumbley Bee, even though the bumblebee stripes were long gone.

Bumbley was the only one of his kind in the tropical Jamaican waters. His natural habitat would typically be anywhere in the Pacific Ocean, from Japan to the Hawaiian Islands. Still, as luck would have it, he was dumped off the coast of Jamaica through a series of mishaps and made his way to Luminous Lagoon, where he met Buzz.

At twenty years old, Bumbley weighed approximately 1600 pounds and was over twelve feet long. He now looked more like a camo-colored 1963 rusted-out Volkswagen Beetle meandering along the ocean floor.

Bumbley spent most of its day cruising around the coral reefs of Luminous Lagoon, looking for small sharks, skates, stingrays, and pretty much anything that looked edible. To look at him, you wouldn't think that something that big could be very agile, but you'd be wrong. One minute, there could be a four-foot Lemon Shark casually swimming nearby, and in less time than it took for you to read this sentence…no shark.

There came a time when Bumbley was under threat of being caught and sold to a wealthy Arab sheik for his private aquarium. The agents of the sheik had captured the gargantuan grouper and were preparing to set sail for other ports of call to gather other exotic marine life when Buzz contacted his old friend Rodin for help.

Rodin and Le Gang de la Clé de Singe sent several teams and a ship to retrieve Bumbley and all the other illegally captured sea life so they could return to their natural habitat.

Bumbley was eventually released off the tiny island of Hon Lon, less than a mile off the coast of South Vietnam in the Vinh Van Phong Sea. Six months later, a 43½-foot Spindrift Sunrise sailboat named The Sweet Mary Jane dropped anchor off Hon Lon island, where Buzz and his *Epinephelus Lanceolatus* friend were once again reunited.

☠☠☠☠☠☠☠☠☠☠☠

Bob Browning, a 66-year-old big game hunter from the tiny village of Phuduhudu, Botswana, claims to have shot and killed over four thousand eight hundred elephants, seven hundred Cape buffalos, seventy lions, ninety hippos, and sixty leopards during his fifty-plus years as a hunter.

Browning, who now resides in Cape Town, South Africa, brands himself as the most prolific elephant killer in the world, a title he relishes. Nigel Williams of the BBC World News recently interviewed him.

"Mr. Browning, the Campaign to Ban Trophy Hunting has labeled you one of the world's most prolific elephant killers; how do you respond to that claim?"

"I'd say they are sadly mistaken; I am not one of the most prolific; I am the most prolific elephant killer in the world, and proud of it."

"You claim that you didn't hunt these animals for sport, but for 'management culling'; however, animal rights advocates point out that elephant numbers are in steep decline and that 'management culling' is used as a cover for trophy hunting."

"That's just a bunch of bullshit by some left-wing socialist liberal activists. Elephants are not an endangered species. Wildlife parks in southern Africa have 10 to 20 times more elephants than they can sustain, destroying the environment."

"The people at the Campaign to Ban Trophy Hunting claim that elephant numbers in southern Africa have declined from 1.3 million to just over 400,000 since the 1980s."

"So?"

'So? One African elephant is killed every 15 minutes, which means that at this rate, the African elephant could become extinct within ten years."

"Those numbers are made up. The problem is that we've got a bunch of liberal experts from the West telling us what to do. I'm a trained university ecologist, so I must know something about the subject. I've published five books on the subject."

"Well, graduating from a college and writing books doesn't necessarily mean you're on the right side of an issue."

"Bugger off!"

"In your book Man, God's Hunter, you say that you believe God gave man dominion over everything on earth. Is that correct?"

"That's right, Genesis 1:26. And God said, Let us make man in our image, after our likeness: and let them have dominion over the fish of the sea, and over the fowl of the air, and over the cattle, and over all the earth, and over every creeping thing that creepeth upon the earth."

"So, you believe that you're doing God's work, slaughtering all these animals?"

"Praise the Lord. It gave me no pleasure to have killed thousands of elephants, but on the other side, I have no regrets. I was doing God's work!"

"Do you believe that it is God's plan for man, the hunter, to kill off everything on earth, the fish of the seas, the fowl of the air, the cattle, and everything that creepeth upon the earth?"

"I repeat, it gave me no pleasure killing those beasts. I was just doing God's work!"

"Right, you just happen to have made a fortune by killing or, as you say, culling hundreds and thousands of elephants, hippos, and lions, among other animals. Plus, you've written several books glorifying your hunting exploits, and you sit here tonight telling me you never received any pleasure in killing any of these creatures; I find that to be rather unbelievable."

"You believe what you damn well want, sir; I believe this interview is over. Good night, sir."

"And with that, Mr. Bob Browning walked out of the studio and our interview. This is Nigel Williams of the BBC World News. Good night."

Isala turned to Rodin and said, "Now, there's a fellow I would really like to meet."

"Well, then you shall, my dear. I'll see if I can arrange a trip to South Africa with the company to visit Mr. Browning."

"I do so look forward to that."

☠ ☠ ☠ ☠ ☠ ☠ ☠ ☠ ☠ ☠ ☠

"Wooch, Rodin here."

"It's been a while; how are you and Isala?"

"We're doing well, and yourself?"

"Doing good; what can I do for you?"

"Bob Browning, you know him?"

"The elephant killer? Yeah, I know him."

"Isala and I would like to, um, meet him. Think you might be able to arrange that?"

"Business or pleasure?"

"Oh, it will be both, I can assure you."

"Send me a postcard."

"Will do, Wooch, and thanks."

"Send my love to Isala."

"Next!" Shouted the custom agent at O•R•TAMBO International Airport, Johannesburg, South Africa.

Rodin and Isala approached the customs man and handed him their passports.

"Welcome to Johannesburg, Mr. and Mrs. Bridges. Are you traveling for business or pleasure?"

"Both," Rodin said.

Isala explained, "You see, my husband is here on some business, and then we're going to take some time for pleasure."

"I see. What kind of business are you in, Mr. Bridges?"

"Actually, it's Doctor Bridges. I am an astrophysicist, and I'm here to confer with some folks at the Wits Planetarium and the University of the Witwatersrand."

"Sounds fascinating."

"Have you ever been to the planetarium?"

"As a kid."

"Did you like it?"

"I did; they had a laser show with Pink Floyd music that was pretty awesome."

"Yeah, you can't go wrong with Pink Floyd, that's for sure."

"Well, enjoy your stay, Doctor, Mrs. Bridges."

"I'm sure we will," Isala replied.

Once out of customs, they made their way to the Woodford Car Hire kiosk, where they rented a silver Mercedes E class 4-door sedan. They headed towards the R24 highway to the Melrose section of town to their hotel, the Hyatt Regency, Johannesburg.

After checking in and taking a few hours to relax and acclimate to the new time zone, they went downstairs to meet Bob Browning in the hotel's oneNINEone restaurant.

Bob Browning looked to have been dressed by a Hollywood wardrobe designer, like the great white hunter in a 1950s jungle movie. He donned a khaki safari jacket, olive green cargo trousers, Courteney Selous Ostrich Safari Boots, and a double terai slouch hat.

"Mr. Browning? Good day. I'm Doctor Bridges, and this is my wife, Julia. We're so glad you could meet with us on such short notice."

"It is my pleasure, Doctor Bridges, Mrs. Bridges."

The hostess greeted and seated them at an outside table in the lush gardens overlooking the courtyard pool. They ordered drinks and dined on Crayfish, baby squid, and sea herbs sautéed in a mushroom broth.

"What can I do for you, Doctor?"

"Julia and I want to go on safari, and we can't think of anyone with whom we'd rather experience such an adventure than you."

"Well, I am flattered, but I have a rather full schedule at the moment."

Isala gently placed her hand on Browning's hand, and, looking very doe-eyed, she said, "We would really appreciate it if you could possibly work us into your busy schedule. It would mean so much to me, Bob."

He looked longingly at her and asked, "How long are you planning on being in South Africa?"

"However long it takes," Isala said.

Browning looked at Rodin, "What are you looking to hunt?"

"I'd like to go for the big five if possible, but definitely an elephant."

"I wouldn't have the proper amount of time to help you attain the Big 5, but I can help you get an elephant."

"That would be amazing," Isala said.

"I won't be available for at least ten days. Is that satisfactory?"

"That will be perfect; that will give us plenty of time to get kitted out," Rodin replied.

'I'll give you a list of items you'll need and where you can obtain them.'

"Perfect."

"It won't be cheap."

"Not a problem."

"All right, then. Well, I must be off; I'll be in touch."

"Thank you again, Mr. Browning. We look forward to going on safari with the best."

Browning started to get up, then sat back down. He looked at Rodin and Isala and asked, "You never asked how much I charge; how come?"

Rodin looked at Isala and said, "Mr. Browning, we believe that if you want the best, you must be willing to pay for the best."

"How refreshing."

"Besides, we believe this will be a memorable adventure that we all will remember for as long as we live," Isala added.

"Quite right, quite right," Browning quipped as he doffed his hat and walked away.

The following day, Rodin received an email from Bob Browning with a list of items he suggested they purchase for their upcoming elephant hunt.

One Holland & Holland Royal Double Rifle .303 British, .303 British cartridges ammunition, a handgun of choice, and appropriate clothing.

They would be required to pay half of the cost of the safari, USD 50,000 up front, the rest to be paid upon the completion of the successful safari. Where most elephant hunts were scheduled for at least ten days, Browning estimated they would be on safari for no more than five days, guaranteeing at least one kill.

They should be downstairs in front of their hotel, packed and ready to go in six days, at 6 a.m., rain or shine.

At precisely 6 a.m., a red 4-door Land Rover pulled up to the Hyatt. The driver got out of the vehicle and announced, "Doctor and Mrs. Bridges, I am Jabulani; I will be your driver today. Please have a seat; I will take care of your luggage."

Jabulani, a man well into his seventies, with a full head of gray hair, sporting a large matching gray handlebar mustache and weighing all of 98 pounds. He was dressed in a black chauffeur uniform, loaded all the luggage, and offered them a thermos of fresh coffee. As he drove away, he said, "It is a four-and-a-half-hour drive, so please let me know if you wish to stop at any time. In two hours, I will be stopping for petrol at Nelspruit, so just sit back and enjoy the ride. If there's anything that you want or I can do for you, please just let me know."

"Thank you, Jabulani. You're very kind, but for now, I think we're good," Rodin said.

The road to Nelspruit was an open four-lane highway. The ride was so smooth that both Rodin and Isala fell fast asleep until Jabulani pulled into the Sasol Emkhatsini petrol station some two hours later. While the attendant serviced the car, Rodin entered the convenience store and purchased a bag full of koeksisters, an Afrikaner confectionery made of fried dough infused with syrup or honey.

They drove for another hour until they reached the Malelane Gate of Kruger National Park. Bob Browning and his safari outfit, consisting of two 4X4 mobile safari Land Rover Defenders and one Toyota Hilux DC 4X4, were waiting for them.

Rodin and Isala said their goodbyes, expressed their appreciation to Jabulani, and watched as their gear was stowed into one of the Defenders. It was after noon when they started to travel into Kruger to begin their first safari, and, unbeknownst to Mr. Browning, his last.

☠☠☠☠☠☠☠☠☠☠☠

Kanacea Island is a volcanic island with seven peaks in Fiji's Lau archipelago. It is 8 square miles with a maximum elevation of 850 feet.

Rutherford Remington Murdochski, the third, a.k.a. Buzz Murdoch, privately owns Kanacea Island.

Buzz purchased the island as a favor to his lifelong friend Todd Styles, a.k.a. Rodin. This was primarily because Rodin's dog, Buster, a pure breed American Leopard Hound, was left on the island after an extended protracted combat mission, which Rodin and his Red Team had to evacuate in a hurry.

After the evacuation, Rodin lamented to Buzz that Buster had been left alone after the mission on the private island.

"Well, after my next mission, I will try and get Buster off Kanacea Island. He's a tough old pooch; he'll be able to survive until I can get back to him. It's a private island, so he shouldn't have to worry about some fool thinking he's vicious or mean. He is only aggressive if I give him the command. Otherwise, he's a sweetheart."

"Who owns the island?" Buzz asked.

"Actually, it's up for sale. I think they're asking twenty-six million for it."

"Does it have anything on it, or is it deserted?"

"Naw, it's over three thousand acres; it has a nice coconut and sugarcane plantation, a bunch of freshwater streams, a large lagoon with a boat opening, and it even has great cell phone signals across the island."

"And they're asking twenty-six million for it."

"Yeah."

"Twenty-six million; Hell, I'll buy it, man."

"Right."

"You think I'm joking? I'm loaded. I inherited over seven billion dollars when my folks passed away."

"Billion with a B?"

"Pretty cool, huh, man?"

"Buzz, you're wearing that exact same fucking Rolling Stones tee shirt that you wore in 1976. Except for this boat, you've got all the same shit."

"Yeah, well, it pays to buy quality, man. Besides, it's just stuff, and I don't need more stuff."

"You're telling me for real that you're worth seven billion dollars?"

"Yeah," Buzz picked up his satellite phone and dialed.

"Hello Reggie, Buzz here. Hey, what's happening, man? Yeah, I'm doing great. I'm just sailing around the Pacific with my special lady friend. Say, Reggie, I'm just wondering what I'm worth these days." Buzz holds the phone out so Rodin can hear.

"Buzz, your net worth is 8.4 billion dollars as of yesterday morning."

Rodin's jaw dropped. Buzz brought the phone back to his ear and said, "Listen, Reggie, I want you to do me a favor; I want you to purchase the island of Kanacea. Yeah, island. It's near Fiji; I hear it's going for twenty-six mill; see what you can do by offering them cash, and call me back and let me know how it goes, okay? Hey, I love ya, man. Thanks, brother."

"Un-fucking-believable."

"Hey man, we got to get you and Buster back together, right?"

"Buzz, you're crazy, man."

☠☠☠☠☠☠☠☠☠☠☠

Buzz and his special lady, Doctor Laura Runnel, a marine biologist, recently moved to Kanacea Island from Hon Lon Island in the Vinh Van Phong Sea off the coast of Vietnam. He had lived on his yacht, the Sweet Mary Jane, for over three years.

He recently lost his dear friend of over fifteen years, Bumbley Bee, a sixteen-foot *Epinephelus Lanceolatus*, more commonly known as a Bumble Bee Grouper.

Bumbley had recently been killed, saving Buzz's life from a Vietnamese gang lord. Since Bumbley's passing, Buzz and Doctor Runnel decided to leave Vietnam and sail to Kanacea Island to live.

Whenever Buzz and the Doc needed to interact with people or if they needed supplies, they would simply sail the SMJ to the main island of Fiji. It usually took them about fifteen hours to make the journey.

Buzz was one of a thousand anonymous benefactors of Le Gang de la Clé de Singe. Occasionally, Wooch or Rodin would visit him by seaplane for various reasons: financial help, advice, or social. This happened a couple of weeks before Rodin and Isala's encounter with Browning.

Rodin and Isala flew in for a long weekend visit on a Grumman G-11 Albatross. Buzz always looked forward to their visits. He had built them their own home on the other side of the island and told Rodin that whenever he and Isala were ready to retire from Le Gang de la Clé de Singe, they would have a permanent place to live on Kanacea.

One night, when the four of them and Buster were sitting on the beach around a bonfire, having a few beers and smoking a couple of doobies, they got to talking about

Woodstock- not the lame recreation, but the original 1969 three days of peace, love, and rock & roll.

How half a million people came together for one magical moment, even though there were some issues that people had to overcome: the rainy weather, overcrowding, and bad acid going around. Buzz kind of recalled when either Wavy Gravy or Chip Monck took the mic and made his famous quote, "The brown acid that is circulating around us is not specifically too good."

"I remember that because I had just taken a tab of brown acid, man," Buzz said, laughing.

"How was it?" The Doc asked.

"It was a real bummer, man. I was freaking out, but they had some real groovy people in the Hog Farm that helped me get thru it.

Did you know they were supposed to have Roy Rogers close the weekend out by singing "Happy Trails," but he declined? That would have been awesome, man.

"Someone told me that you were involved in burning down a hamburger stand," Rodin said.

"That's true, man. The official concession stand was called Food for Love. It turned out to have been run by a cult who were jacking up the prices way up, so me and a bunch of the Motherfuckers, the anarchist group, burned the joint down, man.

"Those were good times. You know I still have a couple of tabs of that brown acid, man. Anybody want to trip?"

They all responded with a resounding, no!

Later, when Buzz and Rodin were alone, Rodin asked, "Hey Buzz, I'll take a tab of that brown acid."

"Oh wow, man. I don't know, that's some real bad shit."

"Oh, it's not for me; it's for this guy I know."

"Must not be a good friend, man."

"Actually, he's a real dick."

"Oh, in that case, okay.

☠☠☠☠☠☠☠☠☠☠☠

Bob Browning's safari caravan drove north on the Malelane-Skukuza Road until they reached the Afsaal Picnic Site, a beautiful spot where they stopped to stretch their legs and grab a bite to eat before going out into the bush to find a campsite for the night.

They drove west along the Voortrekker Road for about thirty miles, then turned off the road to camp by Voortrekker Waterhole. It was the perfect spot to observe a whole host of wildlife coming to the watering hole at sunset: lions, zebras, hyenas, and a large herd of wildebeests.

They had requested an authentic safari, not a day camp safari, where they would venture out during the day and return to a hotel-style lodge at night. Rodin and Isala wanted to be in the wild, even at night, for several reasons. First and foremost, a lot of unexpected things can happen when you're out in the wild, plus you can trek further out into the bush away from authorities and prying eyes.

They had told Browning that they felt it was worth the extra cost to get what they felt was the authentic safari experience, and he was more than happy to take their money. In addition to Browning, they were accompanied by a driver, Rodney, and the driver/cook, Marc, who would be responsible for setting up and maintaining the campsite and driving the vehicles.

After dinner, they all sat around an open campfire drinking cognac while they had their weapons next to them just in case a pack of hyenas got a bit too brazen, but none did. Before everyone turned in for the night, Marc and Rodney went about the camp's perimeter, setting up electric fencing with alarms.

Their tent was quite luxurious. It had a queen-size bed, two cushioned chairs, luggage racks for their bags, vented screened windows with flaps, and Persian rugs on the floor.

There was an air of danger camping out in the bush, even with the electric fence. A hungry pride of lions or a rambunctious pack of hyenas could easily break through the fence if they wanted to, making love all the more exciting for Rodin and Isala.

☠ ☠ ☠ ☠ ☠ ☠ ☠ ☠ ☠ ☠ ☠

Breakfast consisted of Fruit, eggs, sausages, beans, toast, and coffee. After the camp broke down, they headed deep into the bush. Browning intended not to have Rodin kill his elephant on the first or second day since the first couple of days were more of a relaxed trek through the bush, allowing them to observe the wildlife.

During the day, they followed a pride of lions hunting and successfully bringing down an Impala. They saw several different herds of Steenboks, Kudus, zebras, and Gnus. Off in the distance, they saw some giraffes eating leaves from a baobab tree and a family of warthogs rutting around in a mud pit. Browning intentionally kept them from seeing any elephants, as he wanted to save that experience for the day of the kill.

☠ ☠ ☠ ☠ ☠ ☠ ☠ ☠ ☠ ☠ ☠

Rodin and Isala thoroughly enjoyed the day. It wasn’t too often that they got to enjoy such an adventure. Usually, it’s all business, from planning to getting into position, setting up the target, and completing the job.

Marc, the cook, did an outstanding job preparing dinner. He made an avocado vinaigrette salad, tomato bisque soup, and Matoke with beef fillet and salad.

There wasn't too much talk around the dinner table; conversations were saved for sitting around the open fire pit.

"So, Mrs. Bridges, how was your first day on safari? Was it everything you hoped it would be?" Asked Browning.

"It was truly magical," Isala said with a large smile.

"Doctor?"

Rodin replied, "Bob, it was an amazing day. Just being out here with all these magnificent creatures roaming free makes me feel what it must have been like thousands of years ago for primitive man, both beautiful and terrifying."

"Well, tomorrow, you'll really get a feeling of how man has evolved to be the dominant species when you become the master over the largest mammal on earth. There is nothing like the rush you get when you bring down a 6-ton elephant with one shot. By God, man, it's better than sex."

"God, I hope not," Isala said.

"Pardon me, Mrs. Bridges, no offense, sometimes I just get carried away.

"Even after killing almost 5,000 of the beasts, 700 Cape buffalos, 70 lions, 90 hippos, and 60, I still love the hunt and the actual killing. It's still such a thrill."

"Well, let's hope you will get your thrills tomorrow, Bob. I know I will," Rodin said.

The following day, as the sun was starting to rise, the camp was awakened by a chorus of singing by a mixture of Crested barbets, Southern carmine bee-eaters, Dark chanting goshawks, and Black-bellied bustards, all trying to outdo each other.

As usual, everyone was moving slowly. Marc was starting to prepare to make breakfast, but first things first, coffee.

Isala and Rodin stood beside the fire pit, trying to get the chill off their bones. When Isala saw Browning emerging from his tent, she went to the coffee pot and prepared three cups, two for her and Rodin and one for Browning.

"Here you go, Bob, a nice cup of Joe; this should warm you up nicely," Isala said as she presented him with a fresh cup of coffee.

"Cup of Joe?"

"Yeah, Joe, it's American slang for coffee."

"What does…"

"Don't ask, I have no idea."

Browning took a sip, smiled, and held the cup up to Isala and Rodin, "Good Joe."

They ate breakfast, broke camp, and started out to find a herd of elephants.

It took all morning to spot a small herd of cows and their calves; there weren't any bulls. Browning asked if Rodin would be okay killing a cow. Rodin was adamant; he wanted a bull.

"No, I just couldn't kill a cow when her calf was nearby. You can understand, can't you?" Rodin asked.

"Not really. They're just stupid elephants, but we'll find you a bull no matter," Browning replied callously.

As the day went on, Browning acted more and more erratic. He started driving in circles, shooting his revolver at nothing but claiming it had killed a rhinoceros and shouting at people who weren't there. He had fired all six bullets from his pistol at imaginary visions.

They came to a clearing with a large herd of elephants; he stopped the Land Rover, got out, and pointed his S&W Model 29 6 ½" Blue Revolver at Marc and Randy. He said they had been stalking him and planning to kill him. He aimed his Smith & Wesson at Marc and pulled the trigger, but the gun was empty.

As they were all trying to calm him down, he tore off his shirt and began running off into the bush towards the herd of elephants, scaring them and causing them to scatter into the bush.

He was ranting and screaming at the herd when a large bull turned, ran at him, and threatened to attack Browning to protect the cows and calves of the herd.

Browning stood his ground, pointing his revolver at the bull elephant, daring it to charge, which it did. It knocked the man down and proceeded to trample him to death. By the time Rodin got to him, he was no more than a wet stain on the ground.

Rodin suggested that they go back and get the vehicles to retrieve the body. Everyone was in a state of shock. At whatever possessed the most experienced hunter in all of Africa to go mad like he did.

"What was wrong with him? I've never seen him act in such a way. Have you?" Marc asked.

"It was extraordinary; do you know if there is any history in his family with mental illness?" Rodin queried.

"Not to my knowledge."

Isala asked, "Could he been bitten by something that made him act so strange and bizarre? A snake, an insect, anything like that?"

"Nothing I can think of, and I grew up here. Randy, have you ever heard of anything that could cause such behavior?" Marc said.

"No, nothing," Randy replied.

"Well, let's retrieve his body and take him to the authorities," Rodin said as they were almost at the cars. That's when they heard several roars from what sounded to be a pride of lions.

By the time they reached where they thought Bob Browning's body should have been, apparently, the lions had carried his body away. The grass was over waist deep, and none of them wanted to venture out of the vehicles to search, so they all stood atop their cars but could not see anything.

Then they decided that they should each drive around until one of them came across him, and then they would radio the others to their location. Meanwhile, Marc would contact the park rangers and alert them to the tragedy while we continued the search.

Once Marc and Randy's vehicles were out of sight, Rodin and Isala parked their Land Rover under the shade of a sizeable knob-thorn tree, reclined the back seat, and made passionate love like a couple of teenagers who had borrowed their father's car.

Eventually, they started the search for Africa's most proficient elephant killer, which they did find, at least what was left of him. All the lions and hyenas left that they could find were parts of his safari jacket, shreds of his trousers, his half-eaten skull, and what looked to be part of a leg bone.

They radioed Marc, Randy, and the park rangers their location on their GPS and waited, listening to RA Radio, South Africa's classic rock station. It must have been karma when Jefferson Airplane's White Rabbit came on the radio. It was one of the songs they played at Woodstock in 1969. Rodin and Isala looked at each other and smiled. Isala said, "Buzz was right. Don't eat the brown acid, man."

☠☠☠☠☠☠☠☠☠☠☠

The park rangers arrived first, followed by Marc and Randy. Rodin and Isala waited in the Land Rover until the rangers told them it was safe to get out of the vehicle.

Rodin led them to the remains, where two rangers collected what they could find. The rangers did a sweep of the area just to be sure there weren't other parts of Browning's lying about. One of the rangers discovered a half-eaten right hand that a flock of Lappet-faced vultures was picking at since most of the meat had been eaten away.

While the rangers were out scouting for Browning's remains, the lead ranger, Agnes Mbokota, began her investigation by asking the four of them questions.

"What are your names, and what is your position?"

"I'm Randy Mashale. I am one of the drivers and set up the camp."

"I am Marc van Wyk; I am also a driver and the cook."

"I am Doctor Bridges, and this is my wife, Mrs. Bridges; we are the customers; Mr. Browning was our guide."

"Doctor Bridges, what kind of doctor are you?

"I'm not a medical doctor; I hold a doctorate in astrophysics."

"I see. Well, Doctor, could you tell me what happened?"

"I don't actually know what happened. This was our third day on safari; everything was going along beautifully. Mr. Browning had been acting perfectly normal; even this morning, nothing seemed any different. We had the same breakfast as yesterday, broke down the camp, and then went looking for elephants.

"You see, that's one reason we hired Mr. Browning: I wanted to hunt elephants, and he is, I'm sorry, was the best in the world.

"Anyway, after several hours of searching for elephants this morning, he began to act abnormal. He started driving erratically, weaving, swerving, and driving in circles. He was hallucinating, seeing things that weren't there, screaming that insects were attacking him, and hearing voices.

"Then, when we came upon a herd of elephants, he stopped the car, jumped out, and ran towards them, scaring them off- all except this large bull, who turned back and attacked him, knocking him down and trampling him.

"After the elephant ran off, we came to see if there was anything that we could do, but it is evident that he was dead. We decided to get the vehicles and return to retrieve him; I don't think any of us would ever believe that lions would have dragged him off before we could return for him. But they did, and because the grass was so tall, it took us all this time to find him.

"It just so happened that we found him, and that's when we called you."

"Thank you, Doctor. Does anybody else have anything to add?" Ranger Mbokota asked.

Everyone looked at each other, but neither Marc nor Randy added anything; they just shook their heads.

Isala said sobbing, "It was so awful, what a terrible way to die, being trampled to death, then eaten by lions. I can't get that image out of my mind."

Rodin put his arm around her to comfort her.

"Doctor Bridges, why didn't you try to shoot the elephant that attacked Mr. Browning?"

"To be quite honest with you, Ranger Mbokota, I am a bit of a novice in the use of firearms, which is another reason I wanted to go on safari with Bob Browning. And to be quite honest, I have to admit that I was pretty terrified by his bizarre behavior."

"How about you, Mr. van Wyk? You have a lot of experience being on safari; why didn't you take action?"

"I am not a hunter; I am the cook. Both Randy and I indeed carry weapons, but only pistols. They would have no great effect in stopping a charging bull elephant. And as Doctor Bridges said, Mr. Browning's actions were strange; we all looked in disbelief."

"I understand. How about you, Mr. Mashale?"

"I, too, am not an experienced hunter. Sir, the big guns are kept by Mr. Browning. It all happened so quickly; there wasn't any time to think."

"It's quite ironic," Isala said.

"And what is that?" Ranger Mbokota asked.

"That an elephant kills the most prolific elephant hunter in the world, don't you think?"

This was one of the few times that Rodin hadn't proclaimed that Le Gang de la Clé de Singe was responsible for a death it had exacted. He and Isala felt that the elephant deserved all the credit it was due.

The press ate it up, telling how the big game hunter got his just desserts. The New York Post's headline was: Hunter - 5000 Elephant – Won!

☠☠☠☠☠☠☠☠☠☠☠

"Mayday! Mayday! This is Darwin Airways flight two-five-zero to Nadi. Do you read?"

"We read you two-five-zero, over. What is your distress?"

"We have a fire... we're...the engines are flaming out – we're going down!"

"Can you see the runway, two-five-zero, over?"

"Crash landing. We're going in. We're going down."

"Two-five-zero, do you read?

"All hydraulics failed. Mother fuc..."

"Two-five-zero, do you read? Two-five-zero, do you read?"

The commercial cargo airline, Darwin Airways flight two-five-zero, was scheduled to fly from Cairns, Australia, to Mexico City, Mexico. They carried engine parts, wool, coal briquettes, and precious live cargo of indigenous animals from Australia to be shipped to the Chapultepec Zoo, one of Mexico's best-known zoos.

Among the animals on board were fourteen adult kangaroos, twenty-two adult koalas, forty echidnas, twelve tiger quolls, two dozen cane toads, and one wombat.

The pilot tried to land the Boeing 737 nose up so it would hit the water and skid along the ocean surface on its belly. It might have just worked if it hadn't been for the tsunami detection buoy that their right-wing hit. The wing sheared off and created a structural crack in the fuselage, breaking the aircraft in two.

Both the pilot and co-pilot survived, but unfortunately, most of the animals weren't so lucky; the only critter to make it out alive was the wombat. The crate he was transported in was built watertight and just happened to be sealed with marine silicone and polyurethane, making Wally's crate float.

The Fijian Coast Guard rescued the Darwin Airways flight crew two-five-zero and the black box recording device within hours the next day. But Wally the Wombat wasn't saved for another seventy-two hours. It wasn't until when he happened to wash up on the beach of the small island of Kanacea.

The day before the wombat's arrival, Buzz and the Doc had noticed a lot of debris from the crash floating up on their beach. They collected everything and placed it in a neat pile to turn over to the Fijian authorities. Buzz had radioed the Fijian Coast Guard and informed them that he had gathered debris from the Darwin flight and would keep it safe until they came to retrieve the items.

Early the following day, Buzz and Buster were strolling along the beach. Buster noticed the large crate that had washed ashore. Buzz approached the crate with caution. After seeing the movie *Alien,* Buzz developed a phobia of sticking his face over anything that was unknown to be inside of it.

He slowly peered into the crate and saw what looked to be a hairy, pudgy pig with the face of a gopher.

It took him a few minutes to recognize that the little fur ball was a wombat. He dragged the crate away from the beach and onto more solid ground, where he slowly tilted the crate so that the wire grate was on the side, allowing the little bugger to see land and not just sky.

Buzz ran back to the house, gathered an armful of vegetables, carrots, cabbage, celery, and potatoes, and returned to where the crate was. Buster was sniffing at the crate but not being aggressive, so not so frighten, whatever that thing was.

Buzz placed the veggies into the crate and walked away so the wombat wouldn't feel threatened. After several hours, Buzz slowly approached the little marsupial and opened the crate door; Buzz figured if the little guy wanted to hang around him, he would, and if he tried to run away, that was cool, too. Buzz knew there would be plenty for it to eat, and there weren't any predators on the island that it would have to worry about.

Buzz opens the cage door, and he and Buster walk back to the house to tell Doc they have a new uninvited guest on the island. Buzz decides to name it Wally, Wally Wombat.

☠ ☠ ☠ ☠ ☠ ☠ ☠ ☠ ☠ ☠ ☠

Ranger Mbokota had ordered one of her rangers to drive Isala and Rodin back to the Malelane Gate of Kruger National Park in Browning's Discovery Range Rover. When they arrived, a red four-door Land Rover was waiting for them, and the man who had driven them from the Johannesburg Hyatt, Jabulani, stood next to the vehicle.

"Greetings, Doctor and Mrs. Bridges. I am so sorry that we have to meet again like this under such terrible circumstances," Jabulani said.

"Thank you, Jabulani. We never could have envisioned that such a thing could have happened to such a man as Mr. Browning," Rodin said.

Isala, seemingly on the verge of tears, said, "It was ghastly, simply ghastly."

"I can't even imagine," Jabulani uttered almost as if to himself. He loaded the luggage into the Land Rover, and Rodin and Isala helped, seeing how distraught the old gentleman was.

The ride back to the Johannesburg Hyatt was somber; Rodin asked if Jabulani would like to turn on the radio and listen to some music. Jabulani glanced into the rearview mirror and said, "Yes, that would be pleasant. Anything special you'd like to hear, Doctor?"

"We'll leave that up to you."

The old man punched the on button, and classical music began to play Mozart's Piano Concerto No. 23 in A major.

"Very nice," Isala commented, "Very soothing, thank you."

The three of them sat silently for close to an hour, and then, at the top of the hour, the news came on. Nothing was mentioned about Browning, as it was too early in the news cycle for that. There was, however, an interesting story about Mr. George Galooney, a hunter from the city of Vanderbijlpark not far from Johannesburg, who was captured on video shooting and killing a male lion that was asleep.

Apparently, Mr. Galooney decided that he saw an opportunity he couldn't resist, so instead of going after a lion with a sporting chance, he thought he'd take the easy shot. As despicable as that was, it took him five shots to kill and put the poor beast out of its misery. Then, to really get people enraged, he's caught on video laughing.

Rodin and Isala looked at each other and mouthed the name "Galooney silently."

☠ ☠ ☠ ☠ ☠ ☠ ☠ ☠ ☠ ☠ ☠

Vanderbijlpark is an industrial city on the Vaal River. It is home to Vanderbijlpark Steel and Cape Gate, Ltd., a significant player in the copper wire industry.

Hendrik Galooney has held the position of Maintenance and Tooling Supervisor with Vanderbijlpark Steel for over fifteen years. He has been married to Hilda for twenty-one years and has three sons, Hendrik Junior, Harold, and Harvey.

The Galooneys lived in a two-story, five-bedroom home with a pool in a gated community on Bernard Price Street, a charming upper-middle-class neighborhood in Vanderbijlpark SW5.

Hendrik is an avid hunter, so much so that he turned a large portion of his three-car garage into a man cave slash trophy room to display and exhibit all of his kills.

Because of all the adverse reactions to his latest kill, the sleeping lion, he and his family have been receiving hate mail and even some death threats. Hendrik decided it would be best if Hilda and the boys went and spent some time with her mother in Durban. It was the perfect time of year since Durban is on the Indian Ocean, and the boys could spend some time sailing and surfing.

Hendrik would be fine at work and join them in a couple of weeks. Hopefully, by then, this whole mishegoss will have blown over.

☠☠☠☠☠☠☠☠☠☠☠

At ten minutes to nine at night, Hendrik pulled into the Makedonia Trading Store on Beefwood Road to stock up with a couple of six-packs of Castle Lager and his favorite snacks: two king-size bags of Spookies, the chili tomato-flavored maize puffs. This would offer a great combination to watch the Springboks, South Africa's national rugby team, take on the world champions, New Zealand's All Blacks.

On the way to his car after making his purchases, he noticed an attractive woman dressed in a rather revealing black dress having difficulty opening the trunk of her Mercedes. Being the gentleman and the sleazebag that he is, he thought that since the wife and kids were away, maybe he might get lucky.

"Excuse me, dear, having problems?" He asked.

"This stupid trunk is always giving me trouble. The fob isn't working, so you have to use the key, and it just won't open," Isala answered.

"Here, maybe all it needs is a bit of muscle," Hendrik said as he put down his bags of groceries beside the silver C 63S Sedan.

She handed him the key, took a few steps backward, and said, “You’re so kind. I don’t know how I can ever repay you.”

Hendrik was already thinking of several ways she could repay him as he tried to jimmy the trunk lock open.

By now, the supermarket had shut down for the night. The parking lot was empty except for her Mercedes and his red Audi A4. Hendrik was half paying attention to trying to open this bitch’s trunk and contemplating how he was going to parlay his good deed into him getting laid when all of a sudden, the trunk lock clicked, and the trunk popped open.

“There you go,” He said, holding the key up triumphantly. He then offered her the key to her car and asked, “Pardon me for asking, but do you like rugby? The reason I ask is that I’m going home to watch the big match and was wondering if you might be interested in joining me?”

Isala batted her eyes and gave him a sexy smile. “Maybe. You know, I couldn’t help but notice, what is that hanging around your neck?”

He unconsciously brought his hand up to the chain around his neck and felt the large lion canine tooth extracted from the sleeping lion that he shot and killed and he took so much heat for.

“Oh, this. This is a tooth from the lion I recently killed.”

“Ooh, you’re a hunter?” She asked seductively.

“Oh yeah, big game, lions, elephants, rhinos- I hunt them all, “ he said, bragging.

“Is it dangerous, hunting lions?”

“It’s literally kill or be killed. I have several trophies of my kills in my studio. Would you like to see them?”

“Yes, very much,” She purred.

You know, it’s funny how one moment, life seems to be handing you the keys to paradise, and the next moment, your ass is being shoved into the trunk of a Mercedes C 63S Sedan.

☠☠☠☠☠☠☠☠☠☠☠

Rodin opened the electric gate and drove Hendrik's Audi A4 straight into the garage, followed closely behind by Isala in the Mercedes C 63S Sedan.

When Isala opened the trunk of her car, Hendrik was surprised that he was back inside his garage and not in some industrial part of town in a sleazy warehouse to be tortured.

"Okay, lover boy, get out," Isala said, pointing a Glock 9mm at him.

"Just what the fuck do you think you're doing, bitch?" Hendrik shouted as he was climbing out of the trunk of the car.

"Shut up and go sit over there in that chair," Isala calmly said, waving the gun in the direction of the chair where Rodin was waiting.

Hendrik slowly walked over to the straight-back chair, keeping a careful eye on the man standing behind the chair holding some rope. As soon as he sat down, the man began to tie him tightly to the chair. Once the man was finished, he leaned down close to Hendrik's ear and whispered, "What's the code to the house alarm, Hendrik? If you lie to me, I'll not only kill you, but I'll kill Hilda, Hendrik junior, Harold, and little Harvey too, do you understand?"

Of course, Rodin would never harm the wife or children, but Hendrik didn't know that. At this point, Hendrik was definitely scared but also pissed off, so he defiantly said, "Go fuck yourself."

At which point Rodin placed a piece of duct tape across the man's mouth; he ripped the lion's tooth from around Hendrik's necklace and jabbed the canine tooth deep into Hendrik's thigh, causing Hendrik to scream and feel blinding white searing pain to the point of almost blacking out.

"Don't fuck around with us, Hendrik. Now, what is the house alarm code?"

Hendrik looked down at his left thigh, and seeing the tooth sticking out made him want to vomit. He nodded to Rodin that he wanted to say something. Rodin peeled the tape back off his mouth, allowing Hendrik to gasp for air. Eventually, that wave of nausea passed. Rodin let the man have a few minutes to compose himself before once again asking for the code.

"626478#"

"Okay, that wasn't so hard, now was it?"

"Fuck you! What is it that you want?"

Rodin reached into his jacket and pulled out one of Le Gang de la Clé de Singe's yellow ensigns, "Have you ever seen one of these, Hendrik?"

"You're here to kill me."

"I'm afraid so, but in your case, we're going to give you a better chance to live than you gave that lion you shot that was sleeping."

"What does that mean?"

"If you can stay awake and not fall asleep for the next seventy-two hours, you're a free man; we will cut you loose and leave you in peace. But, if you fall asleep, I'll kill you just like you did to that lion."

Rodin looked at his watch and said, "It's 1:10 a.m. go."

"If I can stay awake for seventy-two hours, I go free?"

"That's right, but if you doze off even for an instant, you're dead."

"Why did you want the house code if you're not going to rob me?"

"Because that's where the bathrooms are, dummy."

☠☠☠☠☠☠☠☠☠☠☠

Isala doctored the tooth wound, cleaning it with hydrogen peroxide, applying a local topical antibiotic, and finally bandaging it.

"You wouldn't kill me, would you?" Hendrik asked.

"Fall asleep and find out."

"But I'm a human being!" He stated.

"And that means what? That being human gives us the right to kill anything we want, just because we're humans?"

"It was just a lion!"

"Yeah, it was just a lion, just an elephant, just a rhino, just a zebra until there are no more; then is it just too bad?

"Did you know that in 1930, there were five million elephants in Africa? Today, there are less than three hundred and fifty thousand elephants; a hundred elephants are killed every day; that's one killed every 15 minutes. At this rate, they will become extinct in ten years. There are only twenty thousand lions in the wild in Africa today, so in less than 20 years, there will be no more lions."

"Look, what if I promise never to hunt again? Will you go?"

"Sorry, love. That's not how the game is played."

"So, this is just a game for you?"

"I'm talking about the game of life, Hendrik. There are always consequences for one's actions, some of which are fair and others are not."

"Fucking Bitch!"

"You got that right."

☠☠☠☠☠☠☠☠☠☠☠

At six in the morning, Hendrik was fairly alert; anger and fear would do that. Isala was sitting on the couch in Hendrik's "man cave" opposite her bound hostage, reading a copy of Huisgenoot, the weekly Afrikaans-language general-interest family magazine.

"Praat jy Afrikaans?" Hendrik asked.

"Ja, I speak a little, enough to get by."

"Hoeveel tale praat jy?"

"I speak seven languages. Jou?"

"Drie."

"Three, Afrikaans, English and?"

"Swahili."

"Nice, I've always wanted to learn to speak Swahili. Say something."

"Kwenda kutomba mwenyewe," Hendrik said smiling.

"What does it mean?"

"Have a nice day."

"Really?"

Hendrik grinned and nodded, "Yes."

"Cause I would have sworn you just told me to go fuck myself."

"I thought you said that you couldn't speak Swahili."

"Speak it, no. Understand it, yes."

Rodin walked into the man cave carrying a .375 H&H Magnum rifle. "Sorry, am I interrupting anything?"

Isala, looking at Hendrik, said, "No, we were just discussing the advantages of being multilingual."

Rodin held the rifle up to Hendrik and asked, "Is this the rifle you use to hunt lions?"

Hendrik said nothing, just stared straight ahead.

Rodin placed the rifle next to the couch, sat beside Isala, leaned over, kissed her on the cheek, and said, "Why don't you go lay down? I'll sit here with Hendrik so we can get better acquainted."

Isala rose from the couch, touched Rodin on the cheek, and turned to Hendrik, "It was nice talking to you; I hope to see you again, Mr. Galooney," She said as she left the room.

Once Isala left the room, Rodin picked up the .375 rifle, pulled the bolt back, slid a cartridge into the chamber, and closed the bolt, sealing the cartridge into the chamber and arming the weapon.

"So, how are we feeling, Hendrik?" Rodin asked.

"You and that bitch of yours are a real piece of work, you know that?"

Rodin didn't respond; he stood up, walked to the lighting panel, and lowered the lights. Then he clicked on the turntable, thumbed through Hendrik's vinyl albums, selected one and placed it on the turntable, lowered the tonearm, and in seconds, the mellow voice of Mister Nat King Cole was singing 'Unforgettable.'

"You have a very nice record collection, Galooney."

"Fuck off!"

"That's it, stay mad, Hendrik. You only have sixty-two hours to go."

☠☠☠☠☠☠☠☠☠☠☠

A week after the plane crash, several members from the Fijian Coast Guard came to Kanacea Island to collect the debris that Buzz and Doc had washed up on their beach.

Captain Biuvakaloloma of the Coast Guard Cutter RFNS Kacau told them that the aircraft was carrying nearly a hundred different animals from Australia destined for a large zoo in Mexico City. Thank God the pilot and co-pilot survived.

Buzz thought about telling Biuvakaloloma about Wally but decided not to since it seemed that Wally Wombat had become very attached to Buzz and the Doc. He would accompany them in the evenings when they took walks along the beach, lie beside them when they sat out on the veranda to watch the sunsets and join them at dinner since Wally is nocturnal. Buzz would always fix Wally a big bowl of roots and grass that he would eat next to his newest best buddy, Buster.

Two weeks after Wally landed on Kanacea Island, Wally spent a lot of time hidden. He wouldn't hang around them or play with Buster like he used to. Buzz thought that maybe he was sick. Even though Doc wasn't a vet, she took a look and examined Wally as best she could.

"Well, Doc, what do you think? Is Wally going to be okay?"

"I hate to tell you this, Buzz, but Wally is pregnant."

"Say what?"

"That's right, Buzz, you're going to be a father."

"Far out, a baby Buzz. Buzz junior."

"Think we need to rename Wally?"

"Naw, she's cool, besides what's in a name, right?"

"Okay, now you do know wombats are marsupials, so we won't be seeing baby Buzz for six to seven months."

"Yeah, he's got that whole pouch thing going. I mean she."

"You know Buzz, I think you connecting with Wally is a good thing; I mean, after losing your good friend Bumbley."

"Yeah, I miss the Bee, but I got you, Doc, and you mean more to me than anything, even Bumbley."

"I know, Babe, but losing the Bee left a small hole in your heart that Wally and Baby Buzz just might fill."

"Hey Doc, what 'ya say, feel like taking a little nap?"

"You mean sex."

"Doc, you know me like a book."

"Yeah, a cheap novel."

☠☠☠☠☠☠☠☠☠☠☠

After fifty-six hours of fighting to stay awake, Hendrik was slowly losing the battle. The low lighting, the soft music, and keeping the temperature warm didn't help, and they weren't supposed to.

"You fuckers aren't playing fair, bastards!" Hendrik protested.

"Yeah, fair, like killing a sleeping lion," Rodin answered.

Hendrik was only four hours away from surviving when he semiconsciously heard the rifle being cocked, and in a strange way, he welcomed the end.

The South African police and Interpol were alerted that they would find the body of Mr. Hendrik Galooney in his man cave with a single bullet wound to the heart.

Le Gang de la Clé de Singe claimed responsibility for Mr. Galooney's death. The usual telltale signs were there: the yellow banner with a black skull and crossed monkey wrenches and, of course, the manifesto proclaiming the justification for his execution, the killing of a sleeping lion.

The Internet was abuzz with people on both sides of the issue. Some protested his death as plain and simple murder, and some celebrated his death as a form of justice.

The authorities found no evidence, no DNA. Still, they did find the preverbal, out-of-place single celebrity fingerprint, this time that of the world's most famous lion tamer, Gunther Gebel-Williams.

"Ladies and Gentlemen, I'd like to thank all of you for either attending in person or for those who couldn't be with us; thank you for phoning in for our semi-annual meeting of Le Gang de la Clé de Singe.

"We have a lot to cover today. Today's agenda and discussion topics are in front of you, and I believe we will be able to cover them all today.

"I'd like to take a minute or two to welcome and introduce our two newest members to join the executive committee. First, I'd like to introduce you to Mr. Buzz Murdock, a world globetrotter and one of Le Gang de la Clé de Singes' most valued philanthropists. Where are you these days, Buzz?"

"Hello, Wooch, hello everybody. Sorry I couldn't be there with all of you today. I am currently living with my special lady on Kanacea, a small island off of Fiji Island, man. I invite all of you to come visit; we've got plenty of room for everyone."

"Thanks, Buzz, for that generous offer.

"And now, I'd like to introduce our newest member, Senor Jose Perez of Mexico City. It's good to have you with us, Mr. Perez," Wooch said.

"Thank you, Senor Wooch; I am honored to be part of such a noble cause."

"We're sorry you two cannot join us in person, but we hope you can attend the next meeting.

"Let's just take a few minutes to go around the table and have everyone introduce themselves."

"Good day, I am Marcel Marchand, CEO of ARMCO Petroleum."

"Hello, I am Etienne Archambeau, Vice President with Environ."

"Schönen Tag, my name is Helmut Schneider, I am President of the Berlin chapter of IFAW."

"Hello, I am President of the International Society for Animal Welfare, Mark Peeters."

Over seventy-five members came from all four corners of the world, representing not only environmental and animal rights organizations but also major world corporations. Due to Le Gang de la Clé de Singe's aggressive nature and methods, they wished to remain anonymous.

Commander Brown took control of the meeting after everyone's brief intros, "Thank you all; now I have a couple of items to start with. Number one, one of our senior leaders has alerted me as to his retirement. I am speaking of my personal friend Rodin, who, as most of you know, has been a champion of our cause for many decades.

"He has led many successful campaigns against trophy hunters and safari outfits and has waged war against the worst groups of poachers worldwide.

"Recently, he has taken on the role of, for lack of a better word, assassin against the most egregious individuals. Many of his exploits have made world headlines, as they were intended to do.

"He said that he has two or three missions that he wants to complete before leaving. Ladies and gentlemen, he will be sorely missed, not only as a warrior but also as a trusted friend.

"Now, onto business…"

☠☠☠☠☠☠☠☠☠☠☠

PT Bakrie Salim Tbk is one of Indonesia's largest integrated agribusiness companies. It is also the world's leading palm oil grower, producer, and manufacturer.

PT Bakrie Salim Tbk is responsible for Southeast Asia's high primary forest rate worldwide, which has led to millions of acres being cut down for palm oil monocropping. This is particularly bad in Borneo, where 32% of the mammals are under threat. Most species in these rainforests cannot tolerate oil palms because they are toxic, and the food plants they require are destroyed to plant the palms.

These fragile animals, such as orangutans, Sumatran rhinos, Sumatran tigers, and Asian elephants, are already on the world's endangered species list.

The CEO and President of PT Bakrie Salim Tbk, Ibrahim Rajagukguk, has been quoted as saying that if the death of a couple of monkeys is the price one has to pay for corporate profits, then so be it.

Ibrahim Rajagukguk is a ruthless corporate commander with two passions: his political ambition to run for Prime Minister of Indonesia and his desire to win the America's Cup.

Rajagukguk is a fanatical sailor who wants nothing more than to bring the ultimate sailing prize to Indonesia. He has spent over three hundred million US Dollars developing a radical 75-foot flying monohull, rumored to be the fastest design ever. Team Salim Indonesia is his private entrée into the Cup, and he is known to be in secret trials in the Java Sea off the tiny island of Karimunjawa.

☠ ☠ ☠ ☠ ☠ ☠ ☠ ☠ ☠ ☠ ☠

The Grumman G-11 Albatross landed after buzzing Kanacea Island twice. Rodin's signature pattern was letting his oldest and best friend, Buzz, and his special lady, Doctor Runnel, know they had guests.

It was always a time for celebration whenever Rodin and Isala came to visit. Buzz and Laura didn't get many visitors, which was OK with them. They had their books, tons of projects, and things to do around the island, plus there were Buster and Wally. Of course, Buzz's seafaring ferrets, Groucho and Bosco, kept them company. And now there was a new addition ever since Wally gave birth to Buzz Junior, a chubby baby Wombat who thinks Wally and Buzz are his parents.

"So, what brings you guys to our little piece of paradise?" Buzz asked.

"I've announced to Le Gang de la Clé de Singe that I am retiring."

"That's wonderful," Laura said excitedly.

"Well, I still have a couple of loose ends that I need to tie up, and that's one reason why I'm here. I was hoping that you and Buzz might be up for an adventure."

"No fucking way, man!" Buzz said.

"Oh, I'm sorry, Buzz."

"Hey man, I'm just fucking with you. Count us in. Right, babe?"

"Of course, we're always up for a little excitement," Laura said.

"What do you need?" Buzz asked.

"Are you up for a sea adventure aboard the Sweet Mary Jane?"

"Sure, she's been jonesing for a bit of sea duty. Just need a couple days to get the old girl ship shape. Where we off to?"

"A small island in the Java Sea, Karimunjawa."

"And what's happening there?"

"I have to have a little talk with a corporate mucky muck."

"Oh, you having a little talk is never a good thing."

"Not for Mr. Rajagukguk, it isn't."

"Rajagukguk, isn't he the rich dude trying to take the America's Cup next year?" Laura asked.

"The one and only," Isala answered.

"What's this Rajagukguk guy done?"

"He has been amassing a fortune by destroying thousands of acres of rainforest for the production of palm oil, which is home to dozens of endangered species like Orangutans."

"Greedy corporate bastards!" Buzz said.

Just then, Buster, Wally, and Buzz Junior came running around the corner of the house. Buster was so glad to see Rodin that he jumped into his arms and almost knocked him down. The two Wombats waddled next to Buzz's leg and started making grunting sounds of wanting some attention.

Isala asked, "And who are these two fine-looking fellows?"

"The big one is Wally, and the little guy is Buzz Junior. They were castaways who washed up on our beach looking for a home, so we took them in," Buzz said.

Laura said, "Why don't we all go up to the house and get comfortable? Can we offer you anything to eat or drink?"

Wally and little Buzz made a couple of loud grunts and started running towards the house.

"I wasn't talking to you two!" Laura shouted.

☠☠☠☠☠☠☠☠☠☠☠

Depending on the weather, the journey would take a little over two weeks. Buzz and the Doc hadn't taken the SMJ out for an extended cruise in some time, so Buzz needed to ensure everything was in perfect working order. The last thing you need is for something to go wrong when you are out in the middle of nowhere.

It took Buzz and Rodin three days to complete a systems and equipment check and give the old girl the once over. Everything was in tip-top shape; they spent the last day loading stores and gear for the voyage. The four of them would set sail the following day bright and early, leaving Buster, Wally, and Buzz Junior in charge of the island.

"Red sky in the morning sailor take warning, Red sky at night sailor's delight. Looks like we're in for some smooth sailing in the morning." Buzz announced as he went below deck to the galley where the Doc and Isala were preparing dinner.

They had decided to spend the night on board so they could set sail at first light. Buzz had set a course to sail between the islands of Fiji and Vanaua Levu, then veer south towards New Caledonia and into the Coral Sea. They would swing north and thread the needle between Papua New Guinea and Australia's Thursday Island. Then they'd head out into the Arafura Sea before making their way into the Banda Sea and finally the Java Sea to Karimunjawa Island, which sits off the coast of Central Java. If all went well, they wouldn't need to stop at any ports, although it would be two weeks out on the open sea.

It happened late in the evening, about two days before the Sweet Mary Jane was crossing into the Arafura Sea from the Coral Sea; a mega container ship lost three containers of Nike sneakers overboard off the coast of Papua during a squall. By the time the SMJ sailed into the waters, the weather had cleared up, but unfortunately, the containers had taken on water and were floating just below the water's surface. That's when the SMJ hit one of the containers and punched a hole in the bow just below the waterline.

Water was pouring in, and it was all hands on deck, as they say. They finally got a temporary patch put on but needed to get into a port to repair it properly. It turned out to be a tossup of either going to Daru Island off the coast of Papua New

Guinea or going south to Thursday Island, Australia. The overall consensus was to head to Thursday Island.

Buzz had radioed into Waiben Light Marine Services on the island's northeast corner.

"SMJ to Waiben come in, over. Dusty, this is Buzz. Do you copy, man?"

"Waiben to the SMJ, copy. Buzz, you old sea dog, how the Hell are you, mate?"

"Doing good, got a bit dinged up from a UFO."

"A flying saucer!"

"No, Dusty, not that kind of UFO- an unidentified floating object, you Aussie knucklehead. I was hoping to come in and do some repair work. Can you help me out?"

"You bet, mate; when can you be here?"

"Tomorrow sometime, man."

"Look forward to seeing ya, mate."

"Far out, man. Later."

Dusty Harrington has been a longtime friend since the Jamaica days at Bitchin Studios. Dusty was a backup musician who played with Olivia Newton-John on tour and her records for a long time. After sessions, Dusty and Buzz would head out on the SMJ and get stoned.

Dusty was one of the few people Buzz entrusted with the secret of his friendship with Bumbley Bee. Over the years, after the recording sessions and tours were over, Dusty went back to Australia. He and Buzz stayed in touch with occasional letters, emails, and phone calls. So, it was somewhat serendipitous that the run-in with the container happened, and when it did, it would bring these old friends together.

"Buzz, looking good, mate. How long's it been?"

"Oh wow, man, at least ten years."

"How's Bumbley?"

"Bumbley passed away, man."

"Sorry to hear that, mate."

"Yeah, it was a real bummer, man."

"So, what are you doing, just sailing around the world with some friends, you old geezer?"

"Kinda, hey, let me introduce you to everyone. This is my special lady friend, Doctor Laura, my oldest best buddy, Todd, and his lady, Isala, and everyone; this is an old compadre of mine from my days at Bitchin Studios, Dusty Harrington, a world-class musician, and even more important a world-class guy and friend."

"It's really nice to meet you all, but Buzz flattery isn't going to get you a lower price, mate."

"Damn! I forgot what a cheap bastard you are."

"Where you living these days, mate?"

"On a small island near Fiji, Kanacea."

"Kanacea, hey, I heard of that place. There was a reality TV show shot there, some kind of combat shoot 'em up show. Were you involved in that, mate?"

"Me? No way, man. I'm a lover, not a fighter; you know that."

So, what brings you guys out this way?"

"We're heading to Karimunjawa."

"Where the fuck is Karimunjawa?"

"The Java Sea."

"More importantly, what the fuck is in Karimunjawa, mate?"

"Beats me, man. Todd and Isala have to see some guy about something. So, the Doc and I thought we'd go for a bit of adventure and fun, man."

"So, how's it going?"

"Well, we've been having fun until three days ago when we hit that container and punched a hole in my SMJ, so now we're having an adventure."

"Okay, let's go take a look at that sweet, Sweet Mary Jane."

The SMJ was docked at a small marina not far from Dusty's Waiben Light Marine Services shop. Dusty examined the extent of the damage and the temporary patch job they did.

"Well, Buzz, I got some good news, and I got some bad news, mate."

"Lay it on me, man."

"Well, the good news is I can have you ship shape and on your way in three days."

"And the bad news?"

"The bad news is, I can have you on your way in three days."

"Man, you're messing with my head."

"Listen, mate. Are you sure you can't stick around for a couple more days? I'm sure we can find lots of ways to get into a lot of trouble, mate."

"I wish we could, man, but we have to be in Karimunjawa in a week. But maybe we'll see you on the flip side."

"No worries, mate."

☠☠☠☠☠☠☠☠☠☠☠

They docked the Sweet Mary Jane four days after setting sail from Thursday Island at the Karimunjawa wharf next to Alun-Alun Karimunjawa Park. When they docked, a farmers market and cultural celebration were going on. There were food stalls, musicians and native dancers, and even carnival-type rides. Hundreds of people from all over the island attended the monthly event.

The four of them made their way through the throngs of people to Jl. Dr. Sutomo Street and hailed a bunga taxi to take them to their hotel. It was a five-minute ride to the Breve Azurine Lagoon Resort on the opposite side of the island. Rodin picked this resort because it's the hotel Rajagukguk and his crew are staying at.

The Breve Azurine Lagoon Resort has bungalows. Each bungalow has an ocean view, its own terrace, and a sitting room. The interiors are teak from floor to ceiling and decorated in a Polynesian motif.

There was a restaurant and lounge bar on the grounds, where Rajagukguk and his sailing crew would hang out after practicing racing all day. Their 75-foot flying monohull, Gelombang Pembunuh, which translates into English as Killer Wave, was kept some twenty miles off the coast of Karimunjawa and docked to a secret floating man-made island called KMP. Kelimutu.

Every day, Rajagukguk and his crew would take a speed boat to KMP Kelimutu and do a series of practice runs in complete secrecy. They would have several private armed security patrol boats keeping onlookers away, as Buzz and Rodin found out the hard way.

They casually followed Rajagukguk and crew out to KMP. Kelimutu, and as they were approaching the "yacht club," they encountered one of Rajagukguk's patrol boats.

"Berhenti! Ini adalah area terbatas!" Shouted a man holding an AK-47.

"What?" Buzz shouted back.

"You go!"

"Why?"

"You not allowed!"

"Can't we watch?"

"No! You have no watch. You Go!" he yelled, holding up his rifle to emphasize the point.

"Okay, okay. We're going, but you're going to get a really bad review on Yelp!"

"You go, now!"

And with that, the Sweet Mary Jane turned around and headed back to Karimunjawa's wharf. Their mission really didn't need to see the Gelombang Pembunuh race accomplished.

Just before reaching Karimunjawa, Buzz and Rodin sailed around the small island of Palau Parang to see if there might be a hidden inlet that might serve their purpose; there was one on the north end of the island.

☠☠☠☠☠☠☠☠☠☠☠

Isala and the Doc were waiting for them when they docked at the wharf.

"How did it go?" Isala asked.

"They had a bunch of goons out there with machine guns keeping everyone away, man," Buzz said.

"Yeah, they're serious about their privacy," Rodin added.

"Did you find what you needed?" Asked the Doc.

"Yeah, a small inlet over on Palau Parang, it'll be perfect," Rodin said.

"Hey man, I'm hungry. Is anybody else hungry? I got a bad case of the munchies."

"What are you in the mood for, Buzz?" The Doc asked.

"I could go for a tuna and anchovy pizza and an icy cold beer, man," Buzz said.

"Yuck, that sounds disgusting, Buzz." Uttered the Doc.

"I saw a pizza place not too far from here," Isala said.

The four of them started walking up Jl. Dr. Sutomo Street for about a block and a half until they saw eat&meet Pizza. It had a Polynesian thatched roof, an outdoor patio, an iron horse sculpture, and large family-style tables with benches.

The place had a fair-sized crowd for late afternoon, primarily young people snacking and having beers. They found a table on the patio and placed their order when the waitress swung by.

"Hi guys, I'm Mandy. Can I get you something to drink?" the twenty-something blond waitress asked.

Buzz took charge, “Miss Mandy, my friends and I will each have an icy cold Prost Beer in a frosty mug if you please.”

“Yes, sir. I’ll get those going for you while you look at the menu. Be right back.”

Moments later, Miss Mandy returned with four frosty mugs filled to the brim with ice-cold beer. As she placed the beers in front of each of them, she asked, “Have you all decided on something to eat?”

“I’ll have the tuna and anchovy pizza,” Buzz said.

“Mmm, that’s my favorite,” Mandy replied.

“See, it’s Mandy’s favorite; I told ya it was good,” Buzz chortled.

Rodin and Isala each ordered the House Burger, which consisted of a pure beef patty, tomato, onion, pickles, cucumber, special tomato sauce, double cheese, egg, avocado, and wasabi sauce, with a side of fries.

The Doc ordered the black rice salad with mango and peanuts.

A few minutes later, Mandy returned with bad news, “The chef says he’s sorry, but we’re out of tuna.”

“Oh man, what a bummer. Okay, Mandy, then I’ll have the seafood pizza.”

“Very good, sorry about that.”

“Hey, shit happens.”

“So, Buzz, what’s in the seafood pizza?” the Doc asked.

“Squid, shrimp, pineapple, mozzarella cheese, and anchovies,” Buzz announced proudly.

“Barf city, am I right?” The Doc said she was looking for support from Rodin and Isala, which she got.

“Got to admit, Buzz, it’s a bit out there,” Rodin said.

“I have to concur.” Isala agreed.

“Peasants, I’m dealing with peasants.” Buzz groaned.

Ibrahim Rajagukguk came from the ultra-rich classes of Jakarta's high society. His father was a world-famous heart surgeon, and his mother was a noted Indonesian Supreme Court Judge. Ibrahim was sent at an early age to the finest prep schools in Switzerland, and he then went on to attend Oxford and Cambridge Universities, graduating at the bottom of his class. Ibrahim was a rich, spoiled brat who only did enough to get by, and when he couldn't, he had his parents pay to get it done.

After he graduated, Ibrahim knocked around Europe looking for employment, but to no avail. In every position he landed, his employer soon discovered that Ibrahim was a sniveling, conniving, self-serving weasel, and he would be asked to leave.

It wasn't until he went back to Jakarta and his father bought him a vice-president's position at PT Bakrie Salim Tbk, did Ibrahim find his true calling. The forest management company's board of directors was struggling with global moral and ecological issues such as deforestation, habitat degradation, climate change, animal cruelty, and indigenous rights abuses in the countries where they serve.

Ibrahim found he didn't face those moral dilemmas because, as it turned out, Ibrahim had no moral conscience; in fact, Ibrahim had no conscience at all. He made deals with oil palm plantations to clear their lands by committing to a plan of total deforestation. He got around the laws by paying huge bribes to government officials, thereby doubling and even tripling the company's profits; Ibrahim, like the piece of crap that he was, rose to the very top of the shit pile and soon became the CEO and President.

He wasn't going to let a few orange hairy monkeys or a couple of peanut-loving Dumbo's slow down his corporate rise to stardom. Ibrahim Rajagukguk's name was synonymous with palm oil; he was Mr. Palm Oil. Anyone who wanted palm oil had to deal with Ibrahim Rajagukguk, the Palm Oil King.

Ibrahim Rajagukguk, at the tender age of thirty-four, found himself on the covers of Fortune, Business Week, Forbes Magazines, and unbeknownst to him, on the top ten most wanted hit list of Le Gang de la Clé de Singe.

Being one of Indonesia's hottest and wealthiest bachelors, Ibrahim Rajagukguk was quite taken by himself. It was good that he was wealthy and successful because he weighed over three hundred pounds and had a face that could stop a clock. But young, beautiful women always surrounded him, mostly escorts.

He would treat women like sex objects, grab them by the hair and push their heads into his crotch, lift up their skirts, and try to pull down their panties or pull down their tops to expose their breasts. He had a goon following him with his pockets stuffed with cash, giving the women that Ibrahim Rajagukguk assaulted money to settle their complaints and go away. He just claimed that it has boys being boys, and when he talked to them disparagingly, it was just locker room talk.

Eventually, he grew tired of the hassles of "dating" women and preferred the company of prostitutes. They were easier to degrade, debase, and bully. They would never complain because he paid them ten times what they would have usually gotten, so they kept their mouths shut.

There had been rumors going around that he had raped several underage girls and that they had brought suits against him. He would always have his lawyers counter-sue to scare the young women, and when that didn't work, he used his mother's influence as a Supreme Court Judge to intimidate witnesses and defendants. Eventually, the charges against him were dismissed through a payoff and a nondisclosure agreement.

☠☠☠☠☠☠☠☠☠☠☠

Isala sat outside Masjud Agung Karimunjawa Mosque wearing the traditional al Amira Hijab Scarf, which covered her head and included a partial veil that exposed only her eyes.

Ibrahim Rajagukguk wasn't a religious man at all. Still, one of the conditions that both his parents made whenever they would bail him out of trouble or give him financial aid was to go to the mosque every Friday without fail.

This particular Friday, when he went to the mosque for prayers, he noticed a beautiful woman sitting alone, reading what looked like a copy of the Koran. He planned to stop and talk to her when he finished his parental obligation. It didn't matter to him if she might be married or not, for when you're rich and powerful, it affords you certain advantages.

"Excuse me, Miss. I couldn't help but notice you sitting alone. Are you waiting for someone, perhaps your husband?"

"No, I am waiting for no one. I often come here to read in peace."

"I hope that I am not disturbing you, Miss."

"No, it is all right."

Ibrahim was intrigued as he couldn't place her accent; it was not American, British, or maybe German, and her eyes were very exotic. He made up his mind right there: he wanted her, and he usually got what he wanted, one way or another.

"May I join you?"

She looked at him and seemed to smile. Then she held up her wrist, looked at her watch, and said, "I'm sorry, but I must go. I am to meet some friends, and I am running late."

"May I offer you a ride, Miss."

"You are very kind, but I am only going down the street to the Kirmun Coffee Bar. Maybe some other time."

"May I call you sometime, Miss?"

"I think it might be best if we meet here since we are still strangers."

"Of course, that is very wise. I hope I did not offend you, Miss?"

"Not at all."

"If it wouldn't be too forward, may I ask your name?"

"Adiratna. And you, sir?"

"I am Ibrahim Rajagukguk." He said proudly.

The look on her face told him she had no idea who he was, which both disappointed and exhilarated him. At least she wouldn't have heard of all the disgusting things that he had been accused of and all the disgusting things that he actually had done.

"When do you think you might be back?" He asked.

"I'll try to come tomorrow, but more likely the day after."

"I look forward to seeing you soon, Miss Adiratna."

"Good day, Mr. Rajagukguk."

He watched her walk away, but she never turned around to look at him, which was a bit disappointing. He thought to himself, let the games begin.

Isala entered the Kirmun Coffee Bar and sat at the table where Rodin, Buzz, and Doctor Laura were drinking coffee.

"So?" Rodin asked.

Isala smiled and said, "Let the games begin."

Rodin had requested additional local talent to help carry out the mission. The crew would meet Rodin and Buzz the following morning at the wharf where the SMJ was docked.

Buzz and Rodin were sitting on a couple of captain's chairs on the aft of the yacht, drinking their second cup of coffee, when two young men looking to be in their mid-twenties came strolling up to them.

"Good morning. We're looking for Mr. Jordan."

"That's me," Rodin said with a smile.

"Hi, I'm Andy Sharif, and this is Dewi Huntapea. We understand that you could use some help."

"Come aboard, fellas. This is Mr. Richards," Rodin gestured over to Buzz.

"Can I get you boys some coffee or a cup of tea?" Buzz asked.

"No, thank you, we're good, Mr. Richards," Andy said.

Rodin invited the two men below to discuss the mission while Buzz untied the bowlines and took the Sweet Mary Jane out of the harbor and into the Java Sea. He stayed topside while piloting the SMJ through the flotilla of fishing boats heading out to sea.

"So, tell me a little something about yourselves," Rodin asked.

"We're both going to Gadjah Mada University, majoring in Environmental Studies. I'm a senior, and Andy is in his junior year," Dewi said.

"We've volunteered on a couple of campaigns on board the Bob Barker with Sea Shepherd and are members of Greenpeace. Most recently, we've been going up against the industrial fishing fleets," Andy added.

"Very commendable. What do you boys know about Le Gang de la Clé de Singe?"

The two young men looked at each other with excitement and delight. Andy turned to Rodin and said, "Le Gang de la Clé de Singe, they are the big leagues."

"Andy, Dewi, this isn't going to be like protesting on a college campus, carrying signs and chanting slogans, or throwing bottles of chemicals onto a whaling ship. This is going to be up-close and personal; someone is going to get killed.

"You need to ask yourselves if you're up for this; do you think you can live with yourselves? We're talking about being a part of an assassination, the taking of a man's life, committing murder to save hundreds of Orangutans, Rhinos, Tigers, and Elephants.

"I'm going to go topside for a few minutes to give you time to think. If you decide not to get involved, there will be no hard feelings; you can walk away, no problem. Think about it."

Rodin went up on deck and stood next to Buzz.

"So?" Buzz asked.

"Hard to say, Buzz. Murder isn't for everyone."

Isala didn't return to the mosque for three days since she wanted to wet the marks appetite. Buzz and Rodin had each sat in the general area and observed Rajagukguk going to prayers each day at the same time he spoke to Isala. They could tell he was disappointed she wasn't there, but they also noticed that he always had a bodyguard nearby. That would have to be addressed. It wasn't a major sticking point, but it was just something to consider.

"Hello, Miss. It's so nice to see you again," Rajagukguk said.

"Good day, Mr. Rajagukguk," She answered nonchalantly, not wanting to seem too eager.

"It's such a lovely day. I was hoping I could interest you in a walk along Alun-Alun Park," he said with a toothy grin,

"You mean now."

"Yes, now."

"But you haven't been to salah. You go to salah while I sit here and read."

Salah was the furthest thing Rajagukguk had in mind, but if he had to go into the mosque and pray, he would pray that he would soon be fucking Miss Adiratna's brains out. He had all kinds of fantasies he had been dreaming up for this tender piece of ass.

The prayer service lasted twenty minutes, and as soon as the Imam had finished, Rajagukguk had his Gucci loafers on and out the door.

Isala was reading the Koran when Rajagukguk approached her.

"Shall we take our walk now?"

"All right. Mr. Rajagukguk, but who is that man?" Isala pointed to the man standing nearby.

Without turning, he said, "Oh, that is Abdulla, my bodyguard."

"Why do you need a bodyguard? Are we in danger?"

"Do you really not know who I am?" Rajagukguk asked.

"Should I?" Isala could see that it genuinely bothered him that someone wouldn't know who he was.

"I am one of the most powerful men in all of Indonesia. I am Ibrahim Rajagukguk!" He growled.

"Good day, sir," Isala said and started to walk away.

"No, wait, please. Don't leave, I am sorry. I didn't mean to upset you; don't go," He implored her.

Isala stopped her back still to him and stood motionless as if deciding whether to stay or leave. She then turned towards him and asked, "Why were you so upset that I do not know who you are?"

"I guess when you're so used to people knowing who you are, you sometimes forget that people have their own lives that don't necessarily involve you. Again, I apologize."

Isala smiled and asked, "So, who are you, and why should I know you?"

"I am the president of a large corporation, PT Bakrie Salim Tbk," He said proudly.

She said nothing, just smiled.

"Surely you must have heard of it?"

"I'm afraid not. Mr. Rajagukguk, I am not a sophisticated woman. I've graduated from college, but my parents are elderly and unwell, so I stay home and care for them," Isala said unapologetically.

Rajagukguk seemed genuinely touched by her plight, but all the time, he was scheming how to use her troubles to his advantage.

"Miss Adiratna, may I take you to dinner?"

"Mr. Rajagukguk, I do not feel comfortable going out with someone who feels the need to have a bodyguard."

Rajagukguk thought for a moment. Was this little bitch worth taking a chance on? He should be safe; after all, he was on a dink-ass little island in the middle of nowhere; hell, what could happen?

He gestured for his bodyguard, "Abdulla, you may return to the hotel."

"Are you sure, Mr. Rajagukguk?"

"Yes, you may go."

"Very good, sir."

Rajagukguk turned to Isala, "There, now it's just the two of us. Have you ever eaten at the Royal Ocean View Beach Resort? They have fabulous seafood. We can have dinner and, if you're up to it, a nice walk along the beach afterward."

"That sounds very nice, Mr. Rajagukguk."

"Ibrahim, please."

"That sounds very nice, Ibrahim."

They walked out onto the street, and Rajagukguk hailed a taxi. Rodin, Buzz, Andy Sharif, and Dewi Huntapea were already on their way to the Royal Ocean View Beach Resort since Isala had been wearing a wire. It was decided that Doctor Laura Runnel's assistance wasn't required at this time, so she would stay onboard the Sweet Mary Jane and have everything in order for a speedy departure.

On the taxi ride to the resort, Rajagukguk and Isala made small talk, and Rajagukguk was the perfect gentleman. The resort was on the other side of the island, and the ride took about an hour; by the time they arrived, the sun was close to setting. It looked as if it was going to be a glorious sunset, so Rajagukguk requested a table out on the patio, and he handed the hostess a twenty US dollar bill for the table he required.

Their waiter presented them with menus and handed Rajagukguk the wine list. In the Muslim faith, alcohol is haraam, forbidden. They do not eat foods with ethanol, they don't wear perfumes containing alcohol ingredients, and they stay away from all intoxicating substances. Of course, Rajagukguk drinks like a fish and would have killed for a stiff vodka tonic, but tonight, he was playing the part of the good Muslim. Besides, he wanted to be good and sober when he fucked this bitch. If she refused, he'd rape her if it came to that. Who would believe her; a nobody over him, they never had before.

He returned the wine list to the waiter, saying, "No, thank you. We'll have two ice teas."

When they were alone, Isala asked, "So, what looks good?"

Rajagukguk looked at her and just smiled.

☠☠☠☠☠☠☠☠☠☠☠

Over dinner, Rajagukguk talked nonstop about his favorite subject: himself. He spoke of his fabulous lifestyle and meteoric rise in the corporate world but mostly talked about his bid to capture the America's Cup.

Isala pretended to be mesmerized and captivated by his yammering on and on about Rajagukguk the magnificent, Rajagukguk the all-knowing, Rajagukguk the all-powerful and of course Rajagukguk the powerful love maker. In all their time together, he never asked her a single question.

After dinner, he suggested that they take a walk along the beach. At this time of year, it would stay light until late into the evening, and there was a full moon.

One lone Indonesian traditional fishing boat was beached on the shore. Two young men were finishing tying her off to a palm tree and looked to be leaving it for the night.

"Did you have a good day?" Asked Rajagukguk.

"Not bad," One of the men answered.

"Mind if we go on board?"

"Sure, just be careful."

"Anybody on board?"

"No, we were the last."

He turned to Isala and whispered excitedly, "I've wanted to go on one of these since I was a kid. Do you mind?"

"If you want to," Isala said hesitantly.

Rajagukguk had been on dozens of these old fishing boats. He knew they all had cabins with a couple of beds, perfect for his needs.

They slowly strolled along the deck towards the back of the boat, where the wheelhouse and the main cabin were.

"Let's go in and take a look."

"Do you think we really should?"

"Sure, we're just looking; come on."

Inside the main cabin were two beds on either side of the bulkheads, a small table with a couple of rattan chairs, an area where meals would be prepared, and a door leading into the wheelhouse.

Isala was standing with her back to Rajagukguk, looking out of one of the portholes, when she sensed he was approaching her. She turned to face him, and that's when she noticed he had pants unzipped and he was holding his erect penis. He pushed her onto the bed and said, "Okay, Miss Adiratna, open up wide."

Had Rajagukguk paid a bit more attention to Isala and less on trying to get his dick out of his pants, he would have noticed the lady was holding something in her hand.

He couldn't believe his eyes when he glanced down at her, and she looked at his penis and then up at him and smiled. It was right before she shoved the VIPERTEK VTS 230 Million Volt Self-Defense Stun Gun into his testicles.

☠☠☠☠☠☠☠☠☠☠☠

When Rajagukguk came to, he discovered that he was strapped to one of the straight back chairs on the fishing boat, his mouth had been taped, and his balls felt like someone had used a blowtorch on them. Being a master sailor, he knew they were out in the ocean by how the boat was rocking.

Across from him sat the bitch, who, when he gets free, will split her like a chicken. She winked at him and smiled, "Hey, sailor, new in town?"

"He tried to curse at her, but all that came out was, 'Mmmm! Hmmmm!"

The door to the wheelhouse opened, and four men entered the cabin. The man who looked to be in charge, maybe the captain, whispered something to the two young men that he had talked to earlier. It was the captain, some old hippie, and the bitch in the cabin with him. He looked around and noticed that beside him was a black tin drum with a hand pump and a long rubber hose attached to it.

Rodin walked over and ripped the tape off his mouth. Before Rajagukguk could speak, Rodin held his finger to his mouth, signaling Rajagukguk not to speak.

Rodin said, "Mr. Rajagukguk, I've been dying to meet you. From what Isala tells me, oh yes, her real name is Isala; from what she's told me, you're a big oil tycoon, palm oil. Is that correct?"

Rajagukguk nodded.

"Do you like palm oil, Mr. Rajagukguk?"

Rajagukguk nodded.

"Now that's good because we just happen to have a whole drum of palm oil right here," Rodin said as he tapped the black drum next to Rajagukguk.

Rajagukguk began to say something, but Rodin put his finger to his lips and made a shhh sound.

"Don't talk, Mr. Rajagukguk, not yet anyway. What's the going price of palm oil these days, Mr. Rajagukguk? Okay, you can speak. How much?"

"Maybe six hundred dollars a metric ton." He whispered.

"Oh, I'm sorry, Mr. Rajagukguk. I meant to ask what's the going price of palm oil in Orangutans?"

Rajagukguk said nothing.

"How about in elephants?"

Rajagukguk said nothing but began to sweat profusely.

"Rhinoceroses?"

Rajagukguk just stared ahead.

"Pity, but then a man of your stature and importance doesn't really care about a few fucking monkeys or elephants, am I right, Mr. Rajagukguk?"

"Look, how much do you want? I can pay you anything; just name your price."

"We don't want anything, Mr. Rajagukguk. In fact, we are going to give you something: this barrel of palm oil. Isala, I think you should leave now."

Isala gave Rajagukguk a little wink and a smile before entering the wheelhouse. Buzz ripped off another piece of gaffer's tape and placed it across Rajagukguk's mouth. Then Rodin and he tilted Rajagukguk backward and placed a wooden crate under the legs of the chair so his head was lower than his feet. It wasn't until he was lying backward that Rajagukguk realized that the rattan bottom of the chair was missing.

Rodin grabbed a large fishing knife and slit the seat of Rajagukguk's trousers exposing his bare ass. Rodin stood up, took the end of the rubber hose, and inserted it deep up into Rajagukguk's rectum.

"I think this will be enough, but we have more if necessary. Buzz, care to man the pump?"

Buzz took hold of the handle, looked down at Rajagukguk, and said, "You know, man, the animals of the rainforests have been taking it up the ass for years by assholes like you, now let's see how you like it."

☠ ☠ ☠ ☠ ☠ ☠ ☠ ☠ ☠ ☠ ☠

Two days later the CEO and President of PT Bakrie Salim Tbk, Mr. Ibrahim Rajagukguk was found dead sitting slumped over the helm of his America's Cup challenger yacht, the 75ft flying monohull of Team Salim. The coroner found that the cause of death was due to his body having gone into shock from ingesting too much palm oil. The coroner did make a notation of the trauma and extreme swelling to Mr. Rajagukguk's testicles.

The authorities suspected foul play, especially when they spotted the yellow flag with a black skull and crossed monkey wrenches flying atop Team Salim's 75ft flying monohull mast. They also found the traditional manifesto in one of Rajagukguk's pants pocket, proclaiming that Le Gang de la Clé de Singe found him guilty of being involved in the raping and deforestation of Indonesia's rainforests, along with the killing and displacing thousands of the rainforest's animal population, his sentence, death.

PT Bakrie Salim Tbk, Mr. Rajagukguk's company, is offering a reward of one hundred thousand US Dollars for any information leading to the arrest and conviction of Mr. Rajagukguk's killers.

The only clue or evidence that police have been able to find so far, aside from a rubber tube protruding from his rectum, was a single fingerprint on the crystal of his thirty-five thousand Rolex Yacht-Master 42 watch. It was that of Sukarno, the first President of Indonesia, who passed away over forty years ago. A spokesman for the police told BBC News, "We got nothing."

The Sweet Mary Jane was off the coast of Timor-Leste in the Banda Sea when they picked up the latest news on the BBC.

"Good evening, I'm Nigel Williams, and this is the BBC World Headline News. Our top story this hour comes from the tiny island of Karimunjawa in the Indonesian archipelago, where Indonesian corporate mogul Mr. Ibrahim Rajagukguk, the self-proclaimed palm oil king, was found dead

slumped over the helm of his America's Cup challenger yacht, the 75ft flying monohull, of Team Salim.

"Le Gang de la Clé de Singe, the French eco-terrorist group, has claimed responsibility for the killing, stating that his death was justified due to his company's involvement in the deforestation of thousands of acres of rainforest, thereby causing the death and displacement of thousands of animals, many of them are endangered species.

"Palm oil is a minor ingredient in the world's diet, but more than half of all packaged products consumed contain palm oil. It is found in lipstick, soaps, detergents, and even ice cream and is also used primarily for cooking in developing countries.

"The manner of his death was particularly humiliating and gruesome; authorities have told BBC News that Mr. Rajagukguk's body was injected with palm oil forcefully through a tube inserted into his rectum and subsequently died from anaphylaxis shock.

"Worldwide commendation is pouring in as many..."

Buzz and Rodin were standing topside at the helm when Rodin asked, "Hey Buzz, do you ever use palm oil?"

"No fucking way, man. I'm an olive oil man all the way. Just like Popeye, man."

"Well, blow me down."

"A-gah-gah-gah-gah-gah-gah!" Buzz laughed.

☠☠☠☠☠☠☠☠☠☠☠

"Wooch, here."

"Hey, it's Rodin."

"So good to talk to you. I heard about the terrible news about Palm Oil King."

"Yeah, it's a shame, such a real humanitarian. He will be missed."

"Where are you calling from?"

"Buzz dropped Isala and me off in Cairns before he and Doc Runnel headed back to Kanacea."

"Taking a little R & R."

"No, I wanted to talk to you about an assignment I want to take on."

"What's on your mind?"

"Well, you know I'm on my way out, so I want to go out on a high note."

"Okay, what did you have in mind?"

"The newly elected President of Botswana."

"Amogelang Mooketsi, what about him?"

"I want to kill him."

"Ladies and Gentlemen, I know that this is highly unusual to have a request for an assignment from one of our team leaders. But that's why I've called this emergency meeting so we may discuss the mission proposed by team leader Rodin. I have him waiting in the adjoining office, ready to present his case," Commander Wooch Brown said to the assembled governing body of Le Gang de la Clé de Singe.

"Excuse me, Senor Brown. I have a question. Why is it necessary that team leaders need the council's blessing to conceive their own missions?" Asked Jose Perez, one of the governing council's newest members.

"Please, call me Wooch, Senor Perez. And to answer your question, it is because what we don't want is a bunch of combat guerrillas going off willy-nilly, shooting at anyone who might be mistaken for a target and getting killed; that's how anarchy and chaos ensues.

You see, each of our teams is given specific missions that have been carefully researched, and then we make sure they are allocated the proper equipment, weapons, vehicles, and resources, such as local people who speak the language and know the terrain. Occasionally, while on assignment, they might come across an opportunity, and then they may use their discretion and judgment. However, that's the exception and not the norm.

"Are there any other questions?"

Wooch looked around the room and found there were none.

"Good, then let's hear from team leader Rodin," Wooch said as he pressed a small button on the table that alerted Rodin to enter the conference room.

The door opened, and Rodin entered, wearing khaki cargo pants and a Columbia Tamiami Gulf Stream green shirt untucked. He looked casual and relaxed, but his rugged face showed the wear and tear that a lifetime of war and combat can leave on a soldier. His blonde hair was starting to show hints of gray. He had a military manner about him, and when he entered the room, one could sense his confidence as that of a leader of men.

He carried a small notebook in his right hand as he walked over to the lectern at the head of the conference table. He stood for a moment, looking at everyone sitting before him. He smiled and said, "Amogelang Mooketsi must die."

A buzz of hushed whispers filled the room for a good five minutes; Rodin didn't say anything right away, letting the gravity of his words sink in.

The German Helmut Schneider, the President of the Berlin chapter of IFAW, spoke first: "This is totally unacceptable. We have never been involved in political assassination before. This would be the end of Le Gang de la Clé de Singe.

"Right now, nations denounce us, and some even pursue us, but this would unite all the countries against us. It will be suicide. I say no, absolutely not!"

There was much agreement in the room against the idea. When the room finally went quiet, Rodin said, "Ladies and gentlemen, believe me, I understand your trepidations, concerns, and fears about what I am proposing. Please hear me out; President Mooketsi is planning on lifting the ban on the sale of ivory and elephant hunting.

Like so many other leaders of African nations, he can only see the short-term gains of trophy hunting. For example, today, hunters pay a $2500 fee for a license and $100,000 in addition to the hunting outfitters…and graft.

“So, is the elephant’s value a mere hundred thousand dollars? There are those of us who believe that elephants are priceless, and then there are those who do not like the creature. People who have had their crops tramped, destroyed, and livelihoods threatened hate them. And then some like elephants okay but have never given any thought to their value.

The United States established the IWCC, the International Wildlife Conservation Commission, to develop a report on the benefits of hunting elephants in certain African countries.

Not surprisingly, every member of the IWCC is pro-hunting, and just about all of them are members of either the Safari Club International, the NRA, or Worldwide Affiliates of Safari Partners, better known as WASP. Like so many other pro-hunting groups, these groups value elephants based on the size of their trophies.

From the start, the IWCC was focused on one thing and one thing only: the monetary value of the hunt, not the value of the elephant. What they seem to ignore is that an elephant can only be killed once. In contrast, if kept alive, elephants can be photographed, studied, looked at, and enjoyed over and over by people willing to pay to see a live elephant, who usually lives well over fifty years.

Therefore, it is estimated that a living elephant can produce over 1.5 million dollars in ecotourism dollars in its lifetime through national parks like Kruger National Park in South Africa and Amboseli National Park in Kenya.

$100,000 pales in comparison to $1.5 million for a living elephant, wouldn’t you agree? Yet, 100 elephants are killed every day; Central Africa has lost 64% of its elephants in just a decade.

Maybe killing Amogelang Mooketsi won't stop the killing, but it might slow it down, at least get a conversation started. The current Vice President, Goitsemedi Tebogo, is more of a visionary. He's pro-eco-tourism rather than pro-hunting and has expressed more interest in conservation than devastation."

President of the International Society for Animal Welfare, Mark Peeters, raised his hand and began to speak: "I understand the concept of what you want to accomplish here, Rodin. But have you given any thought to what will happen to us? The whole world united against us?"

"I totally get it, Mr. Peeters, I do, but here's the thing, please don't get me wrong, you and everyone in this room is what makes it possible for me and the men and women that are out there in the field to be able to do our jobs. And for that, we are forever in your debt. But the people I command and work with believe in one thing, and I've said it to everyone we encounter: we are willing to die for what we believe in; the question is, are you?

"We're running out of time, and more importantly, we're running out of elephants. Thank you all for hearing me out; I await your decision."

With that said, he looked to Commander Brown, gave a short nod, and proceeded to leave the conference room. He then made his way back to the Grand Hotel et de Milan, where Isala was waiting for him.

☠☠☠☠☠☠☠☠☠☠☠

The Grand Hotel et de Milan is a small boutique hotel. It is four stories tall with very few balconies and, like just about every building in Milan, is built with sienna-colored limestone. The unassuming hotel has been home to opera composer

Giuseppe Verdi, painter Giorgio De Chirico, Greek soprano Maria Callas, and movie star Richard Burton.

Whenever Rodin stayed in Milan, he would stay at this historic lodge. He loved the hotel's interiors, with their refined, unique atmosphere, enriched over the years with exclusive objects and furniture that are now part of its rich history.

They decided to go downstairs to the Caruso restaurant to grab a bite and wait to hear from Wooch. They shared an order of the Vongole E Cozze Al Guanciale, and Isala had a glass of white Bordeaux while Rodin had a Birra Moretti beer.

After finishing off their clams and mussels, they still had no word from Commander Brown, so Isala suggested they take a relaxing stroll through the Brera Botanical Gardens. On their way over to the gardens, they stopped off at a tiny newsstand, and each bought something to read; Rodin got La Gazzetta dello Sport, and Isala picked up a copy of Grazia. They found an empty wooden bench beside an ivy-covered wall, planted themselves, and waited.

Four hours after arriving, the phone call came just as they were leaving the gardens, "Hey, Wooch, what's the good word."

"After a long and heated debate, you got the green light. I'll give you all the support I can, you know that, but if this thing goes south, it could get very ugly."

"I know, if that does happen, I don't plan on being taken alive. But, hey, keep a good thought."

"Always. Just call and tell me what you need, and give my love to Isala."

"Will do, and thanks again."

"Don't thank me, you sold it. Bye."

"Ciao."

Emirates flight 767 landed at Sir Seretse Khama International Airport at 12:50 pm, a total of 38 hours of travel overnight from Milan to Gaborone, Botswana.

Gaborone is Botswana's capital and political center. Most government buildings are located in the western part of the city, called the Government Enclave. The Presidential State House, where President Mooketsi resides, is not far from the Enclave.

Rodin and Isala, having made their way past customs, were met by Dikledi Mosweu, a forty-six-year-old animal behaviorist specializing in wildlife biology. She is currently a professor and the head of zoology at the Botswana International University of Science and Technology. She had been a Le Gang de la Clé de Singe member for over two decades.

"Mr. and Mrs. Novick, welcome to Gaborone. I am Dikledi Mosweu. I hope you had a pleasant flight."

"Yes, thank you. I'm Robert Novick, and this is my wife, Beverly; it's a pleasure to meet you, Ms. Mosweu," Rodin said as he shook her hand.

"Mrs. Novick, it's so nice to meet you."

"Beverly, please. It is very nice to meet you too, Dikledi," Isala said, hugging Dikledi.

Dikledi gestured to ask them to follow her, "Right this way, my car right outside. Do you need help with your luggage?" she asked.

"No, thank you. I think I can manage. Beverly. Why don't you go with Dikledi? I'll grab the luggage and meet you both outside."

As soon as Rodin walked outside the terminal, he spotted Isala and Dikledi in the parking lot across the street. There were maybe fifteen cars in the whole lot. He placed their suitcase into Dikledi's silver Toyota Noah SUV and entered the backseat, insisting that Isala ride up front. He did this to show Dikledi that he treated Isala as his equal, and secondly, it gave him a better opportunity to start getting a feel of the city.

Once Rodin was buckled in, Dikledi headed south on Airport Road past the SSKA Police Station until they jumped onto the A1 for seven miles. Then, they took the Molepolole Road exit to The Grand Palm Hotel Casino and Convention Resort.

The drive from the airport was mostly filled with chit-chat, nothing too detailed. Dikledi had worked on several missions over the years and knew that she would be told what she needed to know when she needed to know it.

As Dikledi pulled up to the hotel entrance, she said, "I am available to you both and will be able to get you anything that you may need. If I can't, then I know people who can."

"Thank you, Dekledi. We know that we can depend on you. I thank you for your service, and we shall be in touch soon," Rodin said.

"Good day, Robert and Beverly. I look forward to hearing from you soon."

As Rodin and Isala exited the car, the hotel bellman came to take their bags.

"This way to reception," The bellman said.

Rodin and Isala were struck by the contrast between the old-world luxury of the Grand Hotel et de Milan and the glitzy luxury of the Grand Palm Hotel Casino and Convention Resort. One offered elegance, charm, and sophistication, while the other offered slot machines.

On their first day back in Africa, they decided to go out and get the lay of the land, and what better way than as tourists? Rodin had always found that people really don't pay attention to tourists, plus they're forgiven when tourists "accidentally" go places where they're not allowed.

So, they went down into the curio shop in the hotel lobby and purchased loud matching African print shirts and two lime green ball caps with the hotel's logo that only a tourist would wear. Rodin walked out of the hotel armed with a 35mm camera, and Isala led the way with an open oversized city map.

On their first day, they hiked to the top of Kgale Hill, which provided a great panoramic view of the city and the Gaborone Dam- a very touristy activity.

On day two, they took the sightseeing city bus tour visiting the Gaborone National Museum and Art Gallery, the Thapong Visual Arts Center, Gaborone Dam, the National Botanical Gardens, and most importantly, a tour of the government enclave that included the Parliament buildings, the Three Chiefs Monument and the President's house where they met Kgosi Masire.

☠☠☠☠☠☠☠☠☠☠☠

Kgosi Masire, a man in his mid-forties, stood six feet two inches and weighed one hundred eighty pounds. He had a dark complexion and twisted curls. He was a member of the Botswana Secret Service, the official organization's name, Directorate of Intelligence and Security Services (DISS) attached to guarding President Mooketsi.

Kgosi was a sergeant major in Botswana's elite Defense Force f5, serving four tours in Iraq and Afghanistan before joining the DISS. While in Iraq, he met SEAL member Robert Lester, aka the Iceman, and they became fast friends.

When Iceman was later recruited by Le Gang de la Clé de Singe as a combat team leader, he contacted Kgosi to see if he was interested in joining. Still, by then, Kgosi had gotten married, had a baby daughter, and signed up with the Botswana Secret Service.

Although he didn't join Le Gang de la Clé de Singe as a full-time combatant, he had been an agent and a volunteer on several missions, where he had played a significant role in their success.

When SEAL Commander Brown contacted him to see if he would be interested in assisting on this assignment, Kgosi jumped at the chance to work with the legendary Rodin, even knowing the mission's goal was to assassinate President Mooketsi.

"Are you sure you're comfortable with this?" Rodin asked.

'I am sure."

"You know if this does or doesn't succeed and they find out about you, you'll be branded as a traitor."

"I know, but my country's heritage, natural resources, and animals are at stake, and Mooketsi is willing to sell them off for a quick buck."

"When do you think you can meet with me?"

"How about tomorrow at 5 pm in the Botanical Gardens?"

"Sounds good, see ya then."

☠☠☠☠☠☠☠☠☠☠☠

Éfaté is an island in the Pacific Ocean, part of the Shefa Province in Vanuatu. Éfaté Island is the main island of Vanuatu, where the capital, Port Vila, is situated. It is the metropolitan area where most commerce and tourism occur.

Buzz and Doctor Runnel sailed the Sweet Mary Jane into Vila Bay and docked on Iririki Island, a resort island just a stone's throw from Port Vila. It's literally a three-minute ferry ride to Port Vila.

After their adventure with the Palm Oil King, Buzz and the Doc figured they could do with a bit of rejuvenation before heading back home to Kanacea Island. So, Buzz called for a three-day reservation via satellite phone at the Iririki Island Resort & Spa Vanuatu. Buzz booked a premium overwater faré. Their bungalow sat over the bay with a fabulous view of Port Vila Harbor and the city.

Once they settled into their room, they grabbed some lunch at the Azure Restaurant, which overlooks a scenic view of the township. They shared an appetizer of yellowfin tuna Carpaccio. The Doc ordered the seafood risotto, while Buzz had the spaghetti frutti di mare. To top off the meal, they split the twice-baked croissant pudding. Then they headed to the spa for the works: massage, cucumber, yogurt body wrap, facials, and a manicure and pedicure.

That evening, they called room service for a couple of burgers and made an early night of it. The following day, they didn't wake up until well past eleven, had breakfast in bed, and made passionate love. Then they lay in bed naked with the curtains drawn open to watch the boat traffic in the bay.

Later in the day, Buzz learned about coconut harvesting and husking, while Doc took a cooking class on local delicacies from native chefs.

On their last day before heading back out to sea, Buzz and the Doc took the ferry to Port Vila to see the sites, check out the shops and open markets, and even have time for a bit of kayaking around the bay. They had a light lunch at Au Peche Mignon in the heart of Port Vila.

They topped off the evening by going to the Nambawan Café, where they had a pizza, and watched The Big Lebowski at the Moonlight Cinema. A large tarp was stretched outside, and movies were projected onto it. It was sort of a homemade drive-in movie.

The following day, bright and early, they set sail for Kanacea Island; they sailed out of Mele Bay and into the Pacific Ocean. The sea was calm, with a strong wind at their backs, which made for smooth sailing. At one point, a large school of bottlenose Dolphins escorted them for several miles. It had happened many times when Buzz had been out in deep water, but it was still an awe-inspiring and emotional experience every time.

Buzz was standing at the helm when the Doc came from behind, put her arm around him, snuggled up, and whispered in his ear, "I love you, Buzz."

"I love you too, Doc, forever."

"Promise."
"Promise."

☠☠☠☠☠☠☠☠☠☠☠

Kgosi found Rodin reading the Botswana Guardian on a park bench next to a cluster of Moporota trees, commonly known as sausage trees.

"Have you seen this?" Rodin asked, holding up the front page.

"No, but I've heard about it."

"I can't believe that he would do such a thing and that the other Presidents would accept it, unbelievable.

"It was reported in the Botswana Guardian that President Mooketsi gave gifts to the presidents of Zimbabwe and Namibia. They were stools made from the feet of elephants. On the front page was a color photograph of the three leaders smiling, posing with the stools in front of them; Mooketsi made the gifts as a symbolic gesture, letting the world know that he was committed to removing the ban on selling ivory products. He was thereby easing the ban for big game trophy hunters to start pouring in to "culling" the herds.

President Mooketsi was quoted as saying, "We're tired of letting other countries, conservation organizations, and left-wing commies dictate, debate, and make decisions about *our* elephants."

"The dubious proposal, which still must be debated by the parliament before becoming law, would overturn a hunting ban introduced by former president Ndabili Ikgopoleng, a fervent conservationist.

"It's a well-known fact that President Mooketsi either owns or has major interests in several safari outfits and hotel/spas that cater exclusively to trophy hunters. He and his cronies make no secret that he and his stooges will be profiting from this new policy. Of course, he claims that the only reason he's considering it is to save the elephants.

Unfortunately for Botswana, Amogelang Mooketsi won the election by lying, deceiving, dividing the people, and preying on their fears, pitting one segment of the population against another. Just like in some major Western countries, the same thing happened. People were scared and lied about voting against their interests.

One leader of a Western power proclaimed how he loves the uneducated voter. Sadly, people today don't investigate the facts; they just blindly follow. It's a sad truth that you get the government that you deserve.

I'm sorry, Kgosi, for going off into a rant. Please forgive me," Rodin said.

"No, no, it's quite all right. I feel the same way you do. I have been giving it a lot of thought, and I believe there might be one window of opportunity within President Mooketsi's schedule next month. "

"Really?"

"Most of this month, he's tied up with foreign heads of state and meetings with parliament. And he'll be traveling the first two weeks next month, but right now, there's a two-day window, the 23rd and 24th."

"Great, that will give me plenty of time to prepare."

"Here, I have uploaded a detailed diagram of the State House, room by room, a bio, and pictures of all the staff and security guards that work in the building, even my own. Finally, all the security and alarm codes and alarm systems," Kgosi said as he handed Rodin an Apple watch.

"Fantastic. How can I contact you if I need to?"

"Here's my home address. Outside, there are two mailboxes; the one on the left is purely decorative. If you need me or if I need you, raise the red flag on the mailbox and leave a sealed envelope with a message. If I need you, I'll do the same."

Rodin read the address aloud, "Two-ten Kgeengwe Road." He then handed the note back to Kgosi.

"It's right across the street from the Thornhill Primary School that my daughter attends."

"Okay, thanks, Kgosi. I'm hoping that this will be the last time we have to meet. So, if I don't see you again, thank you for everything. I will download the information on the watch and destroy it. And please know that nothing will ever be traced back to you. Goodbye." He stood up, shook Kgosi's hand, and walked away.

Before going to Kanacea Island, Buzz, and the Doc figured they'd stop at Suva to pick up some much-needed supplies since they were passing the big island of Fiji.

Suva is the capital of the South Pacific island nation of Fiji. Its location on the southeast coast makes it ideal for stopping because it's on the way to Kanacea. Buzz had called in earlier to gain permission to dock at the Royal Suva Yacht Club. His buying Kanacea Island granted him certain privileges as a Fijian landowner. Although, it initially didn't start out so privileged.

"Hello, Royal Fiji Yacht Club. May I help you?"

"Yeah, do you have any dock space available, man?"

"Are you a member, sir?"

"No, man, I'm just looking for a place to dock the old Sweet Mary Jane for a couple of days."

"I'm afraid our dock space is exclusively reserved for our members, sir."

"Okay, I'd like to become a member; how much?"

"Excuse me?"

"How much to join your snobatorium?"

"You're joking."

"How much, man!"

"Well, it's a thirty thousand initiation fee and six thousand per yearly dues."

"Cool, do you take American Express?"

"Pardon me?"

"American Express, do you take it?"

"And whom am I speaking with?"

"Buzz Murdock, man. And *whom* am I speaking with?"

"I, sir, am Walter Smythe, the third club secretary."

And with that, Buzz Murdock became the newest Royal Fiji Yacht Club member.

Once the SMJ was docked, Buzz and the Doc went into town. They first made their way to the Suva Municipal Market, an enormous market full of fresh fruits and vegetables, then over to the Rajendra Foodtown for miscellaneous paper products and other essentials. After returning to the SMJ and stowing all their stores and provisions, they went for sushi at Daikoku, the only Japanese-owned restaurant in Suva.

While sitting at the sushi counter, they met several couples that had traveled from Kenya for a big match between the Kenyan 7s and the Fijians 7s. It was a big grudge match for the HSBC Rugby Sevens World Championship. The game was to be played the next day at Albert Park, just a couple blocks away.

Buzz had become a big rugby fan while living in Jamaica, so they decided to extend their stay for another day to watch the match. That meant Buzz would have to deal with Walter Smythe, the third club secretary, to keep the SMJ docked at the Royal Fiji Yacht Club for another night.

Buzz made the necessary phone call as they returned to the yacht club from dinner. When they entered the office of the Royal Fiji Yacht Club, Walter Smythe, the third club secretary, was sitting at his desk.

"Yes, may I help you?" Smythe asked.

"Yes, we'd like to extend our stay for another day," Buzz said.

"I'm afraid that won't be possible, Mr. Murdock," Smythe replied while reading the latest copy of Yachting World magazine.

"Oh, I think it's possible, Mr. Smythe. You see, I'm very good friends with the new owner."

Smythe put the magazine down, looked up at Buzz, and queried, "What new owner?"

Buzzed smiled, "Me."

Just then, the club's phone rang; it was Sir Robert Ackley, the Royal Fiji Yacht Club's president. Walter accidentally hit the speaker button.

"Walter, Robert here. I wanted to let you know that the club has been sold to Mr. Murdock, an American of all people. Can you believe it? What a load of bollocks, damn cheeky Yank."

Before Walter Smythe, the third club secretary, could turn off the speakerphone, Buzz said, "Good evening, Sir Ackley."

"Who is this?"

"This is Buzz Murdock, the new owner of the Royal Fiji Yacht Club or as I'm more commonly known as, that damn cheeky Yank. I was wondering if you might do me a small favor, old man?"

"Ah, anything, Mr. Murdock. Anything," Sir Robert said, all flummoxed and embarrassed.

"Listen, Robby baby, would you be a dear and have all signage, business cards, stationery, website, and anything else with the Royal Fiji Yacht Club's name on it removed and have everything changed to Buzz Murdock's Royal Bait & Tackle Shop and Yacht Club. Thanks, man."

"You're joking, right, sir?"

"Do it ASAP, Robby baby. Ciao," Buzz said as he and the Doc walked out of the office, leaving Walter Smythe, the third club secretary, at his desk with his mouth open in shock.

"Sir Robert, can you believe the nerve of that man?" Smythe said after he regained his composure.

"Walter."

"Sir?"

"You're fired."

☠☠☠☠☠☠☠☠☠☠☠

While waiting for the green light from Kgosi, Rodin and Isala connected with Dikledi Mosweu, who helped recruit and assemble an all-female wildlife ranger team called the Basadi Masole (Woman Warrior). The Rangers are a nonprofit International Anti-Poaching Fund division secretly financed by Le Gang de la Clé de Singe.

The Basadi Masole patrol and protect a 200-square-mile area that was being heavily poached not only of elephants but lions, rhinos, and leopards. Over the years, this area has lost thousands of these creatures to poachers and trophy hunters.

Dikledi had brought Rodin to spend time observing and training these lady warriors for the harsh realities of eco-combat. While out on patrol with a squad of Basadi Masole, they apprehended eight armed men, all of whom had various degrees of wounds. A couple of men had scratches or punctures on their arms and hands. One man had his arm in a sling, and one had a bandage on his forehead. They claimed a leopard attacked them and were thereby justified in killing it.

Killing of wildlife without a permit is a criminal offense. After Rodin and the Basadi Masole examined the so-called leopard wounds based on the injuries being of such a minor nature, they were skeptical that the killing was an attack but more likely a case of poaching. Leopard skin, teeth, claws, and bones are worth hundreds of dollars on the black market.

Rodin approached the eight men, held up the yellow ensign with a black skull and crossed monkey wrenches, and asked, "Do any of you know what this is?"

All the men stared at the ground; none would give him eye contact. He raised his Glock 9mm, clocked it, and fired, killing the first man in line. All the women gasped, and there was mumbling amongst them.

Rodin looked at the squad and said, "Ladies, you have to decide right now how committed you are to saving the lives of these animals. These men not only stole from you, they stole from your children and your children's children.

"You say to yourself, but it is only one leopard. Someday, that's going to be the last leopard. Then what? Extinction doesn't happen overnight; it's one at a time.

"Did you know that more leopards are stuffed in people's homes than left in the wild?"

One of the women shouted out, "Do we have to kill them? Can't we turn them over to the police?"

"You can do what you like, but let me ask you, have small fines and a year or two in jail. Have you seen a decline in poaching?"

"No, sir."

"Ladies, like it or not, you are in a war. Do you think any of these men would have thought twice about killing you to save themselves? They're carrying AK-47 assault rifles for a reason."

Rodin walked over to the woman who asked the question and was holding one of the captured AKs. He took it from her and proceeded to shoot and kill the remaining seven captives.

"You okay?" Rodin asked the young woman.

"It's been a tough day."

"Well, you just fulfilled the first rule of war. Make sure you're still alive after an encounter. Would you rather it be you lying there dead?"

"No!"

"I want all of you to remember this. You hesitate, you're dead, there are no do overs. You are all strong, powerful, and intelligent women; no one is better than you, no one.

"If it helps, do not think of them as men. They are poachers, thieves, murderers, and they are only looking out for themselves. They will kill you and will not lose a wink of sleep."

The squad proceeded to place the yellow flags around each of the poachers' necks and put the letters into their pockets. Once they were well out of the area, they called the police as to the poacher's location.

Before he and Isala left, they took time to meet with each one and thank them for their service and dedication to the cause.

One of the women asked him, "Are you ever scared of dying?"

"Of course, but I can't think of any cause worth dying for more than the survival of the innocent and those who have no voice."

☠☠☠☠☠☠☠☠☠☠☠

Before Buzz and the Doc set sail for home, leaving Buzz Murdoch's Royal Bait & Tackle Shop and Yacht Club behind, he had an impromptu meeting with Sir Robert Ackley and the all-male board of directors.

Sitting at the head of a twenty-foot solid mahogany conference table with six board members seated on both sides and Sir Robert Ackley at the other end was the new owner of the Buzz Murdoch's Royal Bait & Tackle Shop and Yacht Club, Buzz Murdoch.

As Buzz looked down the table, he observed that each member was dressed rather smartly. They wore khaki slacks, a white shirt, club ties, and a blue blazer with the Royal Fiji Yacht Club's crest on their jackets. They all looked very top-drawer.

On the other hand, Buzz was unshaven, with scraggly hair, wearing a faded Grateful Dead t-shirt and an old pair of Levis 501 jeans. Buzz smiled at Sir Robert and asked, "Say, Robby, where's my newest best buddy, Walter Smythe, the third club secretary?"

"I fired him."

"That's a bummer. First of all, gentlemen, I firmly believe in equal rights, so I would like some women and minorities on the board. I also think we should open the membership to some less fortunate yacht owners if such a thing exists.

Of course, the names on all the logos will have to be revised. Instead of just the crown, I would like to see a Bumble Bee Grouper wearing the crown. It still reeks of royalty, but now it won't seem so stuffy. Sorry, that means you'll have to get new blazers; oh well, just send me the bill, the first ones on me.

Thank you, gentlemen. I think this meeting's adjourned," Buzz said as he rose.

"Will that be all, Mr. Murdoch?" Sir Robert snidely asked.

"No, man, I believe that covers it. Oh wait, there is one more thing. From now on, I'd like to be referred to as Commodore. Ciao, kids."

☠☠☠☠☠☠☠☠☠☠☠

Dikledi met Rodin at the Gaborone Game Reserve, located inside the city. The reserve is home to several of Botswana's native species, including zebra, impala, eland, kudu, blue wildebeest, steenbok, vervet monkeys, warthogs, and rock dassies. The park has numerous walking trails and two well-appointed picnic sites. Rodin and Dikledi were to meet at the first picnic site, situated by a large grove of Mopane trees.

Rodin was sitting at one of the wooden picnic tables, where a mother vervet monkey holding a baby was sitting on the end of the table, begging for food.

"I'd be careful. They can get pretty aggressive," Dikledi said.

"I'm hoping she'll leave when she realizes I have no food."

Just then, some tourists showed up with a gaggle of kids, excited to see the monkeys. They started offering the monkeys food, and they were quickly surrounded by the little beggars.

Rodin stood up from the bench and asked, "Care to stroll?"

"Good idea."

The game reserve was a fantastic place. Walking along the paths, they encountered herds of zebra and steenbok or the occasional kudu grazing six or seven feet away, unafraid.

"What can I do for you, Mr. Novick?"

"I have a list of items I hoped you might obtain for me," Rodin said as he handed her a folded piece of paper.

She opened it and scanned the list, "The passport may take a couple of days, but everything else I should have by tomorrow. Do you have a photo for the passport?"

He reached into his sports coat pocket, pulled out an envelope, and handed it to her.

"May I?" She asked.

"Of course."

Dikledi removed the photo, looked at it, held it up to compare it to him, and said, "It doesn't look anything like you."

"It will when the time comes."

"So, Mr. Novick becomes Doctor Livingston just like that."

"Just like that."

☠☠☠☠☠☠☠☠☠☠☠

Isala was waiting for Rodin at the hotel pool. She was napping under an umbrella, having fallen asleep reading a tell-all novel about Le Gang de la Clé de Singe, titled Blood of the Beast.

She woke up when she heard him ask, "Good Book?"

"Yeah, pretty good. You should read it."

"Me? I'm a doer, not a reader."

"Pity."

"Hmmm."

"So, how did it go?" She asked.

"The wheels are in motion. Did you get the drone?"

"Yes, it's ready and waiting for me. I'm leaving tomorrow to meet Roger Badenhorst at the Walterzen Filling Station outside Supingstad. Do you have any idea how long a drive it is?"

"Supingstad is just across the border with South Africa, maybe an hour at the most."

"What time are we meeting with Kgosi?"

"We're meeting him at the restaurant at nine o'clock."

"Well, why don't you go change and take a swim?"

"Sounds good; I'll be back in a few minutes."

"Shall I order you something to drink?"

"Sure, I'll have a Cuba Libre."

When he returned from changing into his swim trunks, Isala was at the end of the pool.

"How is it?"

"Heavenly."

The air temperature was 94 degrees, so the coolness of the water went from shocking to soothing immediately. He dived in and swam underwater the entire pool length to where she was standing. He rose out of the water and passionately kissed her when he emerged.

"I love you." He whispered.

She returned the kiss, "I love you, too."

They stepped out of the pool to where she had been sitting, and their drinks awaited them. As they sat quietly enjoying their drinks and the cool desert breeze, Rodin said, "I can't wait for this one to be over; I really think I'm ready to just sit on the beach and chill."

"I thought you're a doer."

"After tomorrow night, this doer is done. What's the name of that book again?"

"Blood of the Beast."

"Catchy title."

☠ ☠ ☠ ☠ ☠ ☠ ☠ ☠ ☠ ☠ ☠

Kgosi was drinking a beer at the bar when Rodin and Isala walked into Caravela Portuguese Restaurant. A live jazz band was playing on the patio, giving the place a real neighborhood feel. The walls were painted a muted golden yellow, and colorful murals by local artists depicted the Portuguese explorers of the 1400s.

The hostess, who seemed to know Kgosi well, found them a table on the patio, away from the band, where they could converse quietly.

"What do you recommend?" Isala asked Kgosi.

"That depends. Are you in the mood for fish, chicken, meat, or vegetarian?"

"Chicken."

"I recommend the Chicken à Portuguesa,"

"How's the Bacalhau à Gomes de Sà?" Rodin asked.

"That's what I always order."

The waitress came and took their orders, and left them to continue their discussion.

Rodin asked, "Is everything a go?"

"Yes, President Mooketsi will expect you for an informal meet and greet at 10 pm. Afterward, you will have an intimate dinner just the two of you, followed by after-dinner drinks in his private office. This is where the ceremony of you presenting him with an enormous check made out to his charity. Of course, it isn't a charity, just his personal slush fund that people contribute to in return for favors."

"And we will be alone?"

"Well, there will be the photographer who will take the traditional photo of the two of you when you first meet, and of course, the servants will be present to serve dinner. But when you two meet in his office, you will be alone."

"No goons or secret service men?"

"No, just the two of you."

"How much time will I have alone with him before someone will get suspicious?"

"I would say most meetings usually last forty-five minutes to an hour. Anything longer, and someone might get concerned."

"And you'll be on duty?"

"Yes, I have already prepared for the alarms to be deactivated once you enter his office."

"What about the CCTV?"

"I've arranged for a pre-recorded loop to be inserted. After you enter his office, the alarms and the CCTV will be deactivated for one and a half hours, so you need to be finished and out the back exit by 11:45."

"Has the diversion been set?"

"Yes, Ms. Mosweu has arranged for a minor car accident to occur in front of the State House at exactly 11:40. That will draw everyone's attention to the front of the State House."

"Excellent. And you're sure that none of this will come back on you or Ms. Mosweu?"

"No, everything will be traced back to President Mooketsi's twin brother, Boipelo, who covets his brother's position. And is even more of an advocate for killing elephants."

Wally the Wombat, little Buzz, and Buster came running to greet the Doc and Buzz upon arriving at Kanacea Island. The greetings took well over an hour to satisfy the three of them, each more needy and jealous than the next.

After things had settled down, Buzz started to unload the supplies from the Sweet Mary Jane into the house. Once all the stores were put into the house, he returned to the SMJ to clean and straighten her up after such a long journey. He turned on the ship's radio and tuned in to Radio Fiji Gold to catch up on what's going on in the islands. Plus, they play music from the 60s and 70s, but more importantly, no disco!

He was grooving to the Beatles' "For the Benefit of Mr. Kite" when a breaking news story occurred.

"*We interrupt this programming for an important news alert.*

"There has been a rash of piracy occurring in and around the islands of Fiji. The latest attack was against an Australian couple on their 48-foot sailboat as it lay moored in an isolated area off Natovi Jetty on the island of Tailevu yesterday at 030,0 as they lay asleep.

"The couple's boat was boarded, and the husband was severely beaten, and the wife was raped. The pirates stole a satellite phone, a laptop computer, about thirty thousand in cash, and traveler checks.

"Be on the lookout for four men. Two men were described as black, in their forties, wearing long dreadlocks and beards. The other two were white, one was bald, and the other one was wearing a ball cap; both men appeared to be in their forties as well, heavily tattooed with multiple swastikas on their entire bodies.

"If anyone sees any of these men, you are advised to contact the Fijian police; they are armed and considered dangerous."

Buzz finished cleaning the Sweet Mary Jane and then went and told the Doc what he had heard about the pirates.

"You know, Doc, we ought to have a plan just in case we get attacked by these pirates. Tailevu, after all, is the next island over from us."

"I agree; what do you have in mind?"

"Well, thanks to Rodin, we have a pretty decent arsenal of weapons. First, we should get them out and make sure everything is in working order.

"I think if there are four of them, they'll try to enter the house from all sides to see where we're the weakest. So, I propose that we shutter up the house tight like we do when a typhoon is approaching, as well as the SMJ."

"And where are we going to sleep?"

Buzz pointed to the guesthouse on the small hill behind the main house.

"It only has two windows and two doors, and it's made of cinderblock, plus it's on high ground. We'll have the advantage. What do you think?"

"Hopefully, they'll catch these punks before too long, and we won't have to worry about them."

Buzz smiled and said as he unlocked the gun safe, "What'd like, the BAR or the AK-47?"

When Rodin entered the State House at precisely 10 p.m., a man from the Secret Service approached and asked, "May I help you, sir?"

"Yes, I am Doctor Livingston, and I have an appointment with President Mooketsi."

"Please follow me," the man said, walking Rodin over to the guest table. Behind a large wooden table, an attractive woman held up a pen and asked, "Would you please sign the register? What is in the bag, please?"

Rodin signed the register, *Dr. Livingston MD IP*. He handed her back the pens and said, "It is my medical bag; I carry it everywhere. Would you care to examine it?"

"If you don't mind, please," She asked.

Rodin handed her the bag open.

As she went through it, she asked, "And what kind of doctor are you?"

"I am a GP, General Practitioner. What we call in the States as a family doctor."

Rodin could tell by how she examined the bag and the questions she asked that she was more than a receptionist; she was secret service, too.

"Where in America are you from?"

"I have my practice in Gulfport, Mississippi. But I am originally from Kansas City. Have you ever been to America?"

"Sadly, no. Maybe someday," She returned the bag to Rodin, smiled, and said to the secret service man standing by the desk if needed, "Please escort Doctor Livingston to the study. Doctor, it was very nice meeting you; I hope you enjoy your visit with President Mooketsi."

"Thank you, Miss?"

"Thato. Miss Thato."

"Thank you, Miss Thato, it has been my pleasure."

They left the reception area and walked into a room that resembled a library. A tripod with a camera and lights was set up opposite a wall of books where the photo op would take place.

Rodin's escort pointed to a sofa near the camera setup and said, "Please, have a seat; the President will be with you shortly." He then left the room.

There was a mirror on the other side of the room. Rodin assumed it was a two-way mirror, and for the guests, it was there so they could check themselves out to make sure they looked their best for the photo shoot.

He stood up, walked over to the mirror, straightened his bow tie, and ensured his glasses were squarely on. He stood there looking at himself, half believing that it was actually him.

Isala did such a fantastic makeup job, including the wig, beard, blue contact lenses, lifts in the shoes, and super glue on his fingers so there would be no fingerprints.

Once he had made sure he looked suitable for the photo, he glanced at his watch and returned to the sofa to sit and wait.

"Doctor Livingston, I am so glad to meet you, sir," President Mooketsi said as he entered the room with another man, Rodin presumed to be the photographer.

Rodin rose from the sofa and greeted President Mooketsi, "The pleasure is all mine, Mister President."

"Shall we have our picture taken, Doctor?"

"That would be an honor, sir."

"Doctor Livingston, may I introduce Jonathan Cuneo, my personal photographer."

"Hello."

"Good evening, Doctor. Shall I get you in position?"

The photographer positioned Rodin and the President onto the marks he had placed on the floor months ago. The lights didn't need adjusting, but people feel he gives them that personal touch that makes the difference.

Five minutes and ten flashes later, Cuneo said, "I think you're both going to be very happy with these; I shall have prints for you by the time you finish with dinner. Gentleman, it's been a pleasure."

Cuneo had it down to a science; it was as if someone went to the drug store and hit 'print' on the photo machine. The man's biggest challenge was ensuring everyone's eyes were open.

President Mooketsi and Rodin went next door into the dining room. There were two place settings at opposite ends of a twenty-foot mahogany dinner table. Rodin saw that the plates and even the silverware were all made of gold, and placed in the center of the table was a large candelabra made of solid gold as well.

Mooketsi indicated to Rodin at which end of the table he was to sit. Mooketsi sat at the end of the table that didn't have a door behind him. It was well known that he had a phobia that someone would come through a door and kill him from behind. So, he never would sit in any room where there was a door in back of him. If he traveled to meet with heads of state, his men would check out the floor plan and seating arrangements before his arrival.

President Mooketsi sat down, picked up a small golden bell, and rang it. Moments later, two elderly women dressed in black maid costumes with white aprons walked in carrying a bowl of Phane and placed the bowls in front of each.

Phane is Mopane worms that are a staple part of the diet in rural areas and are considered a delicacy in the cities. They can be eaten dry, crunchy like potato chips, or like they were served, cooked, and drenched in sauce.

"I hope you are adventurous with exploring new culinary experiences, Doctor Livingston. These are Mopane worms, a true Botswana delicacy," Mooketsi said.

"They look delicious," Rodin said as he took a bite.

The president watched to see his guest's reaction. Rodin ate the first bite and then took several others before speaking, "Mmmm, very delicious."

"I am so glad that you like them."

The fact is that Rodin, over his career as an eco-warrior, had eaten things most people would never consider eating, like rats, centipedes, roaches, snakes, fruit bat soup, raw tarantulas, white ant eggs, witchetty grubs, and tuna eyeballs, to name just a few. So, a cooked bowl of Mopane worms was tame.

The main course was a dish of Mogodu, the intestines and selected parts of a goat cooked with a pig's foot, along with some tswii and ditloo, served with a side of matemekwane dumplings.

They finished the meal with a platter of Koeksisters, fried dough braided together and drenched in honey.

Few words were spoken over dinner; Mooketsi said early on that he prefers very little conversation during dinner; he believes that it's better for digestion.

After they finished dessert, President Mooketsi stood up and gestured for Rodin to follow him, which he did. They walked down a long corridor to his office. Inside, the walls were covered with the heads of trophies: zebra, kudu, warthog, and lion. In the center of them all was the head of an elephant. On the floors were several animal skin rugs. Behind Mooketsi's massive oak desk was a ledge with sixteen elephant footstools from elephants that he bragged about killing.

Across from his desk at the other end of the office was a large display table with an architectural 3d model of a golf course with a clubhouse and an apartment complex.

"Please have a seat, Doctor Livingston. Would you care for some cognac?"

"Yes, that would be nice."

Mooketsi walked over to a credenza where a sterling platinum and 24-carat gold bottle covered in over 6,000 diamonds sat amongst six crystal glasses. He picked up the bottle and poured a finger's worth into each glass.

As he carried the precious brandy to his guest, he boasted, "This is one of the rarest cognacs in the world; it is Henri IV. It's aged for over 100 years. It is named to pay homage to King Henri IV, but the bottle itself is the only thing rarer than the cognac. It costs 2 million US Dollars."

"Where does one purchase such a rare item?" Rodin asked.

"I honestly don't know, Doctor; it was a gift from a dear friend. Would you like to be my friend, Doctor?"

"Yes, I would like very much to be your friend."

"A special friend?"

"A very special friend, Mr. President."

"Excellent. Now, what can I do for you? Are you interested in obtaining a special hunting license for big game?" Mooketsi asked.

"Yes, I'm interested in hunting big game."

"Well, I think I can arrange that, but you didn't need to meet with me to get what you're looking for. You could have met with my secretary; the price would have been far less. Why did you feel that you had to meet with me?"

"But then I couldn't become your special friend," Rodin said as he picked up his medical bag and placed it in his lap.

Mooketsi held up his glass of brandy and said, "Cheers."

Rodin held up his glass to toast Mooketsi, "Here's to the beginning of a very special friendship."

The President walked over and sat down at his desk.

"And what special gift do you have for me, Doctor Livingston?" Mooketsi asked.

Rodin reached inside his bag and pulled out a yellow piece of canvas tied with a bright purple ribbon from the false bottom of the medical case. He leaned forward from his seat, placed the small package onto Mooketsi's desk, and slid it towards the man seated across from him.

Rodin then sipped the Henri IV cognac, "Mmmm, now that is special."

Mooketsi also took a sip while gazing at the unusual tribute placed before him.

"I must admit that I am intrigued by this curious little offering lying before me, Doctor." He said as he took another sip of brandy.

The President sat there looking at the small parcel, thinking of all the possibilities. No one had ever given him such an interesting gift; usually, it was something like a bag of cash, a large check, or the keys to a Ferrari 488 Spider.

He reached out and picked up the small bundle, pulled on the purple ribbon bow, gently removed it from the folded yellow canvas, placed the ribbon neatly on his desktop, and then began to unfold the yellow sailcloth.

As he began to unfold it, he noticed some black embroidery. He wondered if it might be a message, so he quickened his pace until the whole ensign was revealed. The yellow banner was emblazoned with the symbol of a skull with crossed monkey wrenches.

He smiled at Rodin and asked, "Are you presenting me with a yacht?"

"Not quite. Have you ever heard of an organization called Le Gang de la Clé de Singe, President Mooketsi?" Rodin said as he produced a Glock 9mm handgun with a silencer attached. "Please keep your hands flat on the desktop."

"What is this about?" President Mooketsi asked as he did as he was told, placing his hands flat on his desktop.

"You'll never get away with this; my men will be crashing through that door any minute. So even if you kill me, you'll never get out of here alive."

"Yeah, I don't think anyone will be crashing through that door, but we'll see."

"What is this all about?"

"Well, Mr. President, it's about a lot of things; for one, it's about those sixteen elephant footstools that lined up behind you. It's about selling wildlife game reserve land to the Chinese so they can build that golf course complex you got sitting over there. And finally, it's about your taking a giant leap backward in animal conservation, removing the ban on elephant hunting and selling tens of hundreds of hunting licenses.

"You see, we feel that your VP will serve the people of this nation far better than you and your greedy, self-serving cabinet ever did. You never cared about the people or the wildlife, just what you and your cronies can get for yourselves."

"If that's true, and I'm so evil, why did I win the election?"

"Well, as one of the Presidents of the United States once proclaimed, he loved the uneducated. They're easily manipulated, deceived, and fooled, which is what you count on. You pulled the old bait and switch, and it worked."

Rodin saw on the wall to his left a native shield covered in zebra skin with an authentic spear and a *tiokoa*, a native battle axe crossed underneath.

Rodin looked at President Mooketsi and said, "Say, would you mind rolling up your pant legs?"

☠ ☠ ☠ ☠ ☠ ☠ ☠ ☠ ☠ ☠ ☠

Buzz and the Doc had been preparing for a possible attack from pirates reported operating in and around the Fiji islands for three days. They felt that the odds were pretty good that these thugs would eventually try invading their island since it was privately owned and not heavily occupied. It would seem easy pickings.

The Doc and Buzz had noticed an old Tartan 3500 sloop; she appeared to be about a 35-footer and looked pretty shabby. It had been sailing offshore for the last two days; Buzz and the Doc had gone into stealth mode, not showing themselves during the day and with no lights at night. They felt they would be attacked under cover of night, so they took turns getting some sleep during the day to be alert when the pirates came ashore.

It was shortly before 3 am when the Doc saw the skiff with four men landing at the dock next to the SMJ. Unknown to the pirates, Buzz had Buster locked inside, down below in the cabin. Rodin had trained Buster to remain silent and only attack on command. Buzz had set up an intercom and a couple of GoPro cameras on the main mast pointing down so they could see if anyone boarded the yacht. There were two inside the cabin with a monitor in the guesthouse where they stayed so he could give the attack command if needed.

One man headed towards the Sweet Mary Jane, while the other three headed to the main house. Buzz could see that they were each carrying what looked to be AK-47s.

From the guesthouse window, Buzz aimed the M40A5 sniper rifle with a suppressor at the man out in front, the one wearing a baseball cap, and fired one shot. *Puff* was the only sound. The impact of the bullet hitting the man in the shoulder spun him entirely around and forced him to drop his weapon and collapse onto the ground.

"Where the Hell did that come from?" The man with dreadlock shouted out as he and the bald man behind him started to run toward the main house, firing indiscriminately in all directions.

The Doc opened fire with the BAR while Buzz had switched from the sniper rifle to an AK-47, pinning the two pirates down behind a small Flame tree.

"Save your ammo, babe," Buzz whispered to the Doc.

"How's Buster doing?" She asked.

Once the firefight started, the pirate who was going to break into the Sweet Mary Jane dropped to the deck. Buzz could see that Buster was poised to attack anyone foolish enough to try to break in.

When the shooting stopped, the thief figured his compadres had everything under control, so he took a crowbar that he had brought with him and broke the lock on the cabin door.

Buzz could see from the mast-cam that the pirate broke the lock on the cabin door and was preparing to enter the cabin. He pressed the intercom button, "Buster, attention!"

Attention was the order to get ready to attack. Buster had positioned himself off to the right of the passageway when one was entering from above. He wouldn't be readily seen as he would be hidden from sight. The man turned on his LED headlight headband as he entered the main cabin and held his AR-15 at the ready. Unfortunately, the stairway was too narrow for him to swing the rifle from side to side.

When Buzz pressed the intercom button and shouted, "Attack! Attack! Attack!" The pirate, along with Buster, heard the command and confused the man long enough for Buster to pounce, knocking the man down and causing him to drop his weapon.

Buster was relentless; the harder the man fought, the more vicious Buster attacked, eventually ripping the man's femoral artery in his leg, causing the man to bleed out, screaming in pain.

His two cohorts, who were still pinned down, could hear his screams as he was being attacked. Buzz shouted into the intercom, “Buster. At ease! At Ease!” Buster stopped, backed up, facing his victim, and sat and waited for further instructions.

The two pirates decided to try to make a run for it back to their ship. As they started to fire at the guesthouse to try to give themselves some cover, Buzz and the Doc were ready. As soon as they saw the men starting to make a break from behind the Flame tree, they opened fire.

The two men didn’t make it ten feet before they were brought down in a hail of bullets, killing the man with dreadlocks and fatally wounding the bald man.

Before exiting the guesthouse, Buzz ordered Buster to “come.” Buster bounded up the stairway and made his way to the guesthouse, where Buzz and the Doc were waiting for him. By the time Buster reached them, they both had reloaded their weapons and proceeded down to where the pirates lay dead and dying.

“Doc, why don’t you go call the police? I’ll stay here.”

When the Fijian police arrived, it was almost seven, and one of the policemen described the scene as something out of a Hollywood blockbuster.

Buzz and the Doc recounted the events of the attack. The police searched the pirate’s boat and discovered the property of several of the victims that they had robbed. The police told them that no legal action would be taken against them and, in fact, they probably would receive the President’s Cross for bravery.

When a reporter from the Fiji Sun asked Buzz for a comment, Buzz said, “Far out, man. Far fucking out.”

☠☠☠☠☠☠☠☠☠☠☠

Isala had launched the drone at 10:15 p.m., destination, State House Gaborone. Once it is within two miles, she would take the controls and land it onto the clay court.

The Ehang 184 drone is a silent autonomous aerial vehicle. Basically, it's a drone that's large enough to fit a human passenger. A computer navigates it without the need for any human control. Isala pre-programmed it to fly from the Walterzen Filling Station outside of Supingstad to President Mooketsi's State House.

The Ehang 184 resembled the basic shape of a 'Smart Car,' except it did not have wheels; instead, it had skids as landing gear and no internal combustion engine.

The Ehang is a quad copter. Unlike most other multirotor drones, the 184 mounts its rotor arms from the four corners of the vehicle; it has eight propellers on the four arms. It runs on a 2.6 lithium battery that gives it a 30-minute flight distance of approximately 25 miles, but Rodin modified the power units to be augmented with self-recharging solar batteries that give the 184 a flight range of over two hundred miles.

At exactly 11:35, Rodin left the State House using the rear door of the President's office and made his way to the tennis courts, where the Ehang 184 drone was waiting for him.

Rodin climbed into the cockpit, put on the wireless headset, buckled up the 5-piece safety harness, and switched on the rotors via the iPad instrument control panel digital display screen. He grabbed the stick and rudder and eased the stick towards him. The silent aircraft ascended. He was over South Africa's airspace in under fifteen minutes.

At 11:40 on schedule, there was a major car crash into the State House, causing all the security staff to direct their attention to the accident just outside the front gates. No one was seriously injured. But an ambulance was called, and three people were sent to the Princess Marina Hospital for minor cuts, scratches, and contusions.

President Mooketsi's body was found the following day at 5:45 a.m. by one of the cleaning staff. The police were called, as well as two inspectors from Interpol, Inspectors Morris and Volker from the London office, who arrived later that day.

Interpol was called in because it was a crime perpetrated by Le Gang de la Clé de Singe. When Inspectors Morris and Volker arrived at the crime scene, they knew immediately that it was the handy work of the assassin known as Rodin.

"What can you tell us?" Asked Morris of Chief Detective Ncube.

"President Mooketsi was shot once in the head, slightly above the right eye, with what looks to be a 9mm, and then his body was mutilated, as you can see."

Detective Ncube pointed to the ledge behind Mooketsi's desk where the elephant footstools were lined up. Next to the last footstool were two human feet that had been fitted into tiny stools. President Mooketsi's feet were chopped off with the tiokoa, the native battle-axe, then turned into what looked to be foot stools resembling the ones of the elephants.

There was the traditional yellow ensign placed around his neck and a note in his pocket which read:

"Let it be known that, from this day forth, Le Gang de la Clé de Singe declares a proclamation of war against all Poachers, Big Game Hunters, all Big Game Safari Outfits, as well as anybody anywhere in the world that targets, kills, profits, and/or supports the killing of any animals that are endangered or any animals that are hunted for sport. Be forewarned: do so at your own peril. You will be hunted down and pay with your lives. Be it man or woman, there will be no exceptions and no mercy; we will show no quarter.

"This now applies to any heads of state that feel that they are above reproach and the law; you are not! This especially applies to all nations, not exclusively to African nations.

"Presidents and Prime Ministers, you have been warned."

Inspector Volker looked at Morris and said, "It's a declaration of war."

Morris nodded in agreement. He turned to Detective Ncube and asked, "Did you find any fingerprints?"

"Only one that couldn't be accounted for."

"And?"

"It is that of Doctor Livingston, the 19th-century Scottish physician."

"Are you sure?"

"Interpol confirmed it. And there's a Doctor Livingston who signed the register last night."

"May I see it?"

A police officer brought the register book to Inspector Morris, who looked at it and smiled, "Yeah, it's the work of Rodin, all right; see, he signed it Doctor Livingston MD IP."

"IP? Ncube asked

"IP, for I presume."

☠☠☠☠☠☠☠☠☠☠☠

Rodin touched down at the Walterzen Filling Station at 12:58 a.m. Isala and their local contact, Roger Badenhorst, were waiting for him.

"How did it go?" Roger asked.

"Mission accomplished. And is everything good on this end?"

"I have everything all set for you and the Misses. I've given Isala all the instructions and passports with all the proper documents that you'll need."

Isala gave Rodin a big kiss and a hug, then whispered, "Did it all go as planned?"

"Couldn't have gone better, babe."

"Sir, here's the key to your car, and you're all checked in at the Radisson Blu Hotel Waterfront. Good luck."

"Thanks. Roger, we appreciate all your help. Take care now, bye."

As Rodin and Isala approached the BMW X7, Rodin asked, "Do you Feel up to driving? I'm knackered."

"You bet I'm fresh as a daisy."

"Great. Baby, you're the best."

"Do you know how lucky you are?"

"I'm the luckiest boy in the world."

"That's right, and don't you forget it."

☠☠☠☠☠☠☠☠☠☠☠

Inspector Morris and Volker met with the newly sworn-in President, Goitsemedi Tebogo, to go over their findings as to the assassination of President Mooketsi.

"Well, we're pretty sure we know who the killer is, Mr. President. He's an assassin with Le Gang de la Clé de Singe, who goes by the name Rodin." Inspector Morris said.

"Rodin, like the sculptor?" President Tebogo asked.

"Yes sir, He is a master assassin and of disguise. We've never had a credible photograph of him until last night when he had his picture taken with President Mooketsi."

"But surely he was wearing a disguise last night."

"Undoubtedly, but now we can have the boys in the imaging department try and break down the layers of deception and see what they can come up with."

"We'll find him, Mr. President," Volker confidently stated.

☠☠☠☠☠☠☠☠☠☠☠

"Wooch, go."

"Hey, Commander, it's Rodin."

"Footstools! Really?"

"Hey, I thought it was a nice touch."

"How's everyone taking it?"

"You've really kicked the Hornet's nest this time."

"You gonna be okay?"

"We'll weather the storm. This one's really got people talking."

"Well, talking's a good thing, right?"

"Right."

"What's the buzz?"

"Well, the battle lines are being drawn between the right and the left, the conservatives and the liberals, big business and eco-warriors. It looks like war."

"I'm sorry."

"Hey, we all knew it would eventually come to this. We're ready for whatever comes."

"I just want to say that it's been an honor to have worked with you, Wooch."

"The honor's been mine; you were one of the greats. Now what?"

"Now, Isala and I are gone. We're done. Mooketsi was my last hit. We're going to…'

"No, don't tell me. Just know that if you ever need me, you know how to reach me. God bless."

"Vaya Con Dios."

☠☠☠☠☠☠☠☠☠☠☠

Virgin Australia flight 4747 landed on time at Nadi International Airport, Fiji. Buzz, the Doc, and Buster were waiting at the customs exit to greet Rodin and Isala when they came through the electronic doors.

Buster broke free from Buzz and jumped up on Rodin, nearly knocking him down. It was a ten-minute love fest between man and man's best friend. Once Rodin was able to get Buster under control, they got into a taxi van and headed to where the Sweet Mary Jane was docked.

The taxi ride was a short fifteen-minute ride to Buzz Murdoch's Royal Bait & Tackle Shop and Yacht Club.

"Buzz, are you joking with me? What the fuck is this?"

"It's a long story; I'll tell you all about it on the trip home."

"As they were making their way to the SMJ, Sir Robert Ackley passed by, "Good afternoon, Commodore."

"Afternoon, Robby baby."

"Commodore!" Rodin laughed.

"Oh yeah, man. Hey, did I mention I got a medal?"

"A medal!"

Part Two

If humans killed each other at the same rate
that we kill animals,
humans would be extinct in 17 days.

Iceman

The Diary of an Eco-Warrior

They call me Iceman. I am a team leader with Le Gang de la Clé de Singe, the French eco-terrorist group whose mission is to rage war against all Poachers, Big Game Hunters, all Big Game Safari Outfits, as well as anybody anywhere in the world that targets, kills, profits, and/or supports the killing of any animals that are endangered or any animals that are hunted for sport.

We have been labeled pirates, marauders, outlaws, killers, murderers, and assassins. All of which is true; we hunt down and exact a life for a life. If you are guilty, you will pay with your life, be it a man or woman; there are no exceptions, no mercy. We show no quarter; each of us is willing to lay down our lives to protect and avenge these creatures.

We owe no allegiance to any government, corporation, or organization. Our loyalty is only to any and all creatures that are exploited. It doesn't matter if they live on land, in the sea, or in the air; our mission is to be the guardians of Nature.

I have the honor of commanding a group of dedicated eco-warriors called the Red Team. Every man and woman is committed to protecting wildlife and reaping retribution on those responsible for the death and destruction of Animalia.

I have decided to chronicle our missions and exploits for posterity. Be forewarned that the events I shall recount here are truthful, accurate, and potentially graphically violent.

Iceman

The Republic of the Congo – January 5th

There have been multiple recent postings on Facebook of a mother, Marissa Kimball, and her twelve-year-old daughter hunting big game in Odzal-Kokoua National Park.

The latest report stated that they were last seen in Kellé, located in a district in the Cuvette-Ouest Region of the Western Republic of the Congo, on the edge of Odzal-Kokoua National Park.

We had a contact, Serge Kombo, who is loyal to our cause, report that a local guide, Mamadou Ohakim, would be taking Mrs. Kimball and her daughter along the Lekona River to hunt for elephants.

The Red Team and I have been shadowing a small herd of elephants, made up primarily of cows, juveniles, and two young calves. We originally rendezvoused in the town of Etoumbi, 67 kilometers from Kellé, where Serge acquired and procured our weapons and all our gear needed for the mission. Since we travel separately under false passports and papers, we rely on local supporters and sympathizers to help acquire the items we require.

Serge is a local safari guide who only works for outfits that provide photo and tourist safaris. He won't guide for hunting safaris, even though the pay for hunting safaris is more lucrative. Big game hunting safaris can charge up to $25 thousand U.S. Dollars per person for an elephant hunt. At the turn of the 20th century, there were about 10 million elephants in Africa. Today, there are a little over 430,000. It's estimated that 100 elephants are killed by poachers every day, and on average, 1200 are killed by big game hunters; that's over 36,000 elephants killed a year, and for what?

The Republic of the Congo – January 8th

We have continued to monitor the small herd for the past two days. There are no signs of poachers or Mrs. Kimball and her daughter.

Today, like most days, I have LuWei, my number one drone operator, send up our Ehang Falcon B drone to be our eye in the sky. Not only do we use it to look for poachers and big game hunters, but we also use it to keep track of park rangers and army patrols.

It was early afternoon when Lu Wei spotted what looked to be a Toyota pickup truck with several people sitting in the truck bed with AK-47s. They had just peeled off of Highway P40.

We were already in our Ghillie suits positioned around the grazing herd when I heard on my earpiece, "Red Leader, this is Red Flyer, over."

"Red Leader over."

"I've spotted a red pickup truck headed your way from your left. It looks to be bogies. Over."

"Roger that, Red Flyer."

I then contacted my team and gave them a heads-up.

"Red Leader to Red Team, possible bogies incoming from 10 o'clock; stay sharp."

I received acknowledgments from the entire team.

Today, each member of my team is equipped with an M40A5 sniper rifle, with the exception of Odin, my second in command, who is equipped with a Browning Automatic Rifle (BAR).

We heard the occupants of the truck before we made visual contact. They were firing their rifles into the air in hopes of scattering the herd so they could isolate their target.

I gave Odin the order to open fire on the truck, concentrating on the tires, to disable their vehicle. He fired off a short burst and blew out the front right tire, causing the truck's front end to drop significantly. It forced it to bog down into the sand and come to a complete stop. As the men jumped down from the truck bed and the occupants from the cab, I gave the order to open fire.

Within minutes, it was over, and seven poachers lay dead. I sent Odin and Vulcan out to make sure all bogies were down.

"Red Leader, this is Red 2, all clear."

I gave the signal for the team to advance. When we got to the truck, we found a half dozen elephant tusks that appeared to be freshly extracted, which meant that at least three elephants had been killed.

We proceeded to lay the poachers side-by-side, placing our calling card around each of their necks, a yellow canvas flag with a black skull, and crossed monkey wrenches.

Each poacher had a letter describing their crime placed inside each of his pockets.

Le Gang de la Clé de Singe has declared a proclamation of war against all Poachers, Big Game Hunters, all Big Game Safari Outfits, as well as anybody anywhere in the world that targets, kills, profits, and/or supports the killing of any animals that are endangered or any animals that are hunted for sport. Be forewarned: do so at your own peril. You will be hunted down and pay with your lives. Be it man or woman, there will be no exceptions and no mercy; we will show no quarter. You have been warned.

These men were found guilty of the poaching of elephants and have been sentenced to die.

As we finished this ritual, the small elephant herd meandered off. I radioed Lu Wei, who located them so that we could reconnect with them.

Once we were a safe distance from the poacher's bodies, Lu Wei radioed the park rangers and gave them their position. We left the poached ivory in the truck bed as evidence.

Today was a mix of sadness and joy. We saved many elephants' lives, but we found that the poachers had already killed three of these magnificent creatures.

The Republic of the Congo – January 9th

Heavy rains today curtailed any encounters with big game hunters or poachers. Few venture out on days like today, which is good for the elephants.

The Republic of the Congo – January 10th

It rained again today, and it looks like it might clear out by morning. We took the downtime to review our gear and service our weapons. After two days of heavy rain, tomorrow will be a slog, but spirits are high.

The Republic of the Congo – January 11th

This morning, after periods of intermittent rain, we were greeted by a glorious rainbow, and after a quick breakfast, we suited up and headed out. Lu Wei sent up the drone and has spotted what he believes is our big game safari is in route to engage with our elephant herd.

We reached the herd and took our positions. We deployed a central ambush team and two outlying flanking ambush teams on either side.

According to Red Flyer, the hunting group consisted of four people: the guide Mamadou Ohakim, the driver, Mrs. Kimball, and her daughter. The rest of the safari company, cooks, wait staff, etc., were still back at their base camp.

Mrs. Marissa Kimball and her daughter Jeanette come from a long line of big game hunters stretching back four generations. The Kimballs hail from Winnetka, an affluent suburb north of Chicago. They are old money. Theodore Kimball amassed the family fortune by building and selling large press machines that were originally designed for stamping out automotive frames and fenders for Henry Ford. Today, Kimball presses are used in farming equipment, airline, and industrial manufacturing worldwide.

This isn't Mrs. Marissa Kimball's first solo hunting expedition with her daughter; they have been hunting as a mother-daughter team since Jeanette was eight when she killed her first warthog.

This morning, as the team was in position, waiting for the Kimball hunting party to arrive, we heard a shot ring out and saw one of the mother cows fall down dead. Immediately, the rest of the herd surrounded her to try and assist her while the mother's calf was crying out, but to no avail.

Apparently, Mamadou, the guide, switched their course at the last minute, and we weren't notified in time to adjust. I gave the command to advance, and the entire Red Team, all ten of us, rose from our positions and started to move in.

I gave Fu Hao, our top sniper, the green light to take out the guide, Mamadou. She stood absolutely still, using her partner, Sue-B's shoulder, to steady her rifle. There was a soft puff sound from the silencer on her M40A5, and a split second later, Mamadou Ohakim's head emitted a spray of red mist as the .308 caliber bullet passed through his brain, removing a large chunk of his cranium.

Mrs. Kimball and her daughter were so delighted over the killing of the elephant that they didn't notice their guide was dead, as he was talking a few feet behind them. It wasn't until their driver sitting in the Jeep started screaming that she turned around and saw Mamadou's body lying on the ground.

Jeanette was the first to see people wearing what looked to be plant- and foliage-type suits coming towards them.

"Mummy, there are people dressed as scrubs coming!" She shouted.

I was the first to reach them. They looked dazed, confused, and frightened. The daughter was clinging to her mother, crying.

"Who are you?" Mrs. Kimball asked.

"Le Gang de la Clé de Singe, you have heard of us?"

Mrs. Kimball stiffened up and defiantly said, "I have. How dare you kill my guide, Mamadou. What is it you want?"

"Mrs. Kimball, if you've heard of us, then you know what we want."

"Well, you surely wouldn't kill a mother in front of her child!"

"Just like you wouldn't kill the mother of that one-year-old elephant calf," I said, pointing to the baby calf mourning its dead mother not a hundred yards away.

"But my daughter."

"We don't exact revenge on children, Mrs. Kimball."

I signaled for Sue-B and Fu Hao to take the daughter to the Jeep. She was hysterical, crying for her mother, just as the infant elephant was crying for its mother.

I looked at Mrs. Kimball and said, "Mrs. Kimball, it would be best if your daughter leaves now."

Mrs. Kimball took her daughter by the arm and walked her to the Jeep. She placed her inside, kissed her, and told the driver to get her away from here.

Once the Jeep was out of sight, I removed my pistol and shot Mrs. Kimball once in the head. I then placed the yellow standard around the necks of Mamadou and Mrs. Kimball and the declaration of guilt by Le Gang de la Clé de Singe in her blouse pocket.

I know many of you who are reading this will find our methods to be barbaric and cruel. To that, I say we humans have become so arrogant to believe that we are the only creatures who express emotions. Elephants express sadness, joy, love, jealousy, grief, compassion, and even distress like many other animals. We will think nothing of killing a parent of a species next to its offspring and feel no remorse or sympathy because we believe they feel no emotion and they are inferior to us humans.

Well, the members of Le Gang de la Clé de Singe do not. Each of us has committed our lives to protect these creatures from a useless and wasteful death at the hands of predominantly wealthy, white, narcissistic, self-absorbed assholes. I have come to terms with and am willing to die for what I believe; the question you have to ask yourself is, are you?

After we policed the area so as not to leave any trace of our presence, I radioed Lu Wei and had him call the location of the dead elephant and the bodies of Mrs. Kimball and her guide to the authorities.

By the time we got back to our base camp, Lu Wei and Gianfranco had all our gear loaded onto our two Toyota Land Cruisers, and we headed off to the west, to Gabon.

"Good evening, I'm Nigel Williams, and this is the BBC World Headline News. Our top story this hour comes from the Republic of the Congo, where the bodies of seven known poachers were found shot to death. The eco-terrorist group known as Le Gang de la Clé de Singe has claimed responsibility.

"The men were found with yellow flags bearing the skull and crossed wrenches around each of their necks, along with a letter of declaration of their crimes and guilt.

"Le Gang de la Clé de Singe has also claimed responsibility for the death of wealthy American huntress Mrs. Marissa Kimball and her guide Mamadou Ohakim who were murdered after Mrs. Kimball shot and killed an elephant, according to Jeanette Kimball, Mrs. Kimball's teenage daughter.

"We are told that Interpol has sent a team of inspectors to help. Worldwide commendation is pouring in as many..."

The Republic of the Congo – January 12th

Today is a twelve-hour travel day; the two vehicles travel separately to avoid suspicion. The majority of travel is on dusty dirt roads. Both our vehicles will have drone support to avoid any police or army roadblocks. We are going to Koulamoutou in the coastal country of Gabon, where we will rest and meet with our local contact, Doukas Mbanangoye, a member of the EcoGuard, the Gagonese equivalent of Park Rangers.

It takes about 16 hours to drive from Koulamoutou to our final destination, Loango National Park. Recently, Loango has become known as the "land of the surfing hippos. "

Gabon – January 13th

There was compelling evidence that Boko Haram, an Islamic jihadist terrorist group, was getting funding from ivory poachers in Gabon.

Our job wasn't to do battle against Boko Haram but to go up against and stop the poachers that kill, on average, twelve forest elephants every single day; that's about 5,000 a year. The penalty for the killing of an elephant is five to ten years in prison and five to ten million Central African Francs. We're going to up the ante in the penalty department in Gabon.

Doukas Mbanangoye, our local contact, has been telling us that the rural Gabonese people are either terrified, hated, or go hungry due to elephants eating their crops, so don't expect a lot of support.

Poachers have been entering Gabon from 15 different countries, such as Cameroon and Chad. They'll spend several weeks in the jungle hunting elephants, whose tusks they hack off with axes or chainsaws and then leave. Poachers have killed 80% of Gabon's forest elephants, over 25,000 between 2004 and 2014.

After hearing the depressing news from Doukas, our 16-hour drive to Loango National Park was very subdued and reflective.

Reports in the field indicated that the opposition might be more significant than originally thought, so Iceman had requisitioned some heavy-duty backup. A French Aerospatiale C.22 drone, equipped with two Hero, four Black GoPro cameras, and two Aster missiles in the event that any shit hits the fan. The C.22 could stay up for twelve hours and even has night vision capabilities. Lu Wei had used the C.22 with deadly precision in past expeditions.

Because we are always looking for the element of surprise on this expedition, we will use six Textron Prowler EV IS utility task vehicles. They are electric, silent-running, four-wheel drive all-terrain vehicles with a max speed of 25 miles per hour and a charge time of 12 hours. These help us avoid continually worrying about recharging the batteries, and we have incorporated a KERS system into the engine. KERS stands for kinetic energy recovery system, which is an automotive system that stores recovered energy in a reservoir that is transferred to recharge our batteries. Additionally, each vehicle has been customized with extra heavy-duty framing, special bulletproof Michelin all-terrain tires, and a top-mounted M60E6 machine gun.

We plan to rendezvous in Gamba, a small town on the southern bay of the Ndogo Lagoon, with Doctor Khadija Dabany, the head of the Gabon branch of Le Gang de la Clé de Singe. She is a thirty-two-year-old activist with a Ph.D. in environmental science and works for l'Environnement et de la Protection de la Nature in Gabon's capital, Libreville.

There, she will supply us with all the necessary documents and visas and help us obtain all the extra equipment mentioned above that is needed to carry out our mission.

Of course, if anything goes terribly wrong, such as if one or more of us are either killed or captured, we are totally on our own, and they will disavow any knowledge of our mission and us.

Gamba, Gabon – January 14th

The Laguna Guest House is the place to stay when traveling to Gamba, and by that, I mean it's the only place to stay in Gamba. It sits on Ndogo Lagoon with a nice view of the lagoon. The rooms are sparse but clean, and there is a small restaurant/bar hosted by a gentleman named Jélly Yembité, who, if rumors are to be believed, is one hundred and four years old but acts like a teenager, hitting on the ladies.

We spend all day going over tactics and strategies, trying to plan for every contingency we can think of, knowing that when we're in the thick of it, we'll have to adjust and adapt.

We will load up our gear tomorrow and start the trek up north. There have been reports that a large group of poachers is heading south, having entered illegally from Equatorial Guinea.

Lu Wei will launch the Aerospatiale drone an hour before we head out. If all goes as planned, we shall be in position by nightfall.

Loango National Park – January 15th

We say goodbye to Doctor Khadija Dabany, thanking her for all of her assistance as she heads back to Libreville.

Our caravan of six Prowler EVs has made exceptional time. We have avoided several encounters with park ranger patrols thanks to Lu Wei and the Aerospatiale drone.

Lu Wei has also picked up the group of poachers entering the boundaries of Loango National Park. They appear to be traveling in two groups, each consisting of two Toyota 4Runner 4X4 pickup trucks traveling about five miles apart.

Each truck appears to have four men riding in the bed of the truck; the trucks look to have been fitted with a roll bar and a mounted M240B machine gun, the machine gun of choice for terrorists around the world.

Late in the afternoon, we pick up a large herd of elephants, flank them on both sides and travel with them until sunset, when we decide to make camp.

Lu Wei has developed a line of micro air vehicles, better known as MAVs, tiny flying objects intended to go where humans and other types of equipment cannot. They have the appearance and are the size of a mosquito. Still, they are capable of gathering intelligence through the surreptitious use of tiny cameras, microphones, and various other types of sensors.

They can deploy individually or as a "swarm weapon" sent out by the tens of thousands. The tiny insect drones can deliver a small injection of medicine or, to be more sinister, a disease. Lu Wei has also developed a drone that mimics birds and other insects, such as beetles and bumble bees.

Doukas sat with Lu Wei and translated what the Cameroonian poachers were talking about. We learned that they were planning to attack the elephant herd late morning and take the ivory south to the fishing village of Petit Loango on the coast and rendezvous with a small fishing trawler to transfer their spoils for shipment north to Cameroon.

Loango National Park – January 16th, 4 a.m.

The Red Team got up before dawn and made our way toward the herd; we positioned ourselves into a "Dual-linear" ambush offensive.

The "Dual-Linear" ambush is a modified broadside ambushing technique. Looking down from above, we deploy six two-man teams. The first three will be positioned on the right side of the path the enemy will travel on. Further down the path, we will position the other three teams on the left side of the path.

We will allow the enemy to pass the first ambush teams on the right; the second teams on the left wait until the enemy enters their field of fire and then opens up on them.

The ambushed opposition will usually try to fall back. While they are falling back and trying to fire on the primary ambushing team, the secondary ambush team on the right waits until the enemy arrives in their fire zone. They then open up and finish them off.

It's a tried and true ambush method, but we know anything can happen in battle, so we are prepared to be flexible.

Loango National Park – January 16th

My teams are in position. We are all wearing our ghillie suits and are well hidden among the dibetou, kevazingo, and zingana trees. Lu Wei has the Aerospatiale C.22 drone up, and we are all on the radio, receiving updates.

I have designated the team on the right as the Red Team and the other as the Blue Team. My number two, Odin, is in command of the Blue Team, and I will be in charge of the Red Team.

At approximately ten a.m., Lu Wei informed us that the poachers were on the move and heading our way.

"Red Team, this is Team Leader. It looks like we're a go. Blue Team, get ready; you'll be up first," I radioed.

"Team Leader, this is Team Flyer. Red Team should be having visual contact any second, over."

"Copy that, Red Flyer. Red Team, do you copy?"

I received all affirmatives from my Red Team.

"Blue Team One, this is Team Leader you may fire when ready."

"Copy that, Team Leader," Odin responded.

The first of the two Toyota 4Runner 4X4 pickups traveling over 60 miles an hour came whizzing by us. The second 4Runner was approaching at a much slower speed.

When the first Toyota reached the Blue Team, Odin gave the order for Hazael, the team's most proficient sniper, to take out the vehicle's driver. He popped off one round, hitting the driver squarely in the right temple, killing the driver and forcing the vehicle to careen into a ditch. That flipped the 4X4 onto its side, throwing the occupants who were standing in the truck bed out onto the dirt road.

Once the men were scattered out onto the road, they landed disorientated, dazed, and discombobulated. They soon began to realize that they were smack dab in the middle of a firefight as bullets were whizzing by them.

It seems that whenever we engage in a combat situation, time slows down, and events take on a slow-motion reality even though incidents are occurring in split seconds.

As Odin and the Blue Team were engaging vehicle number one, the second Toyota started to speed up once the shooting started. Our sniper marksman Fu Hao fired, hitting the right front tire, causing the 4Runner to sharply veer to the left, sending it headfirst into a zingana tree.

The man standing with the mounted M240B machine gun in the back of the pickup started wildly opening fire in all directions. Fu Hao, by then, had time to slide another round into the chamber of her M40A5 to take aim and fire the fatal shot, hitting the machine gunner. Since Fu Hao was lying in a prone position, she was shooting at an upward angle. Her round hit the man just below the left side of his jaw, exploding, fragmentizing the entire right side of the man's head. Just as a chicken will continue to run when its head is chopped off, the machine gunner continued to fire as the force of his fatal wound swung around his body. He continued to fire for half a minute until his body collapsed into the truck bed. The remaining members of the poachers took up defensive positions on the left side of the truck.

I could have engaged in a long-standing firefight, but I decided to put a swift end to the assault.

"Team Flyer, this is Team Leader. Do you copy?"

"Team Leader, Team Flyer I copy."

"Do you have eyes on the Blue Team's bandits?"

"Affirmative, Team Leader."

"Team Flyer, take out bandits."

"Roger that, Team Leader."

Within seconds, Lu Wei fired one of the Aster missiles and guided it squarely onto the Toyota 4Runner, disintegrating the pickup and killing all of the poachers.

In all, the conflict lasted less than fifteen minutes, resulting in the deaths of thirteen known poachers and the saving of countless elephants and other animals.

As is our custom, we gathered all the dead and placed them side by side with our standard yellow flag emblazoned with the black skull and crossed monkey wrenches around each of their necks, and placing a note declaring their crime with a warning to others telling that this is the fate that awaits them on their persons.

We carefully policed the area, leaving nothing incriminating behind. Once we left the area, we informed the authorities of the location of the bodies, along with alerting the news media.

When the local police and inspectors from Interpol look for clues and evidence, they will find one clear fingerprint of someone other than that of the poachers. That is Mr. Omar Bongo, the Gabonese dictator who ruled for over 42 years until his death over nine years ago.

Inspectors Morris and Volker from the London branch of Interpol met with the Gabonese Security Forces to aid in the investigation. Unfortunately, there wasn't much they could do due to the lack of physical evidence.

Loango National Park – January 16th

We traveled through the savanna, wetlands, and forest of Loango National Parks, passing several small herds of elephants, buffalo, and hippos on our way to Guidouma, a small town on the N1 road.

There, we rendezvoused with a truck driver named Yaya Abdou-Moussini, who loaded our six Prowler EVs onto his 18-wheeler and transported them 158 miles to the ocean seaport city Port-Gentil. We drove our Toyota Land Cruisers and met him there at the Gabonese Refining Company SO.GA.RA. located on the east side of the Cape Lopez peninsula. There, we loaded all of the equipment and our vehicles onto a 180-foot Burau Veritas class cargo ship named the SS Renard that will take us to our next mission in South Africa.

The president of SO.GA.RA is what we in Le Gang de la Clé de Singe refer to as a ghost, someone who is a secret supporter of our mission. Because we are an outlaw organization, someone still believes in our cause and anonymously supports us financially and with other assistance.

Loango National Park – January 16th

We met Yaya Abdou-Moussini parked down the road from a two-pump Shell petrol station surrounded by nothing. It was a cinderblock box with a tin roof and canopy, no door, two glass windows so filthy that they appeared to be tinted, and, of course, the preverbal stray, half-starved mutt was sleeping by the outhouse.

There was a group of men sitting in front of the petrol station playing Thunee, a local card game, and drinking mass quantities of Tusker lager beer. As the teams drove by, they paid little or no attention to us. A couple of the on-looker's interests were peaked when the six Prowler EVs were loaded into the semi, but they soon lost interest. Even the fact that we were still wearing our ghillie suits and carrying our weapons hardly raised any eyebrows. Having dealt with so many military movements and involvements over the years, a few more troops traipsing around was no big deal.

Loango National Park – January 16th

The semi had been loaded and was on its way to Port-Gentil, taking Yaya all night to make the 158-mile journey. There weren't any decent paved roads to travel.

We will meet him at Mamie Watta, a small diner behind an oil depot on Cape Lopez Bay just off Route de la Sobraga. There, we had some Le Chaud Raclette Bacon breakfast sandwiches with coffee, and I always have a couple of Pain Au Chocolats. I looked forward to it.

Port-Gentil – January 17th

We sat in the parking lot overlooking the bay until Mamie Watta opened. An hour later, around 9 o'clock, Yaya Abdou-Moussini pulled up in the semi. We ate breakfast and drank coffee until eleven; our rendezvous with the cargo ship wasn't until one p.m.

We all ordered sandwiches to go. Most people ordered Le Sandwich Grainé Poulet. I ordered Le Sandwich Polka Jambon Cru and a couple of orders of Le Coeur Brioche Chocolat for the captain and crew of the Renard.

Port-Gentil, SO.GA.RA. – January 17.

When we arrived at the dock, the SS Renard was waiting for us. Captain Philippe Chevrolet greeted us at the bottom of the gangplank.

"Captain, I am Iceman, and these are the members of the Red Team. It's a pleasure to meet you, sir. We are thankful for your help."

"No, monsieur, the pleasure is all mine and my crew. I welcome you aboard the Renard; please let us know if there is anything that we may do to assist you and your team."

It took seven hours to load all the vehicles and gear aboard the Renard, and it cost eighteen hundred U.S. Dollars in duties, tariffs, taxes, and bribes to get the SS Renard loaded up and out of port.

South Atlantic Ocean – January 17th.

We're out to sea, the seas are smooth, and the ocean breeze feels heavenly. There was a slight mist in the air, making me drowsy. But there is no time for naps; I have to meet with the Captain.

"Captain Chevrolet, again, I want to thank you."

"There is no need, mon amie. We are both fighting for the same cause and please call me Philippe."

"So, Philippe, we're off to East London, South Africa. We are going to pay a little visit to one of the largest lion farms in Africa."

"Yes, I have heard of such a thing, and these people actually believe that this is sporting?"

"Sport has nothing to do with it, I'm afraid. Hunters- and I use the term loosely- are willing to pay anywhere from $17,000 to $50,000 for a male lion, depending on how 'old' and 'black-maned' the lion is."

"C'est terrible."

"I agree, these poor creatures are grown in a controlled environment. They're pampered, well fed, and when they reach the age between seven and ten years-old they parade it out into a clearing and the rich, usually white "hunter" shoots it. Sometimes, when the beast is sleeping, then he has the all-important trophy photograph taken so he can post it all over social media to boast what a great hunter he is; women do it too, standing next to the dead animal smiling. Well, Philippe, they won't be smiling for much longer."

"We are 2831 nautical miles to East London. We will be traveling at approximately 12 knots, so if all goes well, we should be in port in 10 ten days."

"Excellent, my team can use the rest."

After another hour of being caught up on the news around the world, I headed down to my cabin to crash. The bunk felt wonderful after sleeping on the ground for so long.

ROBERT LESTER a.k.a. The Iceman

I'm Robert Lester, an ex-Navy SEAL sniper; I'm best known for holding the world record for the longest distance kill in military history, a three-thousand-four-hundred-and-eighty-meter shot. I am a French Canadian and am better known as the Iceman because nothing ever rattles me. Ice water runs through my veins—I am the leader of the Red Team.

I joined the Le Gang de la Clé de Singe after three tours of duty in Iraq. I was looking for something meaningful to get involved with, so I first joined up with Greenpeace right after the Deepwater Horizon disaster. I was among the first to protest big oil rigs drilling in the Arctic Circle and slowing production by jamming their equipment.

Greenpeace did not condone my actions and wasn't prepared to go to bat for me legally. I was arrested for the destruction of private property and vandalizing property; I spent close to a year in Goose Creek Correctional Center in Wasilla, Alaska.

When I was released from Goose Creek, I had nothing but sixteen dollars in my pockets and the clothes on my back from when I was arrested. I walked out the prison gate and headed over to the bus stop, where I caught a ride into Anchorage. Once there, I figured I'd stop at a bar and determine my options. While standing at the bus stop, I was met by a young woman wearing a sweatshirt with the name Sarah embroidered over a Greenpeace logo.

"Hi, are you Robert Lester?"

"Maybe."

"My name is Sammy."

"Your sweater says, Sarah."

"So? My jeans say, Gloria Vanderbilt."

"Okay…Well, are you with Greenpeace?"

"Not exactly. My name is Sammy, and I am with an environmental organization that you might be interested in joining."

"What organization would that be? I have to tell you, I'm a little disillusioned with the whole environmental-activism-thing at the moment."

"Have you ever heard of the Le Gang de la Clé de Singe?"

"Shit yeah—the Monkey Wrench Gang."

"Well, as you probably have heard, unlike other environmental organizations, we don't just protest; we kick ass and take names. We don't ask permission; we ask forgiveness."

"Yeah, you guys do some pretty hairy shit."

"That's us, and, as the Marines say, 'We're looking for a few good men,' interested?"

"Why me, man?"

"You're kidding, right? We're looking for people who are tired of playing by the rules and getting nowhere while the other side cheats, lies, buys politicians, and basically plays by their own set of rules. If you want to make a difference—I mean a real difference—to help stop the world's corporations from ruining the environment for their own personal profit, I have a car right over there. Otherwise, you can stand here and wait for the bus."

I saw the bus for Anchorage approaching its stop; I looked at her and said, "Lead on."

She led me to an old, beat-up, silver Honda CR-V, where I noticed two men seated in the front. I looked at her and asked, "And they would be?"

"My friends, my protection."

"Protection?"

"Yeah, Alaska has the highest rape rate in the country; a girl can't be too careful. Okay?

"Wow, I did not know that."

As we got into the car, Sammy introduced me to her friends, Tommy G and Jimmy the Chew. Both were veterans of many eco-war campaigns for the Gang against corporate America. They would eventually become part of the Red Team. We drove down the Glenn Highway into Anchorage, to West 6th Avenue across Town Square Park, and to Humpy's Great Alaskan Alehouse. We all ordered the halibut fish 'n' chips and a large glass of Hypothermia beer. After almost a year in jail, I said this was the best meal I had ever had. As they sat eating and drinking, Sarah explained what I could expect and what would be expected of me in return.

After several hours and several beers, I agreed to join 'the Gang.' I was given my first solo assignment as a sort of initiation: I was to pose as a National Geographic photographer and make contact with a young woman who hunted big game and endangered species. What made her a person of interest was getting pleasure from torturing the beast before putting it out of its misery. I was given a complete dossier of her social media postings, articles, and affidavits from porters, guides, and other eyewitnesses.

After reading the information, I looked at Sammy and said, "Wow, this bitch is a real piece of work. I'll come up with something special; leave it to me."

Brittany Jones was a twenty-two-year-old Dallas Cowboy cheerleader with aspirations of getting her own television show.

She was hoping that her exploits in big game hunting would give her an opportunity for a hunting show on one of the cable networks that specializes in outdoor programming. She started hunting when she accompanied her father on his big game safaris at the young age of eleven. Killing a rare African white Rhino was her first ever, and it was also the first in her quest to bag the Big 5 African game animals—rhino, elephant, Cape buffalo, leopard, and lion—which she did by the time she was fourteen. Since then, she had continued to kill zebras, White Springbok, hippos, black wildebeest, crocodiles, and giraffes, among dozens of various plains game.

Brittany wasn't the sweet, little, innocent Southern Belle image that she liked to put out to the public; she was a cold-hearted, sadistic killer.

She would shoot her prey with a massive dose of animal tranquilizer, rendering it immobile. Then, when the poor animal would lay there, she would taunt it and torture it. When the beast started to come out of the effects of the tranquilizer drug, she would finally kill it. Having observed her behavior, several of the safari outfits refused to do business with her. Her reputation was starting to spread, so even new safari outfits declined to accept her as a client.

I was given the cover name of Angelo Della Morte, a National Geographic photographer on assignment in Africa on his way home to Atlanta.

It was arranged that we be seated next to each other on Air Namibia Airlines. Brittany, being a bit of a slut seduced me, and we joined the mile-high club several times between Luderitz and Paris, from Paris to Atlanta.

I told her that I was on assignment to shoot a fourteen-foot Anaconda named Bubbles. The Atlanta Zoo had given me permission to shoot the snake after hours, so I invited her to come and observe. I told her that they had an after-hours sexual encounter amongst the Atlanta Zoo's wildlife. The offer was just kinky enough that Brittany couldn't refuse.

We entered the zoo after midnight. I had prepared a special cocktail for her, so I pulled out a flask and asked, "Care for a drink?"

"Sure." She took the flask and took several drinks. "Mmmm, what is it?"

"It's called a Nigerian Chapman. I thought you'd like it."

As we were walking, the air was cool and crisp, but Brittany started to feel warm and then hot. She then felt weak and dizzy, so we stopped and sat down on a bench, where she passed out.

The air was lovely, warm, and humid when she opened her eyes. She realized she was lying down and looking at a large tree branch. She knew that she was inside, but as hard as she tried, she couldn't move; she was paralyzed from the neck down. She tried to scream, but nothing happened. Then, she heard my voice in the distance.

"Ah, you're awake."

She could only lift her head a few inches, but she could see me walking towards her and smiling. Again, she tried to speak, but nothing came out. I was standing over her, looking down at her. "It's no good trying to speak. You see, you've been drugged. I used a drug called Ketamine; veterinarians mostly use it, and it causes you to become temporarily unable to move as if paralyzed. It's also called a Date Rape drug."

I smiled, leaned down closer to her, and said, "No, that's not why I've drugged you. Brittany, have you ever heard of Le Gang de la Clé de Singe, the eco-terrorist group? You see, my real name is Robert Lester, and I've been sent to kill you."

Brittany tried to scream, but nothing came out, not even a squeak. I stood up, looked around, and said, "You know, I had heard a lot about you, how you like to torture animals before you kill them, how you get your jollies from seeing them suffer, how you like to watch them die a slow, agonizing death. Well, guess what, babe? It's your turn. It's payback time."

Her eyes got as large as saucers, and she started to cry and whimper. I knelt down and lifted her body up far enough to show her the fourteen-foot Green Anaconda coiled up about twenty feet away. She began to sob and tried to scream, but nothing happened. She looked down at herself and saw she was naked.

"Don't flatter yourself; you being naked is only, so Bubbles has an easier time swallowing you. Of course, you'll be dead long before that happens. Anacondas always kill their prey before digesting them. I know that it's cruel, but no crueler than you, Brittany, honey. I would recommend that you try not to fight it but just go with it."

I stood up, looked over at the snake, and said, "She will come for you very soon once I leave. Brittany, I just want to tell you that I really enjoyed our time together, and under better circumstances, things might have turned out differently—maybe if you weren't just such a sadistic little bitch. Now, I must go."

She watched me hang a yellow Monkey Wrench Gang flag on the branch of the tree, along with a note proclaiming who was taking responsibility. Then, I left, and I didn't even look back.

As she sobbed, she strained to hear a sound, any sound, any movement, but the messenger of death was silent. She laid there for what seemed to be an eternity, until she felt something smooth touch her leg. She started to cry, hysterically, but there was no sound as she tried to scream. As the snake crossed her body and slid over her pubic area, she could see its green-gray eyes with its black slits. They were cold, dead eyes; as it passed her, it seemed to look into her soul, and she saw nothing, no emotion, nothing. Its whole body passed over her, and then it began to encircle her; its head was next to hers. Once it had coiled itself around her, it slowly started to tighten its grip on her, tighter and tighter. She suddenly noticed that she seemed to have some feeling in her hands; she could move her hands and feet, so she began to resist. But the more she resisted, the more the snake constricted. She began having a hard time breathing. Every time she took a breath, the snake constricted a little more, which made it harder to catch the next breath until, finally, she felt the excruciating pain of her ribs breaking. She began to lose consciousness. Finally, she decided just to let go.

When the Iceman cometh, people die.

Indian Ocean – January 29th

The seas were finally calm again after a rocky trip around the Horn of Good Hope. My team was experiencing severe seasickness, but thankfully, all that's behind us.

East London, S. A. – January 29th

The SS Renard steered us from the Indian Ocean into the Buffalo River in East London so we could dock at the National Ports Authority of South Africa. Several large Ocean Africa container ships were lined up at the northern docks, being unloaded. We were directed to dock on the opposite side of the harbor, where the smaller cargo ships were anchored.

The harbormaster scheduled our unloading for two o'clock this afternoon. I gave a four-liberty to the Red Team to get used to being back on solid ground after ten days at sea. Some would explore Fort Glamorgan, a fort built in the 1800s that is now used in part as a prison. A couple of the guys were heading off to the Naughty Lizard Bar & Grill to soak up some local color and sample a couple of pints of Hansa Pilsner.

We said our goodbyes to Captain Chevrolet and the crew of the Renard, who were setting sail to Madagascar the following day.

East London, S. A. – January 29th

All our gear and vehicles had been unloaded from the Renard and loaded onto a semi to transport north towards the Agatha Forest Reserve. Our objective was the *Impi Ranch,* which means Warrior Ranch in the Zulu language. The ranch is about fifteen miles from Tzaneen and is sandwiched between Agatha Forest Reserve and Woodbush Forest Reserve.

The Impi Ranch is approximately 30,000 acres of tropical and subtropical bush country. At any given time, there are one to two hundred lions in various stages of life, from newborns to male lions seven to ten years old.

They also offer all the other species that make up the Big Five: elephant, buffalo, leopard, and rhino. And for a nominal fee, waiting for the animal of choice to kill, they have a small pond filled with crocodiles that you can either shoot it in the pond or have one of the ranch hands drag it out for you to shoot while it's being restrained on land. Upon leaving *Impi Ranch*, a nice pair of handmade crocodile cowboy boots will be waiting at the desk for you.

The ranch has a petting zoo for the newborns, and they keep a pride of lions on display for the tourists. The breeding stock of lionesses are kept off sight. The females are artificially inseminated so as not to have any male rivalry fights. Don't want to damage the goods. The ranch rears the lions from cubs to maturity, and once the adult lion is fully matured, the buyer chooses his or her trophy. They lure their prey to an open area where the "hunter" is waiting in an air-conditioned blind equipped with a stocked bar and TV that they can watch until their prey is lured to the feeding station. They then walk over to the gun port and kill whichever animal they had paid for.

Afterward, they enjoy a nice lunch and a couple of glasses of champagne while the lion is taken to be skinned, its head removed and sent to the taxidermist. It's all relatively civilized and tidy- no muss, no fuss.

A syndicate of six wealthy hedge fund managers owns the ranch. Five of them live in Johannesburg, and the other one lives in Cape Town. My team and I were going to visit the managers and guests of the ranch while my counterpart Rodin and his partner Isala met with the six owners.

Although *Impi Ranch* is the largest canned hunting club in South Africa, it is by no means the only one- there are seven in total. We believed that the others would get the message if we made an example of the flagship ranch.

We started our journey and traveled north on the N1 Highway until we reached Queenstown. I had arranged lodging at the Gallery Restaurant and Guest House, four-star accommodations, and a restaurant, as this was our last night before the mission. This required our trekking and roughing it out in the bush, so I felt the team could use a little pampering.

Surprisingly, the Gallery Restaurant offered excellent seafood dishes, a top-notch sushi chef, and a fabulous wine cellar.

Queenstown, S. A. – January 30th

We started the fourteen-hour drive to Tzaneen in the morning, where we reconnected with our semi-driver. The trip was uneventful, yet with quite beautiful, lush scenery. We were hitting some high speeds on the four-lane N1, making good time. When we reached Polokwane, we turned onto the R71, a two-lane road through a mostly arid landscape until we reached Haenertsburg at the foot of the Great Escarpment.

The Great Escarpment is the plateau edge of southern Africa that separates the region's highland interior plateau from the narrow coastal strip.

As we traveled along the edges of the plateau, the road became more and more twisty, and we changed from arid to lush green fields of banana, granadillas, and litchi farms, as far as the eye could see. At around 6 p.m., we met up with our driver, Jeffery Govender, at the Allesbeste Nursery and Farm, where the R71 dead-ends into the R36.

Once we unloaded our gear and vehicles, we made our way towards the village of Mokgolobotho, where we would join our guide, Kgabu Bhengu, a Kruger National Park Ranger. He was on a two-week leave of absence.

Kgabu had been a ranger for over thirteen years and had dedicated his life to protecting and preserving the wildlife of South Africa. He joined Le Gang de la Clé de Singe six years ago and has worked on many newsworthy covert operations.

Like the rest of the members of Le Gang de la Clé de Singe, we work in the shadows and claim no glory for ourselves. The survival of the animals we love is its own reward.

Tzaneen, S. A. – January 30th

Afterward, we unloaded the six Textron Prowler EV IS utility task vehicles and placed the Toyota 4Runners, which we retrieved after completing the mission, on the semi. We got off the road to travel undetected and make camp. We were camped a mile away from the lion ranch so that we could hear the occasional roar of a male lion declaring his territory. After a warm dinner, we checked our gear and weapons and then set up the sentry roster.

Impi Ranch, - January 31st

The sky showed a crack of light out of the east as we prepared to head to the lion ranch on foot. Lu Wei had put the Ehang Falcon B drone up to guide us and keep us apprised of any rangers or wildlife we might encounter.

After a two-hour trek, we reached the eastern edge of the lion ranch's boundary and a sixteen-foot-high electrified fence. Odin and Hazael bypassed the circuitry so we wouldn't set off any alarms, and we were then able to breach the fence, ensuring that none of the farm-raised lions could escape. We feared that the lions raised on the ranch might not be prepared to assimilate into the wild since they had spent the majority of their lives in pens.

As we approached the main compound, we heard the lions stirring, preparing for their morning feeding. Attendants walked along the pens, tossing dead chickens over the fences into the lion pens. They kept the lions fat and lazy since they no longer had to hunt for their meals.

We saw that within the pens, there were several female lions with cubs. The females rarely fight amongst themselves, whereas the males have to be kept separate. The ranch owners spend tens of thousands for male lions to sire the lionesses to keep the bloodline pure and to breed the most desired features the hunters want, like size and black manes.

I sent Odin, Hazael, Vulcan, Fu Hao, and Sue B out in the bush in search of any guides and hunters on a hunt while Gianfranco, Venus, Sassoon, Bellator, Cowboy, and I raided the main lodge.

Impi Ranch, - January 31st

We had shed our ghillie suits and were dressed in all black, wearing black balaclavas over our faces as we entered the main lobby. The two receptionists were stunned and shocked to see us. I directed them to keep their hands up and to come towards us. We zip-tied their hands behind their backs and led them into the office, where they were gagged and secured to chairs with their feet bound together. I had Gianfranco, Venus, Sassoon, and Bellator go to the guest bungalows to round up guests and staff and bring them to the dining hall.

Kgabu, Cowboy, and I moved through the main lobby before entering the dining hall, where the majority of the guests were having breakfast. Cowboy and Kgabu entered from the east entrance, and I entered from the west. I fired one round into the air and shouted for everyone to remain seated. Those standing had to lie on the ground. Any disobedience, any defiance, and the offender would be shot.

I had Kgabu and Cowboy collect all cell phones and any weapons. We then separated the hotel staff from the guests, hunting guides, and management. Soon, Gianfranco and the others entered the dining hall with the guests they had collected from the bungalows. All told, we had 24 guests, 12 guides, and six management staff that we detained in the dining hall. The 18 hotel staff members were taken to the office where the two receptionists were being held. They, too, were seated and restrained.

The 42 prisoners' hands were zip-tied behind their backs, taken outside, and lined up in a straight line.

I announced, “We are members of Le Gang de la Clé de Singe, and you have all been found guilty in the participation of trophy hunting of critically endangered and, in some cases, endangered species. This carries the penalty of death.”

Afterward, we placed each hunter and guide next to the animals they were responsible for killing. Each of them had the ceremonial yellow flag, black skull, crossed monkey wrenches placed around their necks, and a copy of the statement of their crime.

Shortly after we finished, Odin, Hazael, Vulcan, Fu Hao, and Sue B wandered into camp.

“How did it go?” I asked.

Odin said, “We encountered three hunting parties. The first was hunting a lion. He and his guide were waiting in the blind, drinking Bloody Marys.

“We got to the second man too late as they had just shot an elephant. The poor thing was crying out in pain, struggling and trying to breathe, while the hunter and guide were standing off to the side, having a smoke. You know what they say: smoking can kill you. Well, they’re right.

“We caught the third one posing for a photograph, smiling, and kneeling behind a spiral-horned antelope that she killed with a bow and arrow.”

“Any problems?”

“Not for us.”

“Okay, everybody, let’s saddle up. Cowboy, do you want to do the honors?”

Cowboy took a metal case out of his backpack, retrieved a small clear plastic card, peeled the paper backing off, and rubbed the plastic onto the window of the door leading to the reception desk. Authorities would later discover that the single fingerprint belonged to P.W. Botha, nicknamed “the Big

Crocodile," the leader of South Africa from 1978 to 1984. It was our way of saying fuck you to the establishment.

Kgabu, Cowboy, and I put on our ghillie suits for the trek back to base camp. On the way, I instructed Lu Wei to notify the authorities and the media. When we arrived, Lu Wei had the camp broken down and the vehicles loaded and ready to go.

Once the local authorities realized that the killings were attributed to Le Gang de la Clé de Singe, they called in the SASS, South African Secret Service, who in turn brought in Interpol.

Not long after the murders were thought to have occurred, Inspectors Morris and Volker were able to discover a small clip of a surveillance video from a petrol station several miles from the ranch showing two Toyota 4Runners passing by.

It wasn't much, if it was anything at all, but they'd been working on case after case of Le Gang de la Clé de Singe killings and had only gathered a handful of evidence, mainly those damn fingerprints. They put out an APB for all of South Africa and their neighboring countries, Lesotho, Swaziland, Botswana, and Namibia.

We headed back towards Allesbeste. We met up with Jeffery, our semi-driver, who was parked in a grove of granadillas trees down a dirt road across the Wheelbarrow Farmstall and a few miles from the Allesbeste nursery. He was hidden in a secluded field far from prying eyes. We loaded the six Textron Prowler EV IS utility task vehicles and unloaded the Toyota 4Runners.

Our next mission was a seven-hour drive to the farming community of Wolmaransstad in the Northwest Province. It was not far from the diamond-mining town of Maquassi Hills, but we would be guarding something more valuable than mere diamonds: the white rhino.

One of the largest captive rhino breeding farms is just 10 miles from Wolmaransstad, hidden down a dirt road. There were over a thousand rhinos, close to 3% of the total global population of white rhinos.

Big Horn Ranch is the brainchild of Tommy Turner, an eccentric billionaire who made his fortune in buying and selling vintage airplanes.

His ranch was kept a secret for years, but word got out, and the poachers got in. On average, they killed over three rhinos a week, even though Tommy and his crew cut off the horns of the rhinos every two years to discourage the poachers, but to no avail. He's tried everything: electrical fences, sensors, aerial drones, even a security detail. Unfortunately, he discovered some people on his security detail were in cahoots with the poachers. Out of desperation, he contacted an old friend associated with Le Gang de la Clé de Singe, and voilà, here we come.

The Members of the RED TEAM

I thought it would be good to introduce you to the members of the Red Team, a finer band of warriors you won't find. They're dedicated to saving the world's precious wildlife. Each one is willing to die for what we all believe.

VERONICA VENTURA aka Sue B and YUM WU aka Fu Hao

Veronica Ventura and Yum Wu couldn't have been more opposite. Veronica was five-foot-eleven, had long, blonde hair and green eyes, weighed one hundred and ten pounds—just plain beautiful—and came from Greenwich, Connecticut. Her father was a hedge-fund banker, and the Venturas were ranked as one of the ten wealthiest families in America. Her father, Jonathan Ventura, was well acquainted with David Leeway, a prominent American real estate mogul who once ran for President of the United States; they usually played golf together once every two or three months at one of the Leeway's golf resorts in West Palm Beach, Florida. Veronica and Sasha Leeway attended the same prep school, the Greenwich Academy. Growing up, they were wildly different in how they saw the world. While Sasha loved killing things, Veronica volunteered at animal shelters, animal rescue centers, and local veterinary clinics.

Years later, it came as no surprise to Veronica to see that Sasha was really into big game hunting, as her family had gone on hunting parties for all of their school breaks. They once opposed each other on the issue of big game hunting while on the school's debate team. It was a spirited debate, each giving as good as they got. Emotions ran high, and what started as a heated debate turned into a personal attack on each other, resulting in Sasha storming off the stage in a rage. That was the last time either spoke to each other, ever.

Sasha went on to graduate from The Wharton School of the University of Pennsylvania and then on to work for her father. Veronica graduated from UCLA and spent three years in the Peace Corps in Nepal, where she joined Le Gang de la Clé de Singe and recruited Yum Wu.

Yum Wu stands five feet four inches tall, has pitch-black hair and brown eyes, and weighs one hundred and eighty pounds. Standing side-by-side, they look like the perfect odd couple but are actually the perfect even pair. Yum was originally from the small town of Jinchang, the People's Republic of China. Jinchang is in the center of Gansu province, bordering Inner Mongolia to the north. It’s known as China's ‘Nickel Capital’.

Yum Wu's father was a miner, his father's father was a miner, and so on, and so on for eight generations. Her mother had died during her childbirth, and Yum and her father lived just outside of town on the West side of Hongshan Crossing, which literally separated the city from the rural community. The property on which they lived was all dirt, as no plants or even trees could grow; it was a depressing existence for Yum. The only pleasure she got was practicing target shooting for

The People's Republic of China Olympic Women's 50m Rifle 3 Positions Team. The event had the athletes shoot over a distance of fifty meters in kneeling, prone, and standing positions.

In the beginning, when Yum began to try out for the team, many of the officials scoffed and laughed at her because of her physical appearance. After only her first try, they were all silenced when she obtained a near-perfect score.

From an early age Yum had gone hunting with her grandfather; she was an excellent shot but didn't enjoy the killing of animals. However, she enjoyed the challenge of the precision and accuracy of hitting a target. She spent hours upon hours practicing target shooting for over twelve years. When she heard that the People's Republic of China Olympic trials for the Women's 50m Rifle 3 Positions Team were being held in Beijing, she and her father made the twenty-two-hour trip to Beijing by bus for the tryouts, which she aced.

While they were in Beijing, they received word that her grandfather and uncle were both killed in a major shaft collapse in the Mojiang Mine, where there had been hundreds of recent complaints from the miners of unsafe conditions. The mine owners just brushed them off as unfounded, and the government backed them, bringing no charges of neglect and stating that the miners were at fault for being careless and not heeding safe practices. When Yum stood with the miners and protested against the government, she was told to stop, or she would be arrested, and she was cut from the Olympic team.

Yum and her father were arrested and spent seven months in prison. She was sent to the Provincial Women's Prison, where she was forced to work in the Jiuzhou Clothing Factory. During her time there, she was systematically beaten and raped by the prison guards.

Her father, Bohai, along with dozens of other protesters, were sent to Lanzhou Prison. It was a high-security prison that included several workshops where prisoners performed forced labor. Prisoners were deprived of food and medical care, and those who did not finish their forced labor tasks were tortured. Bohai succumbed to several beatings and died after five months of imprisonment; his family was never told the truth of how he died, just that he was dead.

After Yum was released from prison, she decided to leave China. She knew that her life would be hell if she stayed, so she made her way through the twelve-hundred-mile journey, on foot, across Qinghai Province to Tibet. Qinghai was a large, sparsely populated province spread across the high-altitude Tibetan Plateau. She mainly traveled at night to avoid being seen and carried a Chinese Hanyang Arsenal Experimental Semi-Automatic Rifle that was her grandfather's. He had owned it since 1918 and kept it in excellent condition. It was the only thing having any sentimental value to her. She was prepared to use it if she had to, as she had decided that she was not going to be taken alive and face prison again.

On day sixteen, she reached Amne Machin, a six-thousand-two-hundred-and-eighty-two-meters-high peak, part of the Kunlun Mountains, and a holy site for Buddhist pilgrims. She was near death from exposure when several Buddhist monks from the monastery Wutong found her and brought her to the monastery. There, she received medical attention and was allowed to stay under their protection for six weeks until she was fit to continue her journey to Katmandu. After another ten days, she finally slipped over the well-guarded border under the cover of a severe blizzard. She didn't make the journey unscathed since she suffered a severe case of frostbite—lost three toes on her left foot and two on her right foot—but she was free.

She eventually found work as a chambermaid at the Hotel Yak and Yeti, a one-hundred-year-old, five-star hotel on Durbar Marg Street in the heart of Katmandu. Here, she learned to speak English. She worked there and, by sheer luck, met Veronica Ventura while viewing the Garden of Dreams, which was created in the 1920s with half a dozen pavilions, several fountains, and hundreds of urns and birdhouses.

During her stay, a couple of young, pre-teenage boys were teasing a dog by a small pavilion in the garden's center. Both Veronica and Yum heard the dog's yelping in distress and went to investigate, each approaching from opposite directions. They arrived almost simultaneously, and each took action to chase the boys away. The combination of a tall, white Anglo woman and a short, stocky Chinese woman joining forces, chasing and yelling, seemed to un-nerve the lads. The boys decided to run off and create mischief somewhere else.

Veronica and Yum hit it off quickly and became fast friends after several days. After Veronica learned of Yum's talents, she recruited her into the Gang. Once the Gang learned about Yum's shooting abilities, she and Veronica were teamed up as a sniper and spotter duo. Veronica had chosen the name Sue-B in honor of her hero, Susan B. Anthony and Yum decided to go by the name Fu Hao, an infamous Chinese female warrior from the Shang Dynasty.

WILLIE TYLER, aka Cowboy

Willie Tyler, who everyone knew as Cowboy, was from Terlingua, Texas. The city's name is from Terlingua (three tongues) Creek, which was coined by Mexican herders, Comanche, Shawnee, and Apaches who lived on its upper reaches.

As a ranch hand, Willie grew up on the Bar T cattle ranch, punching cattle, breaking horses, mending fences, and working cattle drives. The only things Willie owned were the clothes on his back, his saddle, his horse Buck, and a Winchester Model 92 Lever Action Rifle that his father left him on his deathbed.

Like most cowboys in west Texas, Willie didn’t put a whole lot of stock in what all these liberal tree-hugging leftist commie groups with their “Save the Whales,” “Global Warming,” “PETA,” and “Save Endangered Species” crusades. That was until one of the old-time cattle drives, where he drove cattle herd from Terlingua to Fort Stockton. That was a 200-mile trek. The drive took them eight days and was topped off with a Wild West celebration and rodeo. There was also the 10th Annual Texas Coyote Roundup. The object was to see how many coyotes one could kill over the span of a week. The winner received a cash prize of a thousand dollars.

Willie had killed coyotes and even wolves when they threatened the cattle herd, but never for sport. He always felt a little guilty after killing one, but he figured it was part of being a cowboy, watching over and protecting the herd.

Once the cattle were driven into the pens in the stockyards, he put old Buck in the corral and went into town to have a couple of drinks with the boys and maybe find the company of a young lady to spend the night with.

He and his friends went past Historic Fort Stockton and saw the first day's kills. Over 200 coyotes lay side-by-side, and that was just day one. A large crowd of men, women, and children were standing around laughing and joking. That bothered Willie. He felt some respect should be given since coyotes and wolves, unlike humans, don't kill for sport; they kill to survive.

"I've seen enough, fellas; I'm outta here," Willie said.

"What's the matter, Tyler? Do you have no stomach for death?" His trail boss, J.T., teased him.

"Not for sport," Willie said as he walked away from the crowd and headed to the Crazy Mule Saloon.

Willie hadn't noticed that a man and woman had followed him into the bar. He stood at the bar and ordered a Lone Star Beer. While he was waiting, the man who followed him asked, "Are you in the coyote-killing derby?"

"Me? No, I don't abide by killing for sport. I'm okay with hunting for food, but to kill for fun, no. You?"

"Hardly, my friend, Venus here, and I are down here doing a little hunting, but not for sport. Hi, I'm Gianfranco. Did you know that over 400 thousand coyotes are killed in the U.S. every year?"

"No shit!" Willie said after taking a drink.

Venus asked, "You a real cowboy?"

"Yes, ma'am. A bunch of fellas from the Bar T and I drove a herd of about five hundred heads from Terlingua to here in eight days."

After a lot of soul-searching, Willie Tyler decided to try to do something meaningful with his life, to maybe make a difference, after seeing all those dead coyotes that died for nothing other than greed. So, Willie drew his back wages and left the Bar T to join one of those liberal tree-hugging leftist commie groups, Le Gang de la Clé de Singe.

"Glad to have you on our side, Cowboy?"

"Why thank you, ma'am; I do have one concern."

"What's that cowboy?" She asked.

"What about Buck, my horse? I ain't going to just leave him or sell him."

Gianfranco responded, "We wouldn't think of it. There is a farm ranch in the foothills of east Texas, a sort of rescue ranch where Buck will be well cared for. You're more than welcome to visit him at any time."

"Alrighty then, pardner, count me in."

"Welcome aboard, Cowboy," Venus said.

JEAN-PAUL BOUCHER aka Sassoon

Sassoon worked as one of three veterinarians at a private Clinique Vétérinaire in Dakar. He handled everything from domestic animals to farms and the occasional wild animal. The Senegal zoo was too poor to have a veterinarian on staff, so, on occasion, he would be called upon to attend to the animals. He was the newest staff member, as he had just graduated from veterinary school in Paris and wanted to start his career with some adventure and not just attend to cats and dogs.

So when he heard about a position in Dakar, Senegal, he took it. One day, he was urgently called upon to come to the

Parc Forestier et Zoologique de Hann. One of the male lions had been injured. This was to be his first experience working at the Zoo, but when he got there, he could see that the cat had been badly beaten. His attendant claimed that the lion had attacked him while he was feeding him and that he feared for his life. He talked to several witnesses and confirmed that he was teasing the lion and that the man was the aggressor.

After attending to the lion, he noticed many animals had been abused. He went to the proper authorities and lodged a formal complaint, but all he received was the runaround.

It turned out that people at the clinic would get calls to come to the Zoo once or twice a month for an injured animal. He and his fellow doctors continued to complain to the officials and write letters to the newspaper, but to no avail. One day, a man from Le Gang de la Clé de Singe visited him. The man said he had read some of his letters and articles and felt he could help.

Of course, he had heard about the organization and was wary because of all the wild stories he had read about it. Sassoon told him he didn't think he wanted or needed their help. He told Sassoon to think it over and would stop by to see if he had changed his mind.

Several weeks passed when Sassoon received a call from the Zoo saying that one of the chimpanzees had died. He was prepping for surgery on a farmer's ox, so one of his colleagues went there and brought back the body to do an autopsy on the poor thing. They found that the young chimp had been beaten and strangled to death. Two days later, the man from the Gang came by again and decided to ask for their help.

One week passed with no calls from the Zoo, then two weeks, a month, and six months—nothing. Sassoon had heard from people at the Zoo that several of the attendants had quit suddenly and were replaced with more caring and responsible people. It seemed the people who left had been relatives and friends of the Zoo's officials, which was why they were protected. But it was months later that the story of what persuaded them to leave was revealed.

It seems that late one night, the three men who were responsible for the mistreatment of the animals were abducted at gunpoint and taken to one of the lion enclosures at the Zoo. One of the men who was responsible for the teasing and torturing of the lions was stripped naked, bound and gagged, restrained to a chair with his legs spread open, and had honey poured on his genitals. A female lion was released into the cage. The lioness, he was told, went directly to the man and proceeded to maul and nearly castrate him before she retreated into her enclosure. The other two men observed this and were told that if there was any more abuse to any of the animals, they would also face a similar punishment. The next day, all three men resigned, and the man who was mauled was taken to the hospital and soon died of an infection. The case is still unsolved.

Sassoon was later contacted by the man from Le Gang de la Clé de Singe, asking him if he would be interested in joining the group. They always wanted to have people from the medical field, both doctors and veterinarians. He was, at first, uncertain, but the more he thought about how best he could serve abused, injured, and even endangered animals, the more it made sense.

Sassoon has been with Le Gang de la Clé de Singe for over ten years.

LEONOR PESQUERIA aka Bellator

Leonor Pesqueria was always picked on as a child in the small town of Estremoz, Portugal, because she was born with a severe case of facial asymmetry. Facial asymmetry is a condition where one half of the face is not equivalent to or the same as the other half. In Leonor's case, the right side of her face was two inches lower than her left. The condition could have been somewhat repaired, but her family couldn't afford the surgery.

She went through her youth, taunted and made fun of. Then, at the age of fourteen, Leonor took her first karate class at the youth center. By the time she was nineteen, she had earned her Advanced Brown - her first Kyu belt. From then on, no one called her names or teased her after she broke the nose of Vinicius Carneiro, the town bully. This was much to the delight of all of his victims.

At the age of twenty-two, she left Estremoz for Lisbon, got a job at Greenpeace, and, within three years, joined Le Gang de la Clé de Singe. She took the name Bellator, the Latin word for warrior, and everyone who has met her believes that to be true.

MANCO CAPAC aka Gianfranco

Gianfranco is a small man from Peru. He is a direct descendant of the Inca tribes that fought the Spanish explorer Francisco Pizarro when he invaded the Incan Empire in 1532.

Gianfranco came to join the Gang when his father and four brothers all lost their lives in a copper mining accident. It happened because the chairman of the board decided that the cost of rescuing the men would be too cost-prohibitive and would negatively affect the stock price. He felt that the men knew the risks when they decided to become miners, and, therefore, he put in minimal effort for the media.

Two months after the mining accident, the chairman's car brakes failed while going down the 5N towards Oxapama. His car went off the highway at a high rate of speed and careened into Rio Chontabamba. He was unable to get out and ended up drowning. Foul play was expected, but no suspects were ever arrested; the file remains unsolved.

Gianfranco joined Greenpeace and participated in multiple peaceful protests against Peru's mining industry, which had been guilty of excessive air and water pollution, illegal dumping of toxic waste, and poor safety conditions for miners. Growing increasingly frustrated with peaceful protests, he was recruited by Le Gang de la Clé de Singe to get involved in a more aggressive style of protesting.

YELYZAVETA OLIYNYK aka Venus

Venus comes from a small town just outside of Odesa, Ukraine, called Yuzhne; it's a port city on the Black Sea. Her grandfather owned a small fleet of fishing boats; her grandfather's grandfather had handed it down to him. About eight years ago, the government declared that private fishing fleets would become part of a state-owned commercial venture. They had no choice. Those who refused were harassed, and equipment was damaged. So-called 'accidents' happened to crewmembers, and a few were killed—her grandfather was one.

To fight back, a small group of resisters started publicly protesting by marching in the streets and clashing with the police. They tried to bring world attention to their cause, but there was very little outcry worldwide.

It seemed their cause was so small, compared with all the other injustices in the world, that theirs was a lost cause. Some of them started to fight back using tactics that the State had used against them: they sabotaged their equipment and harassed their crewmembers. They were labeled thugs and terrorists and had to go deep underground. One day, a man simply called Mars, like the Roman God of War, came to them and offered them assistance from Le Gang de la Clé de Singe in their struggle against the State.

They formed hit squads against opposition leaders, sabotaged equipment, sunk many State-sponsored ships, and generally wreaked havoc. They exacted an eye for an eye; if one private fishing vessel was sunk, then two of the State's fishing vessels were sunk. If one of the local fishermen were killed, two of the State's fishermen were killed.

For several months, they wreaked holy Hell against the state-run fleet, but soon the Ukrainian government sought help from the Russians. They finally had to disband, so she and several others from Yuzhne left and joined Le Gang de la Clé de Singe.

XING BAO, aka Lu Wei

Lu Wei grew up in Yulin, a prefecture-level city in the Shanbei region of Shaanxi province. His father was a famous porcelain craftsman, well respected and honored until the Cultural Revolution led by Mao Zedong. His father was denounced and sent off to a "reeducation" camp where he was tortured, beaten, and eventually died from malnutrition. His mother committed suicide when she heard of her husband's death.

In 1966, Xing Bao was conscripted into the Red Guard, which at first was considered to be counter-revolutionaries and radicals. Soon, Chairman Mao himself legitimized them.

In order to survive, Xing Bao went along with the madness for ten years until 1976. After Mao's death and the arrest of the Gang of Four, the Maoist policies of the Cultural Revolution began to be dismantled slowly.

Xing Bao made his way back to his hometown, Yulin, to see if he could reconnect with any family members who had survived. But alas, all his family had been dispersed throughout the county, and there were no records to speak of; he was alone.

Xing Bao got involved in animal rights during the June annual dog meat festival celebration. Over 10,000 dogs are killed for human consumption. He and a small band of activists raided the dog compounds and released thousands of dogs when he was promptly arrested, beaten, and sentenced to one year in Guizhong prison. After his release, he was met by Le Gang de la Clé de Singe members to see if he would be interested in continuing the fight for animal rights in China and worldwide.

Xing Bao took the name of Lu Wei, a corrupt politician from his own province, to continually remind himself that absolute power corrupts absolutely.

MIKKAEL EINARSSON aka Odin

Mikkael Einarsson was an Icelander who called himself Odin, after the God of war and death. He was from Reykjavík, Iceland.

Odin became involved in environmental causes in high school by protesting the Japanese whaling ships being allowed refueling privileges. He opposed the building of the Kárahnjúkastífla Dam on the grounds that it caused irreversible environmental damage to the surrounding area. It also devastated the habitat of the pink-footed Goose and reindeer.

He then joined more activist groups like Saving Iceland, where he was involved in making underground protest videos for Anarchy Media. He then joined Greenpeace International and became a Rainbow Warrior, defending the Amazon reef against the world's oil companies for three years, eventually winning. He signed on with Sea Shepherd, where he was on the front lines of Operation Jairo, the battle to save the world's sea turtle population from poachers. They poached nesting adults and eggs, and finally, he yearned for a more aggressive, action-oriented organization like Le Gang de la Clé de Singe.

Since joining, Odin has risen in the ranks and is now the number two on the Red Team.

Big Horn Ranch, - February 1st

We parked the two Toyotas and the semi in the guest parking lot, where Tommy Turner and his sons, Freddy and Frankie, were waiting for us.

“Gentlemen and ladies, I’m Tommy Turner, and these are my two sons, Frankie and Freddy.”

“Mr. Turner, I’m Iceman, and this is my Team: Odin, Lu Wei, Bellator, Cowboy, Venus, Sassoon, Sue B, Fu Hao, and Gianfranco. And this is Kgabu, our guide, and Jeffery, our semi-driver. Now, sir, what can we do for you?”

Turner smiled and said, “Follow me.”

We did, and after a ten-minute walk, we were surrounded by hundreds of white rhinos of all sizes and ages. They are very gentle beasts and very playful.

“These are my babies, all 1300 of them, and I don’t like it when someone sneaks onto my land and kills and mutilates my babies. It makes me angry; this has to stop, understand? Wooch said that you guys are the best. Can you make it stop?”

“We’ll make it stop; it won’t be pretty.”

“Take a look at this, sir,” Turner said as he revealed the mutilated body of a female rhino. Its young calf is still crying for its mother. He continued, “This isn’t pretty either.”

“It’s best that you and your sons remain completely unaware of our actions because when the shit hits the fan, I want you all not to get entangled, understood? You haven’t seen us, and you don’t know us, and you certainly didn’t hire us, got it?”

“You’re like a fart in the wind.”

“More like a fart in a tornado, but you get it. We won’t be seeing us again, but you will know that we’ve been here. Good day, gentlemen.”

“Good day and good luck.”

Big Horn Ranch, - February 1st

We unloaded the six Textron Prowler EV IS utility task vehicles from the semi and loaded the two Toyota 4Runners. Each time we do this, it gets easier and faster.

After swapping out the vehicles and gear, we sent Jeffery to stay at the Tarragon Guest House in the gold mining town of Orkney, an hour's drive from the Ranch. He was to sit tight until he got the call.

After a short discussion, we decided to break up into two teams of five. The Red Team of Odin's would take Bellator, Cowboy, Venus, and Sassoon. I led the Blue Team, including Kgabu, Sue B, Fu Hao, and Gianfranco; Lu Wei was once again our guardian angel, watching us with the Ehang Falcon B drone.

Odin and his team watched the northern half of the ranch, and my team and I took the southern half. Poachers usually strike at night under cover of darkness, so we patrolled in our all-black SEAL sniper uniforms equipped with night vision goggles.

Big Horn Ranch, - February 1st

Both teams had parked the vehicles off into the brush, where we hoped they wouldn't be discovered. We placed a Le Gang de la Clé de Singe yellow flag on each utility vehicle to discourage any interference. Each vehicle had several GoPro video cameras attached so we could monitor them.

Odin, his team, and I took several cursory reconnoiters of our respective areas, staying in constant radio contact with each other and Red Flyer.

Big Horn Ranch, - February 1st

My Blue Team took a bit of R&R. We had some dinner and tried to get a few hours of shuteye before we started our patrols. We each carried our own personally selected MREs. There was everything from chicken pesto pasta to Asian-style beef strips with vegetables and everything in between. I had chosen Spaghetti w/beef and Sauce, just like my mother used to make, except my mother was a lousy cook.

Big Horn Ranch, - February 2nd

We'd been on patrol for two hours when we received a call from Red Flyer. He'd spotted three bogies entering our sector. We were off.

Big Horn Ranch, - February 2nd

We were too late; the three poachers had killed a rhino, removed the small stump of a horn, and were in the process of mutilating the body. I gave the order, Sue B, Fu Hao, and myself, to each select a target, and on my count, fire and the three men fell.

We slowly approached, and each fired a second shot to be sure that the men were dead. We discovered that all three were armed with AK-47s, the weapon of choice for poachers, terrorists, and all-around bad guys.

To drive home the point that we're not fucking around, I took the machete carried by Kgabu and cut off each of the poacher's noses and mutilated their bodies as they had mutilated the rhinos.

We then took their bodies and laid them on the outskirts of their village; the small piece of rhino horn was placed between the bodies, and a yellow flag was placed around each man's neck with a note in their pockets that read, *"Poachers Die!"*

The villagers were in a bit of a pickle if they reported the deaths to the authorities since they would have to admit that the three dead villagers were indeed poachers, which is against the law and carries a huge fine and jail time even for accomplices, be it man or woman.

Big Horn Ranch, - February 2nd

The Red Team reported that there weren't any engagements in their sector. I gave a brief report of our incident and that we were standing down until nightfall. We would implement standard sentinel watches; each member would stand a 4-hour watch while the others would sleep. I took the first watch.

Big Horn Ranch, - February 3rd

Both teams were out in the field on patrol when Red Flyer alerted us that a group of twenty men, many carrying weapons, were approaching the Red Teams sector.

"Blue Leader, this is Red Leader, over."

"Go, Red Leader."

"Red Team is coming; let's keep the chatter going."

"Roger that Red Leader. We're setting up positions now. Over."

"Copy that. Red Flyer, Red Leader, do you copy?"

"Roger, Red Leader."

"Red Flyer direct us to the dance."

"Copy that, continue straight for two clicks, and you'll be in the position to cut off any retreat. Over."

"Copy that, Red Flyer."

The landscape was mainly open fields with minimal brush, with an occasional tree. There was not a lot of cover. We could see the group of men clearly with our night vision goggles as we approached. We definitely had the upper hand, and we took full advantage. The Red Team had dug in and started to engage the poachers as they advanced towards them. Because they couldn't tell where the shooting was coming from, they fired blindly in all directions.

All our weapons are equipped with a 640 Pulsar Trail XP50 Thermal Riflescope, which reads off the thermal signatures of the body. Odin and the Red Team were wreaking havoc with the poachers, killing at least twelve immediately. The group, seeing that they were no match, even with thirty men, they were fighting blind, so they decided to retreat.

Unfortunately, my Blue Team stood in their way, basically trapping them in a box.

It took us almost four hours to transport all thirty dead, mutilated bodies back to their village. We left them in the back of the large Toyota Tacoma flatbed truck with all their noses hacked off, bodies mutilated with yellow flags placed around each man's neck with a note in their pockets that read, *"Poachers Die!"*

Big Horn Ranch, - February 23rd

It had been twenty days since any poacher attempted trespassing onto the Big Horn Ranch. We decided to move on, but before we left, we went around the entire perimeter, posting yellow flags with the black skull and cross monkey wrenches as a warning.

On our departure, we heard several gunshots that stopped us from leaving. I took Odin and Fu Hao to investigate, leaving LuWei to continue packing and preparing to leave.

As we were advancing towards the vicinity where we heard the gunshots, we were aware that there was a pride of lions in the area. We encountered three men who were standing over the dead body of a male rhinoceros; they were in the process of sawing off the horn.

Odin informed me that the pride of lions was approaching, so I decided to wait before we interceded. The three poachers were too involved in mutilating the carcass to notice the lions moving in.

When the lions struck, the poachers panicked and started to run. Unfortunately for them, the lions pursued and attacked. The pride was made up of nine females and an alpha male; the damage assaulting the poachers was pure carnage. The screams from the poachers alerted a pack of hyenas that, when they arrived, decided not to engage the lions but turned its attention to the dead rhino.

After the lions finished with the poachers, they wandered off and took naps under some Jackalberry trees. The only body parts we found were one skull, a small bit of pelvis parts, and three pairs of shoes.

I radioed Commander Wooch and told him about our progress and decision to move on, assuring him we would return if needed.

SEAL Commander William T. Brown, aka Wooch

SEAL Team Commander William T. "Wooch" Brown was best known for spearheading several successful SEAL kill missions against ISIS. The American public will never hear of these, at least not in their lifetimes.

William Brown was born into a military family going back four generations, starting with Captain Robert Archer Brown, who fought with the 7th Ohio Cavalry. He was nicknamed the "River Regiment" because its men came from nine counties along the Ohio River. He fought with distinction in the Battle of Cynthiana and the Battle of Cumberland Gap. He fought alongside General William E. "Grumble" Jones during the Franklin-Nashville Campaign, where he was killed leading a countercharge. That helped turn the tide for the Union when all looked lost.

During the Spanish-American War, his great-great-grandfather, Lieutenant Leonard Archer Brown, fought with Teddy Roosevelt's Rough Riders in the Battle of San Juan Hill. He was assigned to the Gatling Gun Detachment, which Colonel Roosevelt credited with the charge's success. After the war, he taught classes in cavalry tactics and the art of artillery at West Point.

During the Battle of Belleau Wood in World War One, Wooch's great-grandfather, Captain Julius A. Brown, commanded the 3rd Battalion, 5th Marines. After suffering heavy casualties on Hill 204 east of Vaux, the French repeatedly urged them to turn back, but Captain Brown replied, "Retreat? Hell, we don't go backward, only forwards".

While advancing on the Germans, Captain Brown discovered that they had been advancing in the wrong direction. Rather than admitting failure, he pushed ahead across the wood's narrow waist, smashing through the enemy's southern defensive lines. They were often reduced to using only their bayonets or fists in hand-to-hand combat, resulting in finally clearing the forest of Germans. It was considered one of the bloodiest and most ferocious battles U.S. troops would fight in the war.

In 1941, prior to America's entering World War Two, a group of American pilots volunteered to help the Chinese fight the Japanese. They formed a fighter squadron called the Flying Tigers. Under the command of General Chennault, ninety-nine discharged pilots from the Navy, Marines, and Army signed up as mercenaries under a private military contractor, the Central Aircraft Manufacturing Company.

A. William Brown was one of six squadron leaders who flew in the 3rd Squadron Hell's Angels, Flying Tigers. Their primary mission was to protect the Burma Road from Japanese bombing, keeping this vital line of communication open. They were so effective that the Japanese discontinued their raids on the city of Kunming while the Tigers were patrolling the area.

The Curtiss P-40 Warhawk was the aircraft of the Flying Tigers. It was a nimble workhorse, and it could take a beating and usually would get its pilots home safely. Squadron leader Brown flew 26 missions and racked up 12 victories. After the US entered the war, he was assigned to the Eighth Air Force. He was stationed in England, flying P-51 Mustangs as escorts to B-17 bombing raids over Germany. He was shot down twice; the second time, he was captured and sent to Stalag Luft III, where he took part in the so-called great escape. He made it as far as Amsterdam, where he was shot and killed.

William T. Brown joined the Navy SEALs in the fall of 1967. After the grueling training program, he was initially sent to Da Nang, Vietnam, to train the South Vietnamese in combat diving, demolitions, and guerrilla / anti-guerrilla tactics. In 1968, the North Vietnamese launched the Tet Offensive in hopes of breaking America's will to continue with the war, but for Brown and the SEALs, their missions became personal. He and his team were sent north to disrupt the enemy supply and troop movements. He was the team's sniper and earned the nickname "Wooch" when his spotter said that Wooch was the sound its victims made every time he claimed a headshot. By the end of his tour of duty in Vietnam, William T. "Wooch" Brown had racked up a Navy Cross, 2 Silver Stars, 4 Bronze Stars, and 5 Commendation Medals, as well as the rank of Captain.

Captain William T. "Wooch" Brown went on to serve on the ground in Desert Storm, Operation Gothic Serpent, and Operation Red Wings. After 9/11, he was kicked upstairs, promoted to Commander, and sent to work in the Pentagon in planning and operations. He and his team were responsible for dozens of strikes against al Qaeda, resulting in the deaths of more than eighty-seven top al Qaeda leaders. In 2014, in response to the rapid territorial gains made by ISIL, Wooch and his team developed over twenty Quick Reaction Force operations, helping to halt ISIL's advancement.

After 48 years of service, SEAL Team Commander William T. "Wooch" Brown retired quietly and without ceremony with just a dinner at the White House with the President, Vice President, and several of the military's top brass.

His involvement with Le Gang de la Clé de Singe resulted from seeing the cruelty and cavalier attitude towards animals while in the military. The mindless killing of animals out of boredom or sport always repulsed him. After making a speech at UC Berkeley on the subject of 'War and its Effect on Animals,' he was approached by several members of Le Gang de la Clé de Singe. They persuaded him to work with them in the shadows, operating with others like himself, ex-military, corporate leaders, government officials, and private individuals throughout the world, all of whom operated behind the scenes.

Big Horn Ranch, - February 28th

I called Mr. Turner, owner of the Big Horn Ranch and the Park Rangers, and told them about the poaching, the lion attack, and the location where their remains could be found. We told Turner we were going to Cape Town to ride on the *Black Train*. I told him that with our intervention and the news of the lion attack, things should cool down regarding poaching. However, should things pick up, I'd send a team up in short order to quash any resurgence.

I warned him that he would probably be getting a visit from Interpol inspectors and for him to be truthful, but not too truthful. He should say that he only became aware of our presence when we alerted him and the police when the lions attacked the poachers on his property.

Cape Town Station – March 1st

We met up with our driver, Jeffery, who loaded our EVs and pulled out the 4Runners. Then, we headed south to Cape Town, stopping in Colesberg for the night before completing the 11-hour drive.

For the ultimate experience, hunting off South Africa's private "Black Train" Namibia Safari once, a season excursion is high on all big game trophy hunters' bucket lists. It's a ten-day 4000km odyssey, traversing some of Africa's most diverse landscapes and stopping along the way to allow the patrons to experience some of the best hunting in all of Africa.

While traveling in luxury from South Africa's Highveld's open lands to Namibia's calm Atlantic Ocean. There were many highlights. A few of them include the Karoo, Sossusvlei, Kalahari Desert, Etosha Pan Safri, Fish River

Canyon, Windhoek, and Walvis Bay. Of course, the real highlights for the hunters were the three stops in Kruger National Park.

A mere twenty thousand US Dollars per person is a small price to pay for a one-of-a-kind experience. The train passes through Kruger National Park, which has some of Africa's most fertile hunting grounds. This attracts some of the world's Uber-rich hunters. Space on the train is a premium, so the Iceman and three members of the Red Team were fortunate to find passage on board.

The *Black Train* is made up of four Suite cars, two Luxury Suite cars, and two De Luxe Suite cars, accommodating a total of twenty passengers. The suites are the height of elegance with rich wood paneling, opulent marble bathrooms, and deluxe bedding with Frette goose-down pillows and 600 thread-count cotton sateen sheets. A personal butler is assigned for each guest for the entire duration of the journey.

There is a lounge car, resplendent with original works of African art adorning the walls; plush overstuffed leather couches with bouquets of flame lilies accentuate the plush décor. All surroundings make the lounge car ideal for gathering and meetings with fellow travelers.

The Club Car has the relaxed atmosphere of a turn-of-the-century gentlemen's club mixed with a modern cigar bar. Rare, burled wood walls, overstuffed leather wing chairs, a small library, card tables, and a well-stocked bar.

The Dining Car provides only the finest for discerning diners, using the finest silver and crystal service. The *Black Train* is equipped with bone china, cut-crystal glass, and classic silver cutlery with the exclusive Black Train insignia. And, of course, formal wear is required in keeping with the dining car's classical ambiance.

The observation car, which offers large panoramic windows to observe the magnificent scenery, is bringing up the rear. The back of the vehicle provides an outside observation platform with outdoor seating.

Ted Cloche is president of the Safari Society. It's the world's largest organization dedicated to protecting their right to trophy hunt, with well over 800,000 members in the U.S. and abroad. They are a force to be reckoned with.

For this edition of the *Black Train, Tom would be leading* a hunting party of sixteen hunters from around the world. There were eight Americans, four from England, two Germans, and two from China, all members of the SS.

Aside from being President of the Safari Society, Ted was a notable writer of spy novels. His main character is a British aristocrat, Robert Falcon, who fights the forces of evil around the world along with his select group of highly trained mercenaries.

Ted grew up in Greenwich, Connecticut, went to the finest prep schools, and graduated with honors from Yale. He tried his hand in the world of advertising and was very successful, but found that after a while, it lost its allure. So, he turned his talents to writing novels. He wrote several successful detective books but hit the jackpot when he hit upon Robert Falcon super spy. Ted patterns Falcon after himself. The character's physical description fits his unique style of wardrobe, his taste and prowess with women, and even the kind of automobile he drives, the McLaren 720S, a 710 hp twin-turbo, four-liter engine that rockets 0-60 in 2.9 seconds.

Ted has been quoted saying that he wouldn't ask Robert Falcon to do anything that he wouldn't and couldn't do.

Cape Town Station – March 1st

The train was scheduled to leave Cape Town at 11 a.m. We arrived and boarded at 9 a.m. We are shown to our suites. I've chosen LuWei, Sue-B, and Fu Hao to accompany me on this mission. Each team member has the skills that I believe will be needed to bring about a successful mission.

Black Train – March 1st

We all received an invite from Ted Cloche to join him and his party in the Lounge Car for an informal meet and greet. Tea and cucumber sandwiches were served, along with dainty cakes and fresh scones with cream.

As we entered the Lounge Car, Mr. Cloche greeted us. "Greeting fellow travelers. I am Ted Cloche, president of the Safari Society, and these are members of the society. I don't think we need to do formal introductions, as we will have ample time for all of us to get acquainted. Please have a seat and enjoy some tea and light refreshments."

I shook Mr. Cloche's hand and said, "Mr. Cloche, thank you for your kindness. I am Roger Williams, and these are my guests. We look forward to getting better acquainted with you and the members of your society. You're very kind."

"It's always a pleasure to meet people with similar interests, specialty hunters. You folks are hunters?"

"Oh yeah, we're hunters all right."

"Big game?"

"Nothing but the biggest."

"Excellent; I look forward to seeing you shoot."

"Ah, remember that old saying, be careful what you wish for."

For the rest of the tea service we comingled with the members of the Safari Society, getting to know as much about them as possible without appearing to be too nosey. I find that people love to talk about themselves more than listen to you talk about yourself, sometimes to their detriment.

Black Train – March 1st

For our first dinner on board, we were seated with the two Germans, Hans Schmidt and Fritz Müller, both from Düsseldorf, both pilots for Lufthansa and avid big game hunters. They told us that this was the hunting expedition that they were looking forward to getting their big five: lion, rhino, elephant, leopard, and Cape buffalo. They were very enthusiastic at the possibility.

"One shouldn't get too enthusiastic; shit happens, and as Mick Jagger says, "You can't always get what you want," I said.

We started our meal with a glass of Sauvignon Blanc and an order of caramelized foie gras with grilled apples and oriental seafood parcels with a warm fennel salad. The main plates included pepper-crusted springbok with a pistachio lamb cutlet, prosciutto-wrapped monkfish, and seared duck breast. After spending so many days and nights eating MRE, this was indeed the height of luxury.

During the course of dinner, we made small talk with Hans and Fritz and learned a lot about them as well as the other members of the Society. The two Germanic hunters, like the rest of the SS members, believed that African nations relied heavily on money that trophy hunters injected into their economy. But the fact is that the revenue generated from big game hunters in South Africa, for example, was 201 million dollars. It sounds like a lot of money, but that number pales by comparison to the 36 billion dollars in general tourism produced, according to Africa Check.

The African nations are not only letting a minority of big game hunters kill off their most prized wildlife, but they are also allowing them to kill off their future sources of billions of tourism dollars.

Tourists aren't going to come to Africa for the warthogs and wildebeest; people want to see lions, rhinos, and elephants. The only people who genuinely benefit from the fees paid for trophy hunting are the politicians collecting the fees, not the people.

When I brought up these facts that I had portrayed as rumors that I had heard, they, of course, fluffed them off as some sort of liberal commie propaganda and fake news. I didn't want to press the issue because I didn't want to arouse any suspicions, so we ended our evening cordially over cigars and cognac.

Black Train – March 2nd

The guests were invited to tour the Kimberley Big Hole and Diamond Mine Museum today. The Kimberley Mine is an open-pit and underground mine that claims to be the world's first bottomless hand-excavated hole.

I personally declined to go and pay homage to one of the biggest scams in history. Diamonds are the most commonly found precious stones in the world. Yet, through market manipulation and one family's total control and monopoly, diamonds are one of the most expensive, if not the most expensive, jewels. I find it fascinating how, for thousands of years, people have robbed, killed, and died for a rock that has no actual value other than what society places on it. Humans place a higher value on a piece of carbon than on, say, the life of a lion, a rhinoceros, or an elephant. I would rather die saving the life of one of God's creatures than for a thousand diamonds.

Black Train – March 3rd

Our stop today is Pretoria, almost due north of Johannesburg. The guests will have four hours to investigate one of the city's many cultural sites. Pretoria has a plethora of museums, gourmet restaurants, and shops. My team and I decided to take advantage of the city.

Once downtown, we split up and went our own way. It was interesting to see what everyone did. We decided to wait until dinner to disclose where we went and what we did.

Black Train – March 3rd

The Red Team got together in the Club Car for drinks and snacks; we decided to skip the formal dinner in the Dining

Car. Sue B and Fu Hao spent their day going to the Pretoria Art Museum, as well as the Transvaal Museum of Natural History and the Van Tilburg Collection. Lu Wei spent his day watching the South African Springbok's Rugby match against the New Zealand All Blacks. Lu Wei was especially moved by the *Haka* that the All Blacks performed before the match. The *Haka* is a native Māori war dance performed by warriors, traditionally before battle, to intimidate their opponents. The All Blacks execute the *Haka* for intimidation as well as a bit of theater.

"I worked with a New Zealander a couple of years back named Queequeg, like in Moby Dick. We were on the Attila the Hun in the waters off of Antarctica. It was Le Gang de la Clé de Singe's flagship of the anti-whaling fleet. She was an Island Class Patrol vessel, one hundred and ninety-four feet, with a max speed of twenty-two knots, six knots faster than the Azuma Maru, the Japanese whaling ship we were after. The Hun was painted primarily black with blue and white razzle-dazzle camouflage paint scheme. And painted in a bright yellow on either side were twelve-foot letters that read, '*Eat Shit And Die!*'. We flew two flags, the skull and cross monkey wrench flag on a yellow field and a banner flag that read, '*Death to All Whalers.*'

"We had been tracking the Azuma Maru for a couple of days. My initial plan was to put several men on board at night, get to the engine room, set explosives, and blow her up. We had a change of plan when Queequeg found out that he had stage four acute myeloid leukemia, which is cancer of the blood and bone marrow.

"He had gotten the news hours before we sailed out of Australia but kept it to himself. I asked him why he didn't tell me sooner. He said from what the doctors told him that he may have anywhere from a couple of months to a few weeks, and he didn't want to go through with a painful death. He said that he'd rather go out in a blaze of glory. He was going to go all kamikaze on the Azuma Maru, wearing a suicide vest, and take the ship down.

“That night, we set the plan in motion. We created a diversion to distract the crew of the Azuma Maru while I helped him get on board. Once on the ship, he went down to the engine room.

He radioed me, “Iceman, this is Queequeg. I’m down in the engine room. I just wanted to say that it’s been an honor and privilege working with you, the team, and being part of Le Gang de la Clé de Singe.”

“I said, “Queequeg, thank you for your sacrifice. Godspeed, brother.”

“He then proceeded to start his was haka, bent his knees, crossed his arms in front of his chest, and made his scariest warrior face. He opened his eyes wide, contorted his face, and stuck out his tongue as he began vigorous movements and stamping his feet with rhythmic shouting of the All Black haka chant.

“Taringa whakarongo
Kia rite! Kia rite! Kia mau!
Hi!
Kia whakawhenua au i ahau!
Hi, aue! Hi!
Ko Aotearoa, e ngunguru nei!
Hi, au! Au! Aue, ha! H!
Ko kapa o pango, e ngunguru nei!
Hi, au! Au! Aue, ha! Hi!
I ahaha!
Ka tu te ihi-ihi
Ka tu te wanawana
Ki runga i te rangi, e tu iho nei, tu iho nei, hi!
Ponga ra!
Kapa o pango! Aue, hi!
Ponga ra!
Kapa o pango! Aue, hi!
Ha!”

TRANSLATION

"Let me go back to my first gasp of breath
Let my life force return to the earth
It is New Zealand that thunders now
And it is my time!
It is my moment!
The passion ignites!
This defines us as the All Blacks
And it is my time!
It is my moment!
The anticipation explodes!
Feel the power
Our dominance rises
Our supremacy emerges
To be placed on high
Silver fern!
All Blacks!
Silver fern!
All Blacks!
Aue hi!'

"The entire crew of the Attila the Hun was on deck, and all eyes were fixated on the Azuma Maru. We suddenly heard the engines stop, and then we felt a concussion wave, followed by the sounds of the explosions. Then, there was a giant fireball shooting hundreds of feet straight up into the blackness, illuminating the sky as far as the eye could see. And then the Azuma Maru was gone, and there was nothing but silence.

"That night, we all got what we wanted. Le Gang de la Clé de Singe got the death of the Azuma Maru, and Queequeg got a warrior death."

Lu Wei said, "Sue B, Fu Hao, and I were up in the Arctic battling sealers when we heard. It's an amazing story, to be sure."

There was an awkward pause before Sue B asked, "And what did you do today, Ice?"

"I spent my day at SANBI, the National Zoological Gardens. It's the eighth largest zoo in the world, and they even have an aquarium. I found it very relaxing to see animals and know that they won't be slaughtered."

The waiter came by and asked if anyone wanted another drink or something else to eat.

I ordered the kabeljou, snoek, and Knysna oysters for the table. Afterwards, we all called it a night.

Black Train – March 4th, 5th, 6th

We spent the next three days traveling around Barkley West, Warrenton, and Kameel for hunters of game birds. We at Le Gang de la Clé de Singe allow game bird hunting on game bird farms; I have found that 30 to 40% of the birds escape into the wild due to poor marksmanship.

Black Train – March 7th

It all started when the train pulled off from the main tracks onto the private rails of the Kruger National Park, where the big game hunting was supposed to begin later in the day.

I was sitting on the open-air observation platform alone on the Observation Car, having coffee and watching a herd of elephants off in the distance, when Ted Cloche and two of his friends strolled past me carrying hunting rifle cases. I entered the main car and telephoned Fu Hao, asking her to meet me on the observation deck and bring her rifle.

She arrived just as one of Ted Cloche's friends, a man in his mid-fifties with salt and pepper hair. He was sporting a David Niven mustache, wearing aviator sunglasses, and all decked out in a very chic outfit designed by Ralph Lauren. He looked every bit the hunter out of a Hollywood movie.

He and Ted were laughing and joking when the man raised his rifle and took a shot at one of the female elephants in the herd of elephants that I had been watching. The train was moving very slowly since we pulled off the mainline and onto the private tracks of the park. The herd was traveling parallel with the train when the man fired, striking a cow in the spine and causing her to collapse since she was paralyzed in her back legs. She was in considerable pain and struggling to walk as the others in the herd were coming to her aid.

The men were very nonchalant about the elephant's condition and even joked about the man's poor marksmanship while letting the poor animal suffer.

When Fu Hao saw that the men were ignoring the wounded creature, she said, "You just can't let her suffer; you have to do something."

The well-dressed shooter indignantly said, "Who the fuck are you missy?"

She turned to me, and I gave her a nod. She aimed and fired a kill shot to put the poor suffering beast out of her misery.

"Hey, that was my trophy; you had no right to do that!" The man hollered at Fu Hao.

Fu Hao was holding her rifle waist high when she fired a single shot, hitting the well-dressed man below the buckle of his 1800-dollar designer safari jacket. He collapsed onto the floor of the observation deck.

"Oh my God, you shot Douglas! I'll have you arrested, you maniac!" Ted Cloche shouted.

I placed my coffee cup down, withdrew my Glock 9mm pistol, and calmly said, "Excuse me, Ted, may I call you Ted? Ted, we're from an organization I'm sure you may have heard of, Le Gang de la Clé de Singe.

"Remember the night of the party when you asked me if we were big game hunters, and I said the biggest? Well, I think you now understand what I meant. We hunt assholes like you. Now you and your friend drop your weapons."

I went into the Observation Car and pulled the emergency stop cord while Fu Hao detained and disarmed the two men. I called Lu Wei and Sue B and had them force everyone off the train and proceed towards the body of the female elephant that had been killed by the dapper Safari Society member.

Lu Wei had earlier in the day disabled the train's Wi-Fi and all its outside communication capabilities. We also confiscated all of the passengers and staff's cell phones.

We had the entire train staff gathered in the lounge car, with the curtains drawn and watched over by Lu Wei.

After Sue B and Fu Hao placed the yellow monkey wrench flags around the sixteen prisoner's necks, I read to them the letter that would be placed in each of their pockets.

"Let it be known that, from this day forth, Le Gang de la Clé de Singe declares a proclamation of war against all Poachers, Big Game Hunters, all Big Game Safari Outfits, as well as anybody anywhere in the world that targets, kills, profits, and/or supports the killing of any animals that are endangered or any animals that are hunted for sport. Be forewarned: do so at your own peril. You will be hunted down and pay with your lives. Be it man or woman, there will be no exceptions and no mercy; we will show no quarter. You have been warned."

"You all knew the consequences, and yet you chose to ignore the warning; you felt killing big game was worth the risk."

"But I haven't killed anything." A woman shouted out.

"Excuse me, madam. Do you believe we should have waited for each of you to kill something before taking action? Allowing you to take the life of another elephant, lion, rhino, or whatever so you can decrease the population of the species even further. I think that kind of defeats the whole purpose. No, madam, you all were on this train for the express purpose of killing big game, and for that, you all shall be shown no quarter."

Ted Cloche stepped forward and said, "It isn't fair; I'm writing another Robert Falcon best-selling novel; I don't deserve this. To die like this."

I said, "You deserve it more than the elephant lying next to you deserved to die. What makes any of you think your lives are any more valuable than these magnificent creatures? You're so cavalier about killing, you are all so self-righteous, you celebrate their deaths, you take your aggrandizing photographs standing over them, and then you have their heads cut off and mounted them on your walls to remind you how superior we humans are.

"Killing for pleasure is nothing to celebrate. After we're done here, we won't rejoice in your deaths. We won't be taking any photographs. No, we will mourn you and the creatures that you have killed. Death is not to be celebrated.

"You know Ted, we're doing you a huge favor. Because once you're dead, the sale of your books will skyrocket."

Black Train – March 7th

The members of the South African Police Service and Interpol found the bodies of the sixteen hunters lying next to the elephant that "Dapper Dan" shot on the train. They were all found adorned with the Le Gang de la Clé de Singe flags and the proclamations in their pockets.

The train staff all gave police descriptions of the four of us, but of course, we had all been wearing disguises and using South African accents. We told the staff that we had placed explosives on the tracks in either direction so they wouldn't try to move the train. We hadn't used any explosives, but they didn't know that, so they stayed put. We informed them that we would call the police in an hour, which we did.

The police had their CSI look for forensic evidence and found none. However, they did find only one fingerprint other than that of the staff and that of the deceased. That was that of

American railroad magnate Andrew Carnegie. The police and Interpol were not amused.

Xonghile Game Park, Mozambique – March 7th

We made our way to the Phalaborwa—Letsba Road, which runs through Kruger National Park. Odin and the rest of the Red Team picked us up in our 4Runners, and we crossed into Mozambique.

We drove to the Xonghile Game Park, located on the Kruger border, to meet members of the International Anti-Poaching Foundation.

The IAPF and Le Gang de la Clé de Singe had received requests from government officials for our assistance. Xonghile Game Park is one of the continent's hottest poaching areas. The Park is a transit corridor for criminals and poachers entering Kruger in search of rhino horns.

Just in the last two days, there had been three incursions with armed poachers. One poacher was shot and killed with a .458 rifle, and two others were arrested along with the seizure of their vehicle and US$ 10,000 in cash.

We met our contacts at their encampment where the Elefantes River enters the Rio Dos Elefantas Lake. Dr. Kristoffer Spather and Dr. Dennis MacDonald of the IAPF were both veterans of the poaching wars. They told us that poaching in this area had reached epidemic proportions. They were looking for help training the park's rangers in the art of tactical tracking.

We went through our introductions and pleasantries. Dr. Spather and MacDonald told us that they had captured three Nigerians two days ago with a massive haul of the slaughtered game from Kruger National Park, along with elephant tusks, giant snake skins, and the carcasses and heads of various animals. Buffalos and monkeys were loaded into two vans. They also seized a dozen hunting rifles, machetes, five bicycles, and various chemical poisons.

They were holding them in the camp until we could interrogate them.

"Shall we have a go with them now?" I asked.

"Very good, they are being held in a storage shed at the edge of the camp. Follow us," MacDonald said.

Dr. Spather and Dr. MacDonald led the way, and the Red Team and I followed. There looked to be about twelve tents for housing the IAPF Rangers, a mess tent, and a couple of storage sheds. The tin hut storage shed had an armed guard posted outside, and the three Nigerians were sitting on the dirt floor, their hands and feet shackled.

I told the doctors that the guard could go since he wouldn't be needed anymore. I suggested that they might not want to stay as well. Both Dr. Spather and Dr. MacDonald insisted on observing.

Dr. Spather said, "We need to see how you handle the situation. We know that your methods get results, and we're in a desperate situation with poaching having increased 600% since 1974."

"Okay, watch and learn. Don't say anything; let me do all the talking." I said.

We entered the 20 by 20-foot metal hut, and as we entered, the three poachers rose to their feet and glared at us with contempt.

Standing in front of the three men, I reached behind my back and retrieved my Glock. I then screwed on an Osprey silencer and asked where they were taking the stuff and who is their boss?

The eldest of the three spit at my feet and said, "Fuck you, man. You don't scare me, go fuck yourself."

I said nothing; I raised my pistol and shot him in the head once. The force of the bullet sent him backward a good ten feet. The remaining two's eyes got as big as saucers. They looked like a Mutt and Jeff pair, one tall and lanky and the other short and chubby.

Both Doctors took a step forward as if to interfere. Odin raised his hand, indicating them to stop, which they did.

"I said, where are you taking this stuff, and who is your boss? You, fatso, what do you have to say?"

"I don't know nothing."

"That's a shame," I said and shot him in the chest twice, sending him reeling into a stack of elephant tusks that they had poached.

"How about you, sweetpea? What do you know?"

"We were going to Angoche Island." The man said nervously.

"Who were you going to meet and when?"

"His name is Zhang Wei, four days from now at the pier."

"What does this Zhang Wei look like?"

"He is a short, stocky man, not much hair, with large marks on his face, and he wears glasses."

"Have you ever heard of Le Gang de la Clé de Singe or seen this?" I said as I held up the yellow banner.

He shook his head no.

"No? That's too bad." I shot twice in rapid succession, killing him instantly. He, too, fell backward onto the pile of stacked ivory tusks next to his accomplice.

"Doctor MacDonald and I are appalled at your murdering those men!" Doctor Spather said.

"Doctor, I know you'd like to play by some sort of rules, but there are no rules. Do you want to save these animals, or do you want to play nice? Trophy hunting and poaching, in particular, is a dirty business; we play dirty. Either one of those men would have slit both of your throats and wouldn't have blinked an eye.

"I'm sorry to be so blunt, but this is how the game is played. Now, my team is going to remove these three and take them back into Kruger. Then we'll alert the authorities so they will be discovered, and if you like, we will stay and help train your men, or we'll go. It's your decision. What would you like?"

Doctor Spather looked at MacDonald and said sheepishly, "Stay."

"Good. I know it's distasteful, Doctors. War is Hell, but that's what we have here: war. I think a couple of my men and I will head over to Angoche Island and see if we can meet up with this Zhang Wei character.

"I left my number one man, Odin, and several of the Red Team to stay and work with your rangers. If all goes well, we should be back within a week. I will be in contact with the team at all times, so if you need to get a hold of me, you can."

The Red Team gathered the three men up after placing the yellow flags around their necks and putting the message of guilt in their pockets. We then placed them with the items that they poached, drove back into Kruger National Park, and called the Kruger Rangers with the location.

Mozambique – March 8th

The journey to Angoche Island would take us over thirty-three hours and through multiple countries on roads that have no names. Few were even paved, so we relied on our GPS. Driving for hours on end surrounded by miles and miles of nothingness, occasionally, our paths would cross with a herd of elephants, zebras, or wildebeests. The ride was made even more arduous, knowing that we would make the same trip in reverse a few hours after we arrived at our destination.

I brought Sue B, Fu Hao, and Gianfranco with me. We would break up the day by having each of us drive for four hours. About fourteen hours into the trip, Sue B turned on the radio. The only station she found was Radio Moçambique 97.9.

Radio Moçambique is the nation's radio. It broadcasts in Portuguese, which is the official language of Mozambique. Since none of us speaks or understands Portuguese, she continued to find the BBC World Service - Maputo, which she finally did two hours later.

As the sun was setting, we caught the evening news.

"Good evening, I'm Nigel Williams, and this is the BBC World Headline News. Our top story this hour comes from Kruger National Park, where sixteen members of the Safari Society were found murdered. Most notable was that of Ted Cloche, the president of the Safari Society and author of the popular Robert Falcon spy novels series.

"The murders were committed on the "Black" Train Namibia Safari, a private train leased for special clientele. The authorities are looking for four guests who are missing; they are presumed to be members of the eco-terrorist group known as Le Gang de la Clé de Singe, who has claimed responsibility.

"The victims were all found with yellow flags bearing the skull and crossed wrenches around each of their necks, along with a letter of declaration of war. If anyone has any information, the South African police are offering a fifty-thousand-pound reward to the capture and..."

After three more petrol stops, we finally reached Angoche Island a day before the scheduled meeting with Zhang Wei.

Angoche Island – March 10th

After a 45-minute ferry ride from the mainland, we found one of the only three hotels on Angoche Island: Rickshaws Pousada e Cafe.

The hotel is a two-story white stucco Mediterranean-style building sitting right on the water. The outdoor patio has a bright blue sun sail that protects guests from the overhead sun; sitting out for meals and watching the sunset was quite lovely.

When the temperature drops, the guests gather around the fire pit on the patio in the evening to share their traveling experiences.

Not to draw attention to our group, we checked into the hotel as two married couples, Sue B, Fu Hao, and Gianfranco. Our rooms were both furnished with double beds, which made things less complicated.

After dinner, the four of us strolled up the Rus dos Trabalhadores north towards the Museum of the Island of Mozambique. It is located right across from the Il Ponteo pier, where the meeting with Zhang Wei was scheduled for some time in the morning.

There were three men waiting outside the museum; as we got closer, they approached us.

"Boa noite," I said.

The eldest of the three asked, "Você é ingles?"

"Yes, I speak English. Are you from Maputo?"

"No, I'm from Matola. Are you from London?"

"Ayaan. Hi, I'm Iceman, and this is Sue B, Fu Hao and Gianfranco. We really appreciate your help."

"Hi, this is my brother Badru and my cousin Malakai; we are here to help in any way we can."

Ayaan and his brothers all work for the "Save the Rhino" organization in Mozambique. Ayaan is with the park rangers, who are out on the front lines combating poachers in the bush.

Badru, the middle brother, works in the Dog Squad, using dogs to detect the smuggling of illegal wildlife products. The squad also tracks and apprehends poachers and stolen property, and it has been known to help find lost children.

Malakai, the baby of the family, works in the Sumatran Rhino Sanctuary, hand-rearing rhino calves whose mothers have been slaughtered. The poachers usually kill the mothers, butchering them right in front of the infants, and then leave the calves to starve or be attacked by predators. Baby rhinos will stand by their dead mothers, crying and trying to nuzzle them awake. Each of the orphans is assigned a caretaker who feeds them and watches over them.

All three brothers have been working with Le Gang de la Clé de Singe for over eight years on numerous assignments, but this is the first time they have gotten to work together.

I briefed them on the mission and went over the action plan. I told them I wasn't expecting any danger, but they should be armed and ready just in case.

After agreeing to meet at the Convent of São Domingos at 5:30 the following day, we went our separate ways.

Convent of São Domingos – March 11th

When we arrived at the convent, it was still dark outside. A slight sliver of bright orange was visible in the east, and a warm ocean breeze was blowing in from the east.

I had an uneasy feeling, an intuition that we were in for trouble. I tried not to make the team anxious. I could be wrong, but I reminded everyone that we're dealing with notorious villains. Things can turn on a dime, so stay sharp.

The plan was to have Ayaan and his brothers meet with Zhang Wei, lure him off the boat to have him investigate the poached cargo, and we could then capture him. That was the plan anyway. Unfortunately, as John Lennon once said, "Life is what happens while you are busy making other plans." or shit happens.

I always try to prepare for the worst and hope for the best. Today, shit happened.

Convent of São Domingos – March 11th

At 8:48, a twin-engine dark green steel workboat docked at the Il Ponteo pier. Two Chinese men were on deck, the captain and what appeared to be his first mate. The first mate secured the boat to the dock, then walked over to Ayaan and his brothers, who were fishing off the pier, and began to have a conversation.

"How's the fishing?" The sailor asked.

"Nothing today, but it was great a couple of days ago," Ayraan replied.

"Good catch?"

"Unbelievable."

"What do you do with what you catch?"

"We sell them to the highest bidder. Are you interested in buying?"

"Maybe I'll be right back."

As the first mate walked back to the boat, the captain, an older Chinese man, short, stocky, with not much hair, with a large mark on his face, and wearing glasses, was definitely Zhang Wei.

I was further down the dock towards the shore with Gianfranco, pretending to look at the fishing boats tied up along the dock. There were several other people on the dock as well. Sue B and Fu Hao were stationed on top of the Museum of the Island of Mozambique roof, each equipped with a Barrett M1078A1 sniper rifle. Sue B was informing Gianfranco and me of the goings on, as we were trying not to look towards the boat and seem suspicious.

The team and I stayed in communication with wireless radios. Aryaan and his brothers were wired and had tiny radio receivers hidden in their ears so we could communicate with each other.

The first mate and the older man appeared to be in serious discussions for several minutes, pointing to Ayraan and his brothers acting nonchalantly and continuing fishing.

Finally, the two men from the boat approached Ayraan. As they did, Sue B informed us that four men appeared from below deck, all armed.

"Ayraan, whatever you do, don't go on board that boat. Scratch your head if you understand." I said.

Ayraan reached up and scratched his head.

"I understand you fellas have fish to sell; is that correct?" Zhang Wei asked.

"For the right price," Ayraan said.

"What kind of fish do you have for sale?"

"We have several white fish for sale. The meat is ivory white, very beautiful. Very beautiful."

"That sounds delicious. What else?"

"Oh, we have several monkey fish, a couple of giant sea snakes, and a mix of this and that. Interested?"

"Very. Would you and your friends like to come on board and finalize the transaction?"

"Don't you want to see what you're buying? We have our catch in our van at the end of the dock."

Sue B alerted us that the first mate and Zhang Wei pulled out revolvers.

"I don't know who you three are, but I can only assume you're with the authorities. Let's go. On the boat." Zhang Wei demanded.

"Sue B, Fu Hao, take 'em down," I shouted as Gianfranco, and I started to race toward Zhang Wei and the boat.

No sooner than the words had left my lips, Zhang Wei and his first mate's heads exploded like water-filled balloons. It only took milliseconds for the men on the boat to realize what had happened before they opened fire.

Ayraan and his brothers had heard my order for the snipers to open fire, and they had the forethought to dive into the water.

Badru, the middle brother, sustained a bullet wound to his left calf as he was assisting his younger brother, Malakai, who had stumbled and fallen on the dock. Luckily, Badru's injury wasn't severe.

Gianfranco and I were firing at the men on the fishing boat as we ran towards them. Meanwhile, my two fabulous female assassins were making mincemeat of the hoodlums on the boat. By the time Gianfranco and I reached the boat, all the shooters that were on deck had been killed or wounded. I didn't know how many, if any, men were below.

“If there is anyone below and you don’t want to die, you had better come up with your hands where I can see them,” I shouted.

One sacred man in his late sixties slowly popped his head out from below with his hands way up in the air, “Please don’t shoot; I am not armed. I am just the machinist.”

“Up here now, flat on the deck, hands on your head,” I shouted.

The old man did as he was told; I secured his hands behind his back and placed a blindfold on, as he didn’t get a good look at our faces. Gianfranco instinctively jumped off the boat, untied the boat from the dock as I took control of the helm, swung around, and picked up Ayraan and his brothers out of the water. We then headed out into the Bay of Mossuril. Sue B and Fu Hao made their way back to the hotel to wait for our return.

We headed north toward the town of Mossuril; Ayraan suggested that we dock at an abandoned fishing pier just south of the town. Meanwhile, Malakai grabbed the ship’s first aid kit and patched up Badru’s leg. Ayraan called several of his friends to arrange for them to meet us at the pier.

Below deck, Gianfranco discovered a treasure trove of elephant tusks, rhino horns, and several canvas bags filled with pangolin scales, lion’s teeth, and claws. He brought up a couple of tusks and placed them next to the dead sailors. We prepared the dead on the deck with flags around their necks and letters of guilt in their pockets, lying next to the precious ivory they were so willing to die for.

Several minutes later, we spotted the abandoned fishing pier Ayraan had said would be there. Two of Ayraan’s friends were waiting for us in a blue and green two-masted Dhow. After we docked and prepared to leave the boat, I instructed the blindfolded machinist to stay put and that we would call the authorities and alert them to his location.

Angoche Island – March 11th

.

Ayraan's brothers and friends dropped Gianfranco and me off a quarter mile from Rickshaws Pousada e Café.

"Gentlemen, I can't tell you how much we are indebted to you all for all of your help," I said.

"No, thank you. If this can help call attention to the plague of poaching in our country, we are glad to help anytime, anywhere." Ayraan smiled and said.

"Badru, are you going to be all right?" I asked.

"No worries, I'll be at the disco tonight as usual."

Gianfranco and I received handshakes, back slaps, and fist bumps.

"Obrigado. Até logo." I said as we were walking away."

"You're welcome. Até logo," Ayraan said, waving as they headed back out into the bay.

We found Sue B and Fu Hao lying next to each other, sunning themselves on the beach.

"So?" Fu Hao queried.

Gianfranco smiled, "Ah piece a cake."

"Thanks to you two. Nice shooting." I said.

"Glad we could help." Sue B added.

"Any buzz?" I asked.

"Haven't heard anything; what's the plan now?" Sue B said.

"We'll check out tomorrow, not too early, and head back to Xonghile and see how the team is doing."

Angoche Island – March 11th

We were sitting on the patio having dinner, enjoying our peri peri chicken and prego rolls, watching the ships in the bay when four-armed uniformed policemen marched into the veranda and began questioning the guests.

Two men dressed in black suits approached our table.

"Passaportes." One of them demanded.

"Might I ask who you are?" I said.

"I am Inspector Morris of Interpol, and this is Inspector Volker. May I see your passports, please?"

The four of us handed him our passports.

"What is the nature of your visit to Angoche, Mr. Johnston?" He said.

"We are all on holiday, Inspector," I replied.

He looked hard at us and quickly asked Fu Hao, "Where are you from?" trying to pressure her.

"Chicago." She answered.

"What is your occupation, Mr. Verson?"

Gianfranco said, "I'm the sales manager for a water filtration company in Chicago."

"Do any of you have any drugs?" The Inspector asked, rifling through the passports.

"No, sir." We all answered.

"Weapons?" He snapped, trying to catch us off-guard.

"No." We responded.

"And what did you do today?" He asked me.

"We just walked around the island, did some sightseeing and some shopping, and then came back here and went swimming," I said.

He returned our passports and started to walk away when I asked, "Is there something wrong, Inspector?"

He stopped and stared at me before answering, "Why do you ask?"

"Well, you asked about weapons, and with all the terrible things happening in the world today, we…"

He cut me off curtly, "There is nothing wrong."

And that was that they were gone just as quick as they wandered in. The other guests seemed a bit dismayed, so we acted concerned as well.

After we finished our meal, we decided to enjoy the evening around the fire pit, drinking cognac and smoking cigars.

I don't know about the others that night, but I slept with my Glock under my pillow.

Xonghile Game Park – March 14th

By the time we returned to the game reserve, the story had spread across the country: how Le Gang de la Clé de Singe had been involved in a wild west shootout on a pier on Angoche Island; also, the discovery of the bodies of the poachers and the cache they found of the illegal ivory and other products.

The headline in the nation's largest newspaper, the Notícias, read, "A Gangue da Chave de Macaco Mata Oito." *The Monkey Wrench Gang Kills Eight*.

The article went on to describe the shootout on the pier and the discovery of the dead bodies on board an abandoned ship eleven miles away. There were several color photographs of the deceased, all laid out side by side with the yellow flags with the black skulls and crossed monkey wrenches placed around their necks.

There was an interview with the machinist found bound and blindfolded. Mr. Cliften Wazimbo tells how he was sure that in the struggle, he had killed one of the Le Gang de la Clé de Singe members before six of them overpowered, blindfolded, and tied him up. He claimed to be both a hero and a victim.

Mr. Wazimbo had been arrested in connection with the transporting of illegal endangered species, the possession of said products, smuggling, and possibly murder. Mr. Wazimbo pleaded not guilty and has since recanted his story about killing anyone.

Unlike all the other police departments, the Mozambique Defense Armed Forces leaked information about the single fingerprint found at the crime scene other than the victims and Mr. Wazimbo. They announced that it was that of Josina Machel, a Mozambique freedom fighter who died when she was only twenty-five. She is considered a national hero. Police remain baffled, and Interpol remains pissed off.

Odin and the rest of the team, with the exception of Lu Wei, weren't at the compound when we returned; they were out on patrol with Dr. Spather. Lu Wei had stayed in camp with Dr. MacDonald and his assistant Hanifa, who he was teaching the art of the drone.

Of all the rangers, she seemed to have the most aptitude and skills in handling and maneuvering the drone.

Hanifa grew up poor in Beria, the fourth largest city in Mozambique, which is located on the coast of the Indian Ocean. Her father was a fisherman, and she lived with her eight brothers and three sisters in a small shack on the beach. It was on a dirt street with no name in the part of the city known as Area da Baixa.

Every morning before sunrise, her father and the three oldest brothers would take their dhow, a 22-foot single-masted lateen-rigged fishing vessel, fishing in the Indian Ocean. Hanifa, her mother, and her three younger sisters would sell the day's catch in the market square.

As Hanifa was growing up, she remembered her father talking about how the number of foreign trawlers, with their massive fishing nets, were coming into their waters. They were plundering the fishing grounds, leaving them with very little. The Chinese, in particular, and other foreign countries were raping their native fish stocks and selling their catch on the global markets, leaving Mozambique and other African countries with less and less.

Her father and several of the local fishermen were killed when they confronted a Chinese trawler within their waters. Shots were fired, and a firefight broke out, killing seven local fishermen and three Chinese.

The incident became an international scandal; Mozambique barred all Chinese fishing off their coast for six weeks. The Chinese government lodged a formal complaint with the United Nations, which was more for show. They had their fleets sitting in the waters off of Mozambique, ready to go as soon as the ban had expired.

Hanifa's three older brothers took over their father's fishing business. Hanifa became so enraged over the death of her father that she and some of the other families who had lost loved ones organized several protest marches against foreign intervention in the fishing industry. The protests gathered momentum, and as sometimes happens, things turned ugly. What started out as a protest march ended up as a riot.

The police over-reacted and began cracking heads, tear-gassing the crowd, and making arrests, Hanifa being one of them. While in jail, she was approached by members of Le Gang de la Clé de Singe, who were always looking for potential recruits looking for a way to make a difference and a change in the world.

When she got out after three months in jail, she joined numerous attacks against the Chinese fleet out in international waters. She cut their nets, fouled the propellers, and generally made their lives miserable. She used strategies from the playbooks of Greenpeace and Sea Shepherd.

After two years of fighting the Chinese fishing fleet, she participated in dozens of local environmental causes. The most recent was the International Anti-Poaching Foundation in Xonghile Game Reserve, where Lu Wei taught her the art of drones.

She is learning to build, fly, repair, and weaponize drones. Lu Wei is helping her build an armada of drones. She will learn everything about an eight-foot drone capable of dropping bombs and armed with a Ruger AR-556 Automatic Tactical Rifle. She will also learn about a swarm of nano drones for reconnaissance missions that resemble small birds and beetle-like insects.

Xonghile Game Park – March 15th

Doctors Spather and MacDonald had assembled the reserve's Anti-poaching Rangers to the compound so I could present them and go over all the new equipment that Le Gang de la Clé de Singe is donating in their effort to combat poachers. Since the government operates the game reserve, they cannot and will not take any action against big game trophy hunters, only poachers.

There were sixteen rangers standing in a semicircle waiting as I approached, bearing gifts.

"Gentlemen, these are a present, a reward to you for working so hard in a dangerous area.

"It's the beginning of the wet season, so we're giving everyone two sets of boots, so you'll always have one pair of dry boots.

"We have medical gear, so later, we'll be making up some personal medical kits you'll carry out in the bush.

"We also have new vests, each equipped with a radio, a baton, hand restraints, pepper spray, a pair of binoculars, a stun gun, two ammo clips, and a pair of night vision goggles. Finally, you will each be issued a new Steyr Aug A3 SF assault rifle so that the playing field will become a little more level. Thank you, and good luck."

Dr. Kristoffer Spather said, "I know that I speak not only for Dr. MacDonald but for everyone here. We thank you and your organization for your assistance, training, and these well-needed gifts."

Xonghile Game Park – March 16th

A patrol radioed in; they found a breach in the fence at the 39-meter marker and had discovered two sets of spoors leading out of Kruger National Park and into Xonghile. They're looking for backup.

I called the Red Team together, "Saddle up! We're on."

We loaded everyone into one Toyota 4Runner and headed out to marker 39. When we arrived, we found the four-person patrol waiting for us.

"Whadda we got?" I asked the patrol leader, Akbar.

He showed us a set of footprints that looked to be heading out of the South African side of the fence coming into Mozambique.

I saw that they were actually a set of decoy prints. The poachers try to walk backward to deceive us into thinking that they are leaving Kruger, but they are actually going into the park to kill a rhino. I pointed out to them that they could discern the difference by the pressure of the footprints.

When one walks forward, the pressure is on the heel of the footprint, and when one walks backward, the pressure is on the toe of the footprint.

"I think they hoped we'd follow this decoy spoors away from here. I believed that they were still in Kruger and would come out towards us after they killed something.

"I know you can't go into Kruger, but we can. Odin, you, Sassoon, Sue B, Fu Hao, and Gianfranco stay here and set up an ambush. Bellator, Cowboy, Venus, and I will go into Kruger and either catch or flush them back to you."

Kruger National Park – March 16th

We headed into the killing fields dressed in camo fatigues and balaclavas, each carrying an AK-101 assault rifle. This was where over 1175 rhinos were killed by poachers last year, not counting those killed legally by trophy hunters.

Cowboy led the way, as he is the best tracker in our group. The terrain was a heavy brush with clumps of marula trees, which made for slow movement. As we moved along at a snail's pace, Cowboy suddenly gave us the drop-down signal. We were so close to our poachers that we actually heard them speaking.

We slowly advanced towards four men, all of whom seemed to be in their late forties or early fifties. Two were carrying AK-47s, and the other two held machetes for the mutilation of the rhinos. They apparently had spotted an adult black rhino and were preparing to slaughter it. We didn't have a clear shot of the four, but I didn't want to wait until they killed the beast before firing.

"Fire!" I shouted, and the four of us opened fire, trying to concentrate our shots in the general area that we believed them to be as we advanced towards them through the brush.

There was some minor return fire, but it was from just one of the poachers who fled towards the 39 marker, where the other members of the Red Team and rangers were waiting. When we reached the poachers, two were dead; the third was withering on the ground, wounded in the shoulder.

Dr. Spather made a request of me before we left that if any of these poachers were captured alive to please return them to stand trial to set an example to others.

I gave him my word, and I honored it. We field dressed the two dead poachers with our yellow banners, as well as the traditional letter of guilt placed on their persons. Then we forced marched the wounded man back to Xonghile Park to be arrested and taken into custody.

When we reached marker 39, the fourth poacher had also been apprehended. He was sitting on the ground with his hands restrained behind his back.

After questioning the prisoners, we determined that they were looking to obtain a rhino horn for their village's witchdoctor to use in various rituals and medicinal potions.

We turned our wounded prisoners over to the park rangers and left them to bring them to the authorities. We then called in the position of the two poachers that we had left in Kruger.

Xonghile Game Park – March 17th

"Ice. Go," I answered my secure cell phone.

"Ice, this is Wooch. How's it going?"

"Real good. I think we're mission accomplished here. They seem to be in a good place."

"Glad to hear it. Is your team up for another assignment?"

"Wooch, you know we're always ready to rock and roll. Whadda got?"

"The Ibhino Gang."

"Aren't they one of the most notorious and slippery criminal rhino-poaching rings in all of South Africa?"

"They were. They are three brothers who were finally brought to justice after seven years of evasion. They were the South African el Chapo of poaching."

"Well, if they've been captured, what do you want the Red Team to do, kill them?" I said jokingly."

There was a brief silent pause, and then Wooch said dead seriously, "That's exactly what I want."

"You're joking," I said.

"These three brothers were found guilty on 177 counts in 55 separate poaching incidents during just the last three years. These creeps are facing lengthy jail terms, but we don't believe that their punishment fits their crimes.

"We want to send a clear message: Le Gang de la Clé de Singe shows no mercy. We want everyone to know that if you poach, you die."

"Where and when?" I asked.

"They're being held in the Port Elizabeth jail; they're scheduled to be transferred to the correctional services prison at Fort Glamorgan in three days."

"Security?"

"Shouldn't be too heavy. They will be transported in an RG-12 armored personnel carrier."

"You know those puppies carry anti-personnel mine, grenades, firebombs, and small arms protection?"

"Ah, piece of cake."

"More like shit."

"Listen, you and your team make your way down to Grahamstown, and I'll have Kgabu meet you there with whatever you think you need. Just text me as soon as you know."

"Tell Kgabu that we'll be there early tomorrow morning. It's about a twenty-hour drive. If we get there tomorrow, that will give us two solid days to work out a plan."

"Keep me posted, Ice."

We said our goodbyes to Dr. Kristoffer Spather, Dr. Dennis MacDonald, and the rest of the Xonghile Park Rangers, wished them well, and told them to contact us anytime they needed us.

Xonghile Game Park – March 17th

We were off for a twenty-hour killer road trip, literally. On the way down, in the two 4Runners, we all took turns behind the wheel to share the misery. We made two petrol stops, the first just outside of Pretoria and the second in Bloemfontein.

South Africa – March 17th

Twelve hours in, Odin and I had finally worked out a plan. I called Wooch and gave him the list of equipment that we needed. One of our main objectives is not to injure any South African police escorting the Ibhino brothers. This would be a major disaster.

South Africa – March 18th

My turn driving: we had been at it for seventeen hours. Everyone had been asleep for hours. It was a dangerous time to travel at night. You really had to be alert for animals near or on the roads. It wasn't like you might hit a raccoon or even a deer; there are animals that weigh hundreds, even thousands of pounds, roaming around at night.

"How ya doing?" Cowboy asked from the back seat.

"I'm good, how are you feeling?"

"Ready to be there."

"I know what you're saying. You should try and go back to sleep."

"I'm up. You know."

"Yeah, I know."

"So, how, after all this time, did they finally nail these guys?"

"Well, apparently, the case revolved around the events one night in August a year ago. The brothers were arrested at a resort outside Alexandria, not far from Kikuyu Lodge Game Reserve. Two white rhinos had been murdered, slaughtered, and dehorned. Found in the brother's possession were 100 kilos of rhino horn worth over $700,000 on the black market, plus various tools, a dart gun, tranquilizers, saws, machetes, and a stolen Holland & Holland Royal Double Rifle worth about a hundred thousand dollars.

"Evidence from the rhino horns in the case matched the DNA from the two dean rhinos at Kikuyus, and the saw was discovered with the gang at the time of their arrest. A forensic paint expert confirmed a match to a paint chip from the saw's handle to one found at the crime scene."

"But they're going away to jail; why kill them?"

"We want them to fear death more than jail time, even long jail time. Now, try and get some sleep."

Not long after I finished my sentence, I heard Cowboy snoring softly.

Oak Lodge Grahamstown – March 18th

When we arrived, Kgabu was waiting in the Oak Lodge's parking lot. He had arranged for our rooms and had all of our keys.

We each grabbed our keys and headed up to our rooms for a couple of hours of restful sleep. We were all to meet in the parking lot at noon.

The Rat & Parrot – March 18th

We made our way to the Rat & Parrot for some burgers and beers. Kgabu had arranged for us to get the back room all to ourselves. The owners are Le Gang sympathizers, and they gave us a safe house to talk over the plans for tomorrow's attack.

Kgabu has obtained all the equipment that Odin and I had requested. Later that afternoon, we all headed out to the location where the strike would take place, so we were able to see it firsthand and set up our positions. Maps, even satellite maps, give only limited information; things change.

The plan was to attack the police vehicle just after they passed the Hunts Hoek Safaris Game Farm and crossed the bridge for the Groot-visriver River on the N2 highway; there is a long stretch of empty road that is rarely traveled. We would stage an automobile accident that appeared to have multiple injuries and several vehicles involved blocking the road.

We'd been informed that the RG-12 armored personnel carrier would be leaving the Port Elizabeth courthouse at 1 p.m. Our sources tell us three officers will accompany the prisoners, so our hope was that at least two officers would vacate the transport to give assistance, and if we were lucky, all three would. We were preparing for all possible contingencies.

Oak Lodge Grahamstown – March 19th

Everything seemed to be in order; everyone knew his/her job and was ready. We headed out to our position; I had decided to send Lu Wei and Venus down to Trumpeter's Drift Game Farm, turn off the N2, and have them put up a drone to keep us posted on the armored personnel carrier's progress. We would be informed exactly when the police van left Port Elizabeth, then once Lu Wei and Venus picked them up with the drone, that's when we set the stage for the accident.

The N2 Highway – March 19th

We just received word that the police van had just left the Port Elizabeth courthouse with three police officers and the Ibhino brothers on board. The clock was ticking.

The N2 Highway – March 19th

Lu Wei spotted the van and estimated it was traveling at approximately 100 kph—the estimated time of arrival was 3:56 p.m.

The N2 Highway – March 19th

We started to set the stage for the accident. A Nissan NP200, a Chevrolet Ute, and a P-Series Scania delivery truck were strategically placed, giving the impression that the delivery truck had hit the Chevrolet Ute from behind, flipping it over upside down and forcing it into the opposing lane hitting the Nissan, and trapping the occupants of the Chevy, Sue B and Fu Hao were inside with a fire starting to spread.

The N2 Highway – March March 19th

"Help! Help! We're stuck. For God's sake, help us!" Sue B shouted.

Cowboy jumped out of the delivery truck and ran to the overturned car, starting to try to extinguish the fire. Odin and Bellator leaped out of the Nissan and crawled under the Ute to try to get to Sue B and Fu Hao.

When the RG-12 armored personnel carrier arrived, the police officer in the van's "shotgun" position got out to investigate.

"Please help us! We're trapped, God help us! Fire!" Fu Hao screams.

Odin, Bellator, and Cowboy were all trying to overturn the car so they could get the women out before the fire spread.

"All together, push!" Cowboy shouts.

The three men groan as they try to turn the car over.

"Again, on three. One. Two. Three!"

The car rocks back and forth, but there just isn't enough force to flip it.

Odin saw the police van and ran up to the officer who was out of the van and shouted, "There are two women trapped in that car, and it's on fire. Help us get them out."

The officer waved to the officer driving the van to help. As the driver exited the personnel carrier, Lu Wei and Venus pulled up behind the police van, blocking them from going backward. Venus turned on a radio-jamming device to block any distress call that the police van may try to send.

Lu Wei and Venus got out of their car and up past the police driver to join the others to help the two trapped women.

"Don't worry, ladies. We'll get you out of there. Stay calm," the police driver assured them.

The delivery truck and overturned Chevy were locked together to prevent the Ute from easily flipping over. The police officers were the only ones trying to overturn the car.

The Red Team was pretending so the third officer would feel compelled to leave the police van and help.

"Help! Help us, please, we can't get out! Our seatbelts are jammed!" Sue B cried out.

The officer, who was the driver, slid under the car to see if he could somehow undo their seatbelts, but to no avail.

He returned to the personnel carrier and retrieved a fire extinguisher to put out the fire. He shouted over his shoulder for the third officer to come help, which he did.

As the officer with the fire extinguisher put out the fire, Cowboy got into his delivery truck and eased the truck back slowly to unlock the Chevy from the truck. With the two vehicles now separated, the people turned the car on its side, and then, with one last big push, the Chevy Ute finally sat upright.

With all three officers out of the personnel carrier, Sassoon, Gianfranco, and I each took aim with our tranquilizer rifles and fired, successfully hitting our marks. In seconds, the officers were on the ground unconscious.

The N2 Highway – March 19th

Officer Adriaan Badenhort, the driver of the RG-12 armored personnel carrier, woke up with a splitting headache sitting behind the wheel of the van with his seatbelt on. Sitting next to him was Officer Grobbelaar, looking around in a state of confusion. They were parked on the side of the N2, engine running. They could hear the police dispatcher on the radio, "One Delta One, One Delta One, do you read me? Come in One Delta One, over."

Officer Badenhort reached for the mic, "This is One Delta One; come in. Over."

"Badenhort, where the Hell have you been? Over."

"We were assisting a 10-50 on the N2 just passed Grahamstown. Over."

"Is everything all right? Do you need assistance? Over."

From the back of the armored carrier, the third officer, Officer Van der Westhuizen, who had just recovered from his state of unconsciousness, yelled out, "Oh my God, they're gone! The Ibhino brothers are gone!"

Officer Badenhort, dazed, stared out of the front windshield and quietly asked Grobbelaar, "Where is the accident? Where are the cars, the delivery truck, and the people? What the fuck is going on?" The road was clear, not a sign of any accident, nothing.

Grobbelaar took the mic and spoke to dispatch, "Dispatch, this is Officer Grobbelaar. Do you copy?"

"Grobbelaar, this is Captain Durban; what the Hell is going on?"

"Captain, the Ibhino brothers have escaped; send help immediately."

Within an hour, sixteen patrol cars were there. They brought in three K9 units, four plain-clothes detectives, eight CSI lab techs, Captain Durbin, and two helicopters.

Blue Lagoon Hotel, East London – March 19th

We made it safely to East London and checked into the Blue Lagoon Hotel on Nahoon Beach around eight pm. We decided to meet at nine o'clock in the Highlander Restaurant next door after we had a chance to clean up.

The Red Team cleaned up the crash site in record time, under a half hour. We safely placed the officers back into their vehicle after extricating the Ibhino brothers.

The brothers Ibhino thought we were breaking them out and setting them free until we revealed who we were when we placed the yellow ensign with the black skull with crossed monkey wrenches around their necks. At that point, they begged us to leave them in the armored carrier, pleading for us to allow them to do their prison sentence of twenty years each, which they said that they deserved.

The police received an anonymous call that they would find the bodies of the Ibhino brothers in an abandoned farmhouse with a red tin roof. It stood on the edge of the tiny town of Gqumashe, just outside the city of Alice, sixty miles north of Grahamstown.

The police found that each of the brothers had been shot once in the head, execution style, and a letter placed in their prison jumpsuit pocket that read,

"Let it be known that Le Gang de la Clé de Singe declares that the sentence passed down by the judiciary of South Africa against the Ibhino brothers for their multiple acts of poaching was woefully too lenient; Le Gang maintains that nothing but the death penalty would be justified.

"Be forewarned: to all Poachers, Big Game Hunters, all Big Game Safari Outfits, as well as anybody anywhere in the world that targets, kills, profits, and/or supports the killing of any animals that are endangered or any animals that are hunted for sport, you do so at your own peril. You will be hunted down and pay with your lives. Be it man or woman, there will be no exceptions and no mercy; we will show no quarter; not even prison can save you. You have been warned."

The Port Elizabeth Police CSI team did the usual sweep for any evidence of the people who carried out the assault and kidnapping of the police officers as well as the murder of the Ibhino brothers. But aside from the fingerprints of the officers and the prisoners, they only found one clean fingerprint belonging to Percival Guy Tunmer, a South African ex-Formula One racing driver who was killed in a motorcycle accident over twenty years ago.

When Inspector Morris heard about Tunmer's fingerprint, he asked Volker, "Ever wonder where they get these fucking fingerprints? We've been chasing these killers all over the world for over five years, and in practically every case, there's always one unexplained celebrity fingerprint. HQ has yet to crack that nut; it just drives me crazy."

"To tell you the truth, Morris, I'm getting tired of chasing my tail with these fuckers, and I think HQ is beginning to lose faith in us."

"What have you heard?"

"These are just rumors, but you know as well as I do that there's always a kernel of truth in every rumor."

Highlander Restaurant – March 19th

The twelve of us basically took over the whole restaurant. For starters, I ordered a couple of Springbok Carpaccio, Garlic Snails, and Calamari for the table.

Since we were right on the Indian Ocean, just about everyone ordered seafood. I had the Shrimp Kingklip. The only two meat eaters that night were Kgabu, our guide, and Jeffery, our semi-truck driver. Kgabu had the Grilled Ostrich Steak, and Jeffery ordered the Chicken and Rib Combo.

After dinner, I informed the team of our next assignment, Tsavo, Kenya. We were going to help stem the eradication of the dwindling giraffe population.

Unlike the slaughter of elephants and rhinoceros by poachers, the decimation of Africa's giraffes has been overlooked. Africa's giraffe population has plummeted by 40% in the last thirty years. There are less than 5000 Kordofan and Nubian giraffes, and they are now listed as critically endangered. The Maasai and Rothschild giraffes comprise the remainder of Kenya's giraffe population and have declined over 67% in less than fifty years. Due to climate change, human encroachment, land management, trophy hunters, and poachers, time is running out for these magnificent creatures.

I told the team that we were going to Kenya by sea. We plan to sail on board the SS Renard with our old friend, Captain Philippe Chevrolet. We will board the SS Renard tomorrow morning at 8 a.m. at the East London Harbour Pier on Lower Esplanade Street.

Unfortunately, we will sadly say goodbye to Kgabu and Jeffery for all of their help and assistance. I told them I'm sure we will call upon them again soon. The struggle against poaching and trophy hunting will sadly continue.

SS Renard – March 20th

Captain Chevrolet was standing on the bridge when we arrived at the harbor.

"Ahoy!" He shouted.

"Permission to come aboard?" I hollered.

"Permission granted."

He made his way down to the gangplank to greet us.

"Welcome aboard; it's good to see so many familiar faces," He said as he shook our hands and led us on board. "Don't worry about your gear and vehicles; everything is being taken care of. Atticus, my first mate, will show you all to your staterooms; just follow him. Let's all plan on meeting for dinner tonight."

And with that, Chevrolet was gone, back up to the bridge to supervise the loading of our vehicles and gear. I was shown to my room and plopped down on the bed when I noticed a radio beside it. I turned it on and started to listen to CapeTalk radio out of Cape Town. There was a lot of discussion about the abduction and murder of the Ibhino brothers.

"Hi, and welcome back to Charles in the morning. Go ahead; you're on CapeTalk. What's your name?"

"Hi, Charles, I'm Don, and I think those poachers got what they deserved."

"So, you're in favor of vigilantes taking the law into their own hands?"

"No, I'm not, but I don't consider Le Gang de la Clé de Singe a vigilante group."

"What would you call them, if not vigilantes? Don?"

"Defenders of the defenseless. Guardians for those that have no voice."

"Very poetic, but what about the rule of law? Don, we are no better than animals without the rule of law."

"Charles, I just wish we were no better than animals. Animals don't kill for fun, animals don't kill so they can have their picture taken with the corpse, and animals don't cut off heads and skin to place in their dens as trophies. And as far as the rule of law, I say when people don't act like animals, they deserve the law of the jungle.

"The Ibhino Gang wanted to have it both ways. They were happy to apply the law of the jungle to kill helpless animals, but when they were caught, they wanted the rule of law to apply to them.

"They wanted to play in the arena of king of the jungle when it suited them. But as a wise man once said, sometimes you eat the bear, and sometimes the bear, well, he eats you. Le Gang de la Clé de Singe is one mean mother of a bear."

"Well, thank you for your call, Don. You definitely have some strong opinions on the subject. Now, we have Sally on the line."

"You're welcome, Charles." I hung up the phone and took a nap.

SS Renard – March 20th

I had dinner with Captain Chevrolet, Atticus, the first mate, and my team. It was good catching up with old friends and sharing stories. Chevrolet told us it would be a twelve-day journey to Kenya, and he expects smooth sailing all the way to Mombasa.

We were scheduled to dock at the Boss Freight Terminal in the Kilindini Port, where we picked up our vehicles and had gear unloaded once again. Our guide, Maynard Olukayode Fasola, a planner for the Department of

Grazing Management for the Lumo Community Wildlife Conservancy, will meet us at the docks and escort us to Tsavo West National Park.

Tsavo National Park is made up of two separate parks, Tsavo East National Park and Tsavo West National Park. It is one of the largest national parks in the world, and the park is split into two due to the railway going from Mombasa to Kenya's interior.

Tsavo East National Park is primarily flat with dry plains. Tsavo West National Park is more mountainous and is known for its wildlife: black rhinos, Cape buffalo, elephants, lions, hippos, leopards, and Maasai giraffes.

Kilindini Port – April 2nd

Heavy rains and thunderstorms made unloading more tedious and longer. I hope it's not an omen. We had twelve days of beautiful sailing on board the Renard with Captain Chevrolet and crew, and then it rained.

As our gear and Toyota 4Runners were unloaded, we said goodbye to Captain Chevrolet and crew until the next time.

Maynard, our guide, told us that the trip to Tsavo West is normally five and a half hours, but due to the rain, we should expect it closer to seven and a half, maybe eight.

Tsavo – April 2nd

The entire journey was to be on the A109, or as the locals call it, the Mombasa Road, until we reached Voi, where we turned off onto the A23, which would take us to Tsavo West.

Maynard had set up camp a couple of miles outside the town of Mwatate. By the time we got to the camp, the rain had finally stopped. We settled in and unpacked our gear while Maynard and his assistant Absko prepared a warm dinner.

We learned from Maynard that the Sheldrick Wildlife Trust had deployed thirteen De-Snaring Teams in partnership with the Kenya Wildlife Service (KWS), undertaking anti-poaching operations to protect the wildlife of Tsavo National Parks.

We had to remain vigilant and ensure we didn't interfere with their operations. Our mission was to help them fight poaching, not hinder them.

Tsavo – April 3rd

Maynard told us that the poachers slip into the park in the dead of night and make their way to a watering hole. They make themselves a blind to hide from the animals when they come for a drink in the morning; they wait until the animal is drinking, then use a bow and arrow not to spook the herd or to alert any Rangers that might be in the vicinity. They dip their arrows into poison and aim them at the animal's stomach. It then dies a painful death.

The poachers of giraffes usually chop the animal up to sell as bushmeat. They sell severed heads and bones, which earn them up to 140 dollars for each. Giraffes are also occasionally killed to feed the people who are poaching elephants and rhinos.

Lu Wei and Venus sent up a couple of drones to observe any herds of giraffes, poachers, or trophy hunters.

They spotted several KWS De-Snaring Teams in the vicinity, which will curtail our activities. We didn't want to interfere with their operations or let them know of our mission. We were posing as a photo safari group interested in photographing the wildlife of the Tsavo and the natives of the Maasai tribe.

Tsavo – April 13th

Every day for ten days, we hadn't been able to engage with any poachers or trophy hunters. The thirteen KWS De-Snaring Teams had been working primarily in and around the areas where we ventured. It said a lot about their capabilities and effectiveness as a force to be reckoned with.

Tsavo – April 14th

Absko brought news of a large hunting safari outfit based out of the settlement of Maktau, approximately thirty miles northwest of our camp. It's been rumored that there are six hunters involved looking to kill elephants, lions, and giraffes.

Absko had heard the safari would travel east towards the Mwanda settlement in the foothills of the Taita Hills. The land consists of dozens of farms, ranches, and estates. There are some 48 forests on the hilltops that are favorite grazing lands for the big game that the hunters would be searching for.

Tsavo – April 14th

We were suited up in our ghillie suits, checked our gear, and were off. In the meantime, Lu Wei and Venus had launched two drones: one to keep an eye on the progress of the safari outfit and one to keep an eye on us.

Venus radioed us that she had discovered a large elephant herd comingling with a small herd of giraffes in the forest area above Mwanda. Maynard told us this area is a favorite hunting spot for safari outfits because of the abundance of vegetation and a nearby water hole.

Taita Hills – April 14th

The Red Team is in position; we've had plenty of time to customize our ghillie suits to match the environment. You'd be hard-pressed to spot us even if you knew we were here; we've blended in perfectly.

Lu Wei radioed us, alerting us that the safari outfit was approaching.

"Red Leader, this is Red Flyer, over."

"Red Leader, over."

"Bogies approaching at ten o'clock, over."

"Roger that. ¬ Headcount, over."

"Eight total, over."

"Roger that over."

"Red Team, Red Leader, do you read?"

I received eight affirmatives.

"Eight bogies approaching from 10 o'clock. I will assign targets over."

An enormous tan 4X4 Toyota Land Cruiser slowly crept towards us through the brush. The two guides were in the front two seats, and seated behind them were two rows of three hunters each, six men and two women.

The Cruiser came to a stop one hundred feet from the Red Team. The guides began instructing the hunters to be quiet as they exited the vehicle and began gathering their weapons.

As the hunters stood in a group checking their weapons, the guides started their instructions about protocol; I assigned a Red Team member to an individual target. I assigned the two female hunters to Sue B and Fu Hao, and I told Maynard not to participate; I would take his shot.

"Red Team, on my mark, over."

Again, I received eight affirmations.

"Ready. Aim. Fire."

It was as if there was but one shot. All eight figures dressed in fatigues seem to fall in unison in what looked to be a macabre choreographed dance of death.

We waited for Red Flyer to give the all-clear before we emerged from our positions. Once given, we dressed the fallen in yellow flags and letters.

On our way back to camp, Venus and Lu Wei kept us out of the way of any KWS De-Snaring Teams and other safari outfitters.

Once we were safely back in camp, I radioed the positions of the fallen hunters. We then split the camp into two separate encampments, so we didn't seem like such a force. It was decided that we'd move camp north to Mtito Andei since it was clear to us that the KWS De-Snaring Teams were covering this area quite sufficiently.

Odin, Sassoon, Bellator, Cowboy, Venus, and Maynard comprised one group, while Lu Wei, Sue B, Fu Hao, Gianfranco, Absko, and I would make up the other. We would have separate camps within the same general area and coordinate any strikes and operations.

Taita Hills – April 14th

Each group headed north on the A109 to Mtito Andi. We staggered our departure so as not to appear to be traveling together. We decided to head off-road and west, then camp in Chyulu Hills, since we'd received information that there had been an outbreak of giraffe poaching in that area.

Chyulu Hills – April 14th

We pitched our camp in a clearing straddling the Makueni and Kaliado county border in the Aberdare Forest. Our other group set up camp outside the village of Umoja; it is unique in that the village is an all-female matriarch. It is a sanctuary for homeless survivors of violence against women and young girls running from forced marriages.

Umoja – April 15th

Sue B, Fu Hao, and Venus asked, and we were granted the day to visit the village of Umoja. The residents in the community must wear the traditional clothing and beadwork of the Samburu people. Men are permitted to visit but are not allowed to live in the village.

The residents earn their living by creating traditional crafts, which are sold at the Umoja Waso Women's Cultural Center. Every woman donates ten percent of her earnings to the village to support the school and other needs.

Sue B, Fu Hao, and Venus came to me and asked if I could arrange for them to donate their pay for this mission to the women of Umoja; I told them absolutely not because the Le Gang de la Clé de Singe would donate three times their salary to the village.

Aberdare Forest – April 15th

Lu Wei launched one of our Ehang Falcon B Series drones equipped with night vision into the skies over Aberdare Forest. It wasn't too long before we spotted a group of poachers setting wire snare traps in the forest nearby.

Sue B, Fu Hao, Gianfranco, and I decided to investigate. Wearing all back from head to toe, we headed east to engage the poachers. Each of us was equipped with night-vision goggles and an M40A5 Sniper rifle, topped off with a Schmidt & Bender rifle scope and suppressors.

Having Lu Wei watch over us with the drone was the difference between our success and failure and our being killed and surviving. He not only guided us through the jungle, but he also spotted a pack of hyenas out for the hunt.

"Red Leader, Red Flyer over."

"Red Leader, go."

"You are closing in on the bogies; they are approximately 1500 yards due east. Over."

"Copy that, Red Flyer. Over."

"You also are being pursued by a large pack of what looks to be about twenty hyenas coming in from the west. They are about a klick away. Do you copy over?"

"Copy Red Flyer. Please keep me up-to-date. Over."

I radioed my team, "Red Team, Red Leader. We need to form a defensive star. Over."

Forming a defensive star meant that we grouped together facing outward, so we were able to protect the group from every direction. We would then advance forward in a slow rotating circle.

Sue B had spotted the poachers just as Lu Wei radioed us.

"Red Team, Red Flyer. You are within striking distance of three bogies. Do you see them? Over."

"Copy that Red Flyer. Where are the hyenas?" I asked.

"About a quarter mile from you, closing fast."

We were well within firing range of the poachers. I had us all kneel, still in our star position. Fu Hao was facing the poachers, Gianfranco was to her left, me, then Sue B.

I told Fu Hao, "Red one on my order wound one bogie. Over."

"Copy that, Red Leader."

I was able to observe the hyena pack heading toward us, and when they were a hundred yards from us, I gave the order.

"Red One fire."

Fu Hao fired a single shot, hitting one of the poachers in the thigh, causing him to cry out in pain, drawing the hyena's attention. Once they picked up the scent of blood, they were onto the poachers and passed us by.

The other two poachers, having laid their rifles down to set wire traps, were caught off guard and unprepared to defend themselves.

"Red Flyer to Red Leader, you are clear. Over."

"Copy that Red Flyer. Bring us home. Over."

Lu Wei guided us safely back to camp. The team thanked Lu Wei for watching over us.

"Excellent job, Red Flyer," I said to Lu Wei.

"Thanks, Ice, that must have been quite harrowing."

"Yeah, it wasn't any laughing matter."

Aberdare Forest – April 16th.

Maynard was listening to Radio Citizen while preparing breakfast when the music was interrupted by a news bulletin.

"We interrupt our regular programming to bring you this news bulletin. The remains of what appears to be the bodies of three men who were attacked by hyenas were found early this morning after their families reported them missing.

"The men, Alhaadi Mwangi, Gacoki Otieno, and Oluuch Kariuki, were all known poachers. According to authorities, it appeared that the men were in the process of setting wire snare traps when they were attacked and killed.

"Captain Manhry of the Mtito Andei Police warned again of the dangers of poaching and urged people not to engage in this illegal and dangerous activity.

"In related news, Le Gang de la Clé de Singe has claimed responsibility for the deaths of six hunters and their guides in the Taita Hills above Mtito Andei. Police and park rangers are actively on the hunt for the killers.

"If anyone has any information, please call the police. A reward has been posted.

"Now, back to our regular programming..."

Aberdare Forest – April 16th.

Shortly after breakfast, we were visited by eight of the parks Rangers.

"Good morning." I said, welcoming the Rangers, "Can we offer you some coffee?"

"No, thank you. Do you have a permit to camp here?" the group leader asked.

"Of course, Maynard, would you be so kind?"

Maynard proceeded to produce our camping permit.

"How long have you been camping here?" He asked.

"Two nights," I replied.

"What is the nature of your visit?"

"We are photographers; we've been photographing the magnificent wildlife, the natural beauty of your country."

"Do you have any firearms?"

Maynard said, "I do, as a registered Park Guide."

He entered his tent and brought out his Winchester Model 70 and permit.

The lead Ranger asked, "Did any of you hear any disturbance last night? Three men were attacked and killed by a pack of hyenas not far from here."

We all feigned shock and ignorance for not hearing anything.

"It is very dangerous to be camping so far away from everything."

"Thank you, Ranger; I believe, in light of what you've told us, that we will definitely be moving our camp to a safer area."

"You don't look like a photographer; you look like a hunter."

"Me, I don't like guns. I do all my shooting with my camera."

"I would like to see some."

"Sure." I walked to my tent and retrieved a Nikon D850 35mm digital camera. I handed the camera to the Ranger, who started to click through dozens of photos of elephants, giraffes, lions, and Maasai natives.

He looked at me and handed the camera back to me without saying a word.

I took the camera and said, "We'll be leaving as soon as we break camp."

"Good." He said, and with that, they left.

I had a bad feeling that the Rangers didn't totally believe that we were a group of photographers as we claimed. It could have turned ugly if they had requested to search the camp; sometimes discretion is the better part of valor.

We slowly began to break down our camp, making sure that the Rangers had left. Then we contacted our other group and gave them a heads up to break camp and planned to rendezvous at Campi ya Kanzi at 2 p.m.

Campi ya Kanzi – April 16th

Campi ya Kanzi is an award-winning eco-luxury community project that supports the Maasai Wilderness Conservation Trust. Located in the shadow of Mount Kilimanjaro, the camp helps fund the preservation of the land by protecting wildlife through anti-poaching initiatives.

We checked into the six Luxury Tented Cottages. Usually, we wouldn't have been able to get in, but thanks to Wooch, who pulled a couple of strings and called in a lot of favors, we were able to stay.

Campi ya Kanzi – April 16th

Our tented cottages were separate from the main house, which afforded us privacy. After dinner, we adjourned to my cottage to plan our next move.

We weren't able to claim last night's encounter with the poachers and hyenas as a victory for Le Gang de la Clé de Singe. We needed to send a clear message from Le Gang de la Clé de Singe that we don't tolerate poaching. We had success with the safari outfit, but we needed a positive outcome with poachers.

Campi ya Kanzi – April 17th

Lu Wei and Venus had been flying our drones for five hours and hadn't found any targets. I called it and told everyone to stand down and we'd try again tomorrow.

Campi ya Kanzi – April 20th

We hadn't spotted any poachers in the last couple nights. I guessed the hyena attack had really put the fear of God into them. In a way, that was good news; I consider that a win. Every day, there aren't any poachers, and the animals win.

Campi ya Kanzi – April 21st

Lu Wei sent up a drone and discovered a safari outfit heading towards a herd of giraffes. They were too far away for us to reach them before they reached the herd and started killing.

I had an idea. I had Venus place one of our Yellow flags onto a drone and fly it over to where the safari group was hunting. She brought the drone down and began to "buzz" the hunters, making sure that they could see it was the ensign of Le Gang de la Clé de Singe.

While Venus's drone distracted them, Lu Wei brought his observation drone back. She sent out our new experimental drone, the TIKAD weaponized drone, armed with an SR/25 automatic rifle with a silencer.

The TIKAD can take the full recoil of the weapon's discharge and compensate for its force with a unique suppression firing and stabilization solution, letting the operator fire accurately and deadly accurately.

While the four hunters and their guides were busy trying to knock out Venus's drone, they were completely unaware of the killer drone that was silently speeding their way until it was all too late.

Lu Wei proved to be a master of delicately maneuvering the TIKAD. The way he manipulated the drone swept in and around the tree canopies, popping up from the bushes while dodging enemy fire. His capability of swooping up and down with dance-like precession while firing and hitting his targets with sheer accuracy was indeed a thing of beauty.

The hunters and their guides were totally overwhelmed. Once they became frustrated by their inability to fight back effectively, they panicked. Instead of coming together and fighting back as one unit, they overreacted, became terror-stricken, and started to run to try and save themselves. The whole encounter took less than fifteen minutes.

I saw the future of combat unveiling before my eyes; it would forever change the entire concept of combat. Basically, it eliminated the need for the foot soldier. War is now being fought by kids with joysticks.

Campi ya Kanzi – April 21st

Bellator, Cowboy, Venus, Sassoon, and I went out to where the hunters and guides lay dead to prep them Le Gang de la Clé de Singe style, yellow banners around their necks and letters of guilt on their persons.

I decided to send Odin, Bellator, Cowboy, Venus, Gianfranco, and Sassoon south just over the border to Arusha, Tanzania, to wait for Sue B, Fu Hao, Lu Wei, and me. I felt things were heating up, and it made sense to cut the group down so we didn't draw too much attention to ourselves. We planned to join them in the next couple of days after we made a big noise taking down a poacher.

I waited until I heard that they had safely crossed into Tanzania before calling the authorities to ask about the hunter's and guides' whereabouts.

Campi ya Kanzi – April 25th

Sue B, Fu Hao, Lu Wei, and I were summoned to the owner's office by the police. They were interviewing everyone at the resort in conjunction with the multiple killings of the hunters.

Before I left, I placed a small piece of paper at the bottom of the door as I left. If the door had opened in my absence, I would know that the police had searched my room.

They interviewed each of us separately, along with all the other guests staying at the resort. I went into the manager's office, where there was a high-ranking police officer and an officer with sergeant's stripes on his uniform.

"Please have a seat, Mr. Rawlings. I am Captain Manhry of the Mtito Andei Police, " he said as he held and looked at my passport.

"Is there anything wrong, Captain?"

"We've had a series of unfortunate incidents involving several big game hunters and their guides; we're asking everyone if they might have seen or heard anything unusual, Mr. Rawlings."

"I really can't think of anything strange, Captain. My fiancé and friends are here on holiday, and we've been taking a ton of pictures and just enjoying this lovely facility."

"Well, thank you for your cooperation, Mr. Rawlings. I'm sorry to have inconvenienced you."

"Not at all, Captain; I just wish I might have been some help."

I walked out of the manager's office and found that other officers had already interviewed Sue B, Lu Wei, and Fu Hao. We returned to our cottages, and that's when I noticed the paper on the door was now on the floor, telling me that the police had searched our rooms while we were being interviewed.

Years of training have taught us not to leave anything incriminating in your room, other people's rooms, but never yours.

Sue B told me that she overheard a couple of the police officers trying to figure out how the hunters and guides were shot from such a high angle. The theory is that someone must have been firing down from a helicopter.

They were looking into all scheduled helicopter flights and radar from all local airports to see if they could possibly triangulate where the chopper might have come from.

Campi ya Kanzi – April 25th

I thought this would be our last night, no matter what. If it happened, it happened. Lu Wei launched the drone, and the search began.

Three hours later, he found two men who appeared to have begun setting wire snare traps in a heavily wooded area not far from the resort. Giraffes are known to visit this location.

Fu Hao, Sue B, and I slipped away from the resort under the guidance of our drone master, Lu Wei. It only took us forty minutes to arrive where the men were; we observed that these men were actually dismantling the snare traps.

Under the careful watch and cover of my two feminine snipers, I approached the men, making my presence known as I approached.

Wearing all black, including black camouflage covering my face, I must appear a frightful figure. With my hands raised in peace, I say to them in Swahili, "Uiogope, maana yangu hakuna madhara." Reassuring them I mean no harm.

They were initially frightened, but they saw I meant no harm. I asked if they spoke English.

"Forgive me if I've frightened you."

"You gave us a scare."

"What is it you are doing?"

The older of the two men said, “We are removing these wire traps to keep our animals safe. We bring back these wires to the people of our village, who take the wire and make them into pieces of art.”

“We want to give our people the ability to provide for their families without having to resort to poaching, " the younger man added.

“That is truly amazing,” I said. But why are you out in the dark? Why not wait until daylight, when it’s safer?”

“It’s the nighttime when the animals are most likely to get caught.” The older man said.

“Gentlemen, I will leave you alone. I’m sorry that I scared you. Like you, I am a saver of wildlife.”

“You are with the Mchimbaji wa Tumbili Tribe, no?”

“Yes, I am with the Monkey Wrench Gang.”

“We like your bendera.”

“You like our flag? Here.” I reached into my backpack and gave each of them one.

I said, “Be careful; people are scared of that and can do bad things to those who carry it.”

“We understand. Thank you. My name is Auni, and this is my son Badru.”

“My name is Barafu Mtu.”

“Ice Man.”

“Goodbye Barafu Mtu.”

“Goodbye, Auni, Badru. Mungu Akubariki.” I said as I walked back towards my guardian angels.

“God bless you, too.” The father said softly.

Campi ya Kanzi – April 26th

Returning from our encounter with Auni and Badru, we got a call from Lu Wei.

“Red Team, Red Flyer, over.”

“Red Leader, Go.”

"Looks like you have two bogies at three o'clock. Over."

"Copy that."

As we approached, we could plainly see that, unlike Auni and his son, these two were setting traps, not disabling them. One was setting the traps while the other was watching guard with an AK-47. We observed for fifteen minutes just to be sure that we weren't mistaken, and unfortunately for them, we weren't.

"Red Leader to Red One and Red Two, take them out. Over."

"Red One, Take out AK. Red Two take out the wire. On my mark, three, two, one, fire."

There were two soft pops, then two clouds of red mist.

We dismantled the wire traps and dressed our two poachers with the Mchimbaji wa Tumbili Tribe's yellow bendera around their necks, with a letter for each of them in their pocket with the snare wire coiled next to them.

Arusha, Tanzania – April 28th

We arrived in Arusha last night after crossing through the Taveta Border Crossing. They were stopping everyone. We had to stop the 4Runner in front of a white two-story British Colonial building, where two uniformed crossing guards made a cursory search of the vehicle while asking us typical customs questions: What was the nature of our visit, business or pleasure? Do we have any drugs, wildlife, or weapons?

We were also asked the same questions on the Tanzanian side. Once through, it was a three-hour drive from the border to Arusha on the A23. The drive was majestic, passing Mount Kilimanjaro National Park, which flowed right into Arusha National Park.

We checked into the Kibo Palace Hotel around eight o'clock, where the rest of the team were waiting for us. After settling into our rooms, we went down to the lounge bar for drinks and snacks with the team. Odin had received a message from Commander Wooch Brown that I should contact him about our next mission in the morning.

Odin and I were the last of the team still drinking when they closed the bar at 1 a.m., so we headed upstairs to our rooms and called it a night.

Arusha, Tanzania – April 29th – 8:00 a.m. 29th

"Wooch, Ice here. What's up, sir?"

"We've just gotten a lead from someone with the BBC News Investigation on a secret network of wildlife traffickers selling baby chimpanzees."

"Fuck me, man; what the fuck is wrong with people?"

"We're told that they've uncovered a notorious West African hub for wildlife trafficking, known as the "red room." We want your team to go there and put an end to this trafficking ring. Handle these individuals with extreme prejudice, understood?"

"Understood."

"Good, all flight arrangements have been made. You'll be flying out of Kilimanjaro International on separate airlines at different times so as not to draw attention.

"You all have reservations at the Sofitel Abidjan Hotel Ivoire using code name "Jade" passports."

"Yes, sir."

"Ice, these men are armed and dangerous."

"So are we, Wooch."

"I know, just be careful."

"Okay, I'll touch base once we get settled."

"Ice, there's been a development."

"And that would be?"

"I got a message from Morris; Interpol has replaced him and Volker."

"Why?"

"The brass feels like that haven't produced any real results, so they've replaced them with two new inspectors."

"Do we know anything about them?"

"Yeah, we know that neither one of them is a fan of ours, so watch yourselves."

"Who are they?"

"Inspector Schneider, a German and an Italian, Inspector Ferrari. I hear they're out to make a name for themselves by nailing your team."

"You know me, Wooch. I don't scare, and I don't run. We're here to get the job done, whatever it takes."

"I know Ice, I know. Just be careful."

"Okay, Wooch. Thanks for the heads up."

"Talk soon. Have a safe flight."

Arusha, Tanzania – April 29th

I've called the Red Team to my room to review the mission.

"I've just talked to Wooch; we're going to Abidjan in the Ivory Coast. We're after a trafficking gang that is smuggling baby chimpanzees.

"Their usual tactics used by these poachers is to shoot as many of the adults in a family as they possibly can. This prevents them from resisting the capture of the babies, and their bodies are sold as bushmeat. To capture just one infant alive, they'll slaughter at least ten adults.

"After their capture, the baby chimp is shuffled through a sophisticated chain that starts with the poachers and leads to a middleman, who arranges false permits and transportation to the buyer. There is a high demand in China, Southeast Asia, and the Gulf states. Buyers will pay top dollar for these animals and don't mind paying additional fees to bypass international controls."

"What happens to these baby chimps when they grow up?" Fu Hao asked.

"When the chimp ceases to be cute, 90% of the time, it gets locked up and stuck in a cage or killed because it has outlived its cute baby stage."

"I'm assuming people are paying big bucks for these baby chimps," Sassoon said.

"They can go as high as twelve grand, maybe more. They're usually sold to wealthy homes or forced to perform in a crummy out-of-the-way commercial zoo."

"Are we going after the poachers or the middlemen?" Odin asked.

"Both."

"When do we leave?" Sue B inquired.

"We're staggering our flights. Some will leave today, some tomorrow, and a couple will leave the day after. Remember, we will be traveling using code "Jade." Check your email to find your travel information. If there aren't any questions, we'll meet for breakfast at the hotel restaurant, Le Gourmandise. Save travels."

Kilimanjaro Airport – May 1st

I was booked on Qatar Airways flight 1354. It was a two-stop, thirty-plus-hour flight to Abidjan, or as I call it, the flight from Hell. Don't get me wrong- Qatar Airways is a fabulous airline- but it's just a lot of time sitting on a plane and having to deal with two stops. It gets old fast.

My first stop was Doha, Qatar. From there, we stopped in Casablanca, Morocco, and finally, the Port Bout at Airport Abidjan. I was looking and feeling my best, NOT.

Sofitel Abidjan Hotel – May 3rd

I arrived at the Sofitel Abidjan Hotel Ivorie just before midnight, where Odin met me in the lobby.

"Welcome to Abidjan, Ice."

"Everyone get in, okay?"

"Yeah, you're the last. Let's go ahead and get you checked in; I know it was a killer flight, so after you check in, go to your room and crash. I've set up a breakfast with the team for 9 a.m."

"Thanks, brother. See you in the morning."

I left an eight o'clock wake-up call, then went to my room on the 14th floor. I saw that I had a nice view of the Erie Lagoon, but I was too tired to appreciate it. I dropped my bag on the floor and collapsed onto the bed. I was asleep even before my head hit the pillow.

Le Gourmandise – May 4th

Wooch had left a message for me last night at the reservation desk that I was too tired to read. In the morning, I read it, and it let me know that he'd arranged for a couple of local people, Yacouba Kouassi and Affoue Koffi, to assist us with this operation. Yacouba is an Abidjan police detective, and Affoue is a park ranger with the Abokouamekro Game Reserve.

Detective Kouassi is an imposing figure; he's six feet tall, weighs 245, has dark skin, has a shaved head, and always wears black. To look at him, you'd think him a nightclub bouncer or a professional bodyguard. He has been with the Abidjan police for over twelve years, and for the past two years, he has been working on breaking up the wildlife trafficking ring.

Yacouba is married with three kids; he's dedicated, loyal to his fellow officers, and tired of seeing his country's natural resources being stolen and decimated for greed. He has seen his investigation compromised time after time by payoffs and bribes. He has asked for help from Le Gang de la Clé de Singe so he can have the opportunity to work with the Iceman.

Ranger Koffi has been a park ranger for eight years and has a master's degree in environmental science. She has seen the decimation that poachers and trophy hunters have reeked upon the wildlife populations within the game reserve. She's helped Le Gang de la Clé de Singe in the past on a different operation and wants to help stop this trafficking of baby chimps after seeing the slaughter that these people do.

Affoue is just the opposite of Detective Kouassi; he is petite, five foot two, 110 pounds, with long black hair. She is single and white. Together, they make quite the odd couple.

Today, Odin, Lu Wei, Venus, and I are going out to check Abokouamekro Game Reserve and meet with Affoue. It's about a three-and-a-half-hour drive out there. We are going to get familiar with the lay of the land and scope things out.

Abokouamekro Game Reserve – May 4th

We took the A3 north to Yamoussoukro. As we entered town, we turned right onto Route De Mamie Adjoin. Once we were out of town, the road was unpaved and had no name. We traveled the road for an hour until we came to a fork. This is where we met Affoue, who was waiting for us.

She led the way into the game reserve, and we passed several native villages as we went deeper into it. Once past the villages, we pulled off onto a dirt trail, where we stopped.

"I thought that this would be a good place for Lu Wei and Venus to send up the drones to do an aerial scout. But first, let me take you where the latest slaughter of chimps occurred." Affoue said.

While Lu Wei and Venus went about launching their drones, Affoue took Odin and me on foot to a cluster of acacia trees about two and a half miles from where we parked the vehicles. All around us were spent cartridges on the ground. The trunks of the trees were riddled with bullets, and it must have been total chaos for those poor chimpanzees. It always boggles my mind how cruel and heartless people can be, not just to animals but also to each other.

We returned to where we left Lu Wei and Venus, and they were packing up from their drone tests.

"Everything okay?" I asked.

"Yeah, no problems," Venus said.

"We did a cursory search and scan of a five-mile radius. We saw jackals, hyenas, panthers, elephants, hippos, and a troop of chimps, but no people," Lu Wei added.

"Good, we'll start tomorrow. Now, we should start getting back. Affoue, will you be joining us?" I asked.

"No, thank you. I have other things to do. What time tomorrow do you want to get started?"

"You tell us."

"Poachers usually get started early when they're going after chimps."

"We'll be out around 4 a.m. I guess we'll be setting up a camp out here. We can't travel back and forth from Abidjan; it's just too far. Would this be a good spot for our camp?"

"I'll see you here tomorrow at 4 a.m. I'll bring the proper papers."

Sofitel Abidjan Hotel – May 4th

We had a team meeting tonight with Detective Kouassi. We decided that Odin, Lu Wei, Venus, Sue B, Fu Hao, and Gianfranco would set up operations in the Abokouamekro Game Reserve and work with Affoue to see if they could intercept and destroy the Chimpanzee poachers. At the same time, Bellator, Cowboy, Sassoon, and I would stay here and work with Detective Kouassi to see if we could smash the traffickers of these endangered chimpanzees.

"Detective Kouassi, do you want us to try to capture any of these poachers for interrogation?" Odin asked.

"No, thank you, Mr. Jeffers." Answered the detective.

"Okay, then, Randy. I think you and your team should be good to go. Keep me posted. Good luck to you all, and good hunting," I said to Odin.

Prefecture de Police D'Abidjan - May 5th

The building looked more like an army compound than a police station. Surrounded by a tall concrete wall painted beige with blue trim, the entrance was secured with a matching blue ten-foot fence. There were two armed sentries, one on the outside and one on the inside.

Once inside the compound, the police station and jail are housed in an unassuming three-story concrete box with no windows. It is, too, painted beige with a blue trim motif.

I arrived outside the compound at eight o'clock to meet with Detective Kouassi. He glanced at me with no interest as I approached the guard outside.

"I'm here to see Detective Kouassi," I said.

"Your name?"

"Robert Zimmerman."

"Detective Kouassi, he is expecting you?"

"Yes."

"Your name?"

"Robert Zimmerman."

He turned around and gestured to the guard on the inside, who slowly sauntered, looking bored.

"This man is here to see Detective Kouassi."

"What is his name?"

"Roger Zummerman."

The inside guard looked down at his clipboard, then replied, "We have no Roger Zummerman."

"That's Robert Zimmerman, Robert Zimmerman to see Detective Kouassi, not Roger Zummerman," I said.

"Wait," the inside guard said as he slowly walked over to a telephone stand and made a call, presumably to Detective Kouassi. Ten minutes later, the gate creaked open, and I was allowed in.

"Do you know where I can find Detective Kouassi?" I asked.

The guard didn't utter a word; they just pointed to the building and went over to talk to the outside guard.

As I approached the building, there were two doors, one entrance marked Police and one marked Prison. I chose Police, and once inside, there was the typical uniformed sergeant's desk, all abuzz with activity. I waited patiently until it was my turn, “Detective Kouassi, I have an appointment.”

“Your name?”

“Robert Zimmerman.”

The Sergeant looked down at his clipboard, pointed to his left, and said, “Second floor.”

I walked over to the elevator, pushed the up button, and waited. A uniformed policeman with a man in handcuffs walked up and stopped. The policeman leaned over and pushed the button, giving me a look as if he had the magic touch. The prisoner made a remark under his breath that I couldn't make out, but I guess the cop did. He gave him a hard punch to the kidney, making the man cry out in pain.

“I told you to shut up!” The policeman growled.

The elevator doors opened, and two men dressed in suits got off. I let the cop and his prisoner get on first. I got on and pushed the button for the second floor. I looked at the officer. “Three, " he said.

The ride up to the second floor took a good five minutes. When the doors finally opened, I stepped out into a bare hallway, except for a small plastic sign with pointing arrows for the department that you're looking for.

There were arrows for homicide, burglary, robbery, and narcotics, and at the very bottom was an arrow for wildlife pointing to the left.

Prefecture de Police D'Abidjan - May 5th

The detective's office for wildlife was small and cramped. There were boxes stacked all over the office, piled up almost to the ceiling, four desks with papers and folders so high you couldn't see the person sitting there.

"Hello?" I'm looking for Detective Kouassi." I announced.

A moment later, I saw a hand go up in the back of the office. Then Detective Kouassi stood up and gestured for me to make my way to his desk. It took some maneuvering not to knock anything over, but I eventually managed to get there.

"Good morning," Kouassi said.

"Morning. Wow, either you guys are really good at faking it or incredibly busy."

"Unfortunately, incredibly busy. Everyone, this is Robert Zimmerman, an expert in anti-trafficking operations who is here to help us take down and stop the Chimpanzee traffickers.

"That's Detective Kone over there by the door, Detective Ouattara to my right, and Detective Okeke."

"Gentlemen, it's my pleasure. I look forward to working with you all." I said.

"Robert, we have received a tip from a reliable informant on the location of the "red room" and that there will be a major buy tonight for several endangered animals, including six baby Chimpanzees that are getting ready for shipment.

"We would like you and your team to be involved. Could you and your team meet us outside the station at 1 a.m. this evening? We will then all go together for the raid."

"Whatever you need, Detective Kouassi."

"Yacouba, please."

"Whatever you need, Yacouba. We'll be here."

I said goodbye to the detectives and made my way out onto the street and back to the hotel.

Sofitel Abidjan Hotel – May 5th

Bellator, Cowboy, and Sassoon met in my room to go over the raid for this evening. As is my policy, I leave one man back as the designated survivor.

If anything happened to Bellator, Cowboy, and me, Sassoon would go to each of our rooms and collect our "life bags," which are small red bags that contain all of our passports, personal documents, cell phones, and any personal items that we don't want to be captured.

The "red bags" are designed to be opened by their owner, and only its owner; any attempt to open it without the proper code will release a liquid acid that will destroy everything contained in the bag within seconds and release a deadly toxic gas, that if breathed will kill immediately.

The only other way to open the bags is by contacting a special number that has a record of the owner's personal codes. The survivor can also use the special number to get help if a member finds himself or herself in danger to get immediate assistance.

We went over the fact that Detective Kouassi and his squad were going to take the lead; we would serve as backup. With any luck, we could put an end to one of the most successful animal trafficking rings in Africa.

In the meantime, I told the team to use the rest of the day to relax because they needed to be sharp. Things could get harry tonight since we weren't in charge, so we had to be prepared for anything.

Abokouamekro Game Reserve – May 5th.

I received a message from Odin that Lu Wei had spotted a suspicious group of men heading toward a known troop of Chimpanzees. Affoue and the Red Team were going to intercept them before they reached the Chimps.

Odin said he would report back to me after they encountered the poachers.

Abokouamekro Game Reserve – May 5th

Odin had become a master tactician. He split his team into three teams, one on either side of the poachers, with the third behind them.

Nine times out of ten, when a force is attacked, it will try to retreat from the direction it came from because it is familiar.

The poachers were moving slowly. It seemed to Lu Wei that they weren't in any hurry; they appeared to be joking around and having a good time. This gave the Red Team time to get into position.

Odin played it smart and split up his two snipers, Sue B, and Fu Hao, one on each team. There were eight men in the group of poachers. The two men out front appeared to be the trackers. Odin radioed his snipers to take them out first.

"Red One, Red Two, you have a green light; take your shot when you can," Odin said.

"Red Two, Red One here, take target in ball cap, Over."

"Red One copy."

"Red Two on my mark. Three. Two. Fire!"

The way the two men were hit and fell, it appeared to the others in the group that they tripped and fell. At first, the others were laughing and making fun of them until it became apparent that they had been shot.

Panic set in as the Red Team began to pepper them with heavy machine gun fire from both sides. Five of the poachers tried to take cover and started to return fire. One lone man tried retreating but ran straight into Gianfranco and Venus.

The firefight lasted less than twenty minutes. It took longer to dress them with the yellow flags and guilty notes. In the end, eight poachers were slain, with no casualties on the Red Team.

Once the team had finished with their death ritual, they had Affoue call in the position of the poachers while they booked a flight north to the capital city of Yamoussoukro. They checked into the Hôtel Président.

Yamoussoukro – May 5th

The Red Team had accomplished their mission successfully and had taken refuge. I briefed Odin on our mission here in Abidjan about the evening's raid. Since the raid wouldn't happen until well after midnight, I told him that he probably wouldn't hear from me until the morning.

I congratulated him and his team on their success and told him to relax and enjoy the evening. I will talk to him tomorrow.

Abidjan – May 6th

Bellator, Cowboy, and I met Detective Kouassi and his squad of detectives, along with two other plain clothes and six uniformed officers, outside the Prefecture de Police D'Abidjan building as planned. The seventeen of us piled into three police vans and headed west to a large, poor suburb of Abidjan called Adiopodoumé.

We stopped at an intersection of two streets with no names. On either side of the roads were shanty buildings, some made of cinderblocks, others of tin and baling wire; most had some form of a roof, but many did not.

There were no streetlights; the only illumination cast onto the street came from the naked bulbs from the shacks lining the road.

I could see a uniformed police officer had a man handcuffed standing by the side of his police car in the middle of the road, with dozens of people standing around. The handcuffed man looked to have been beaten and was bleeding from a wound to the head.

Detective Kouassi approached the man, pulled a pistol from his shoulder holster, pointed it at the man, and said, "Where is it?"

The man said nothing.

Kouassi pulled back the hammer back to cock the gun, still pointing the pistol at the man, and again asked, "Where is it?"

The man stiffened and answered, "Route de Dabou, next to Chez Zongo."

Detective Kouassi pulled the trigger, and the gun went 'click,' empty chamber. He laughed and told the officer to take the man to the station. Kouassi turned to us and said, "Won't be long now, come."

Everyone got back into the vans, and we were driven down dark, unlit, narrow suburban streets until we reached a main avenue, Route de Dabou. We rode down the street until I saw a flashing neon sign that read Chez Zongo. All the vans stopped, and everyone jumped out of the vehicles; I heard Detective Kouassi shouting, "Go. Go. Go."

Everyone ran towards a small cinderblock house with a pitched tin roof. The uniformed officers surrounded the house while Detective Kouassi and his squad calmly walked into the courtyard, where a chained dog began to bark; Detective Okeke pulled his revolver and shot the dog dead, then proceeded to kick in the door of the house.

I turned to my guys and said, "Watch yourselves; I've got a bad feeling about this."

Before we met up with Detective Kouassi, I made sure we all had radio communication with Sassoon back at the hotel, just in case we needed assistance.

Once we were inside the house, the police gathered all the residents and, brought them into the living room, and made them lie down on their stomachs with their hands spread out to their sides. Over a dozen people lived in the house, mostly women, children, and four adult males.

Detective Ouattara grabbed the eldest man and demanded, “Where is the red room!”

“There is no red room.”

Ouattara punched the man hard in the stomach, “Where is the red room?”

The man doubled over in pain and answered, “We have no red room.”

Detective Kouassi removed his pistol again from his shoulder holster and pointed it at the old man’s head. He looked at the man’s son and asked, “Where is the red room?”

The man began to answer, “We have no red…”

Detective Kouassi pulled the trigger of the gun; this time, instead of a click, there was a loud boom that thundered through the house. The old man’s brains were sprayed against the wall as he dropped to the ground.

The women and children on the floor all began to scream, cry, and wail.

Kouassi pointed the gun at the old man’s son and asked in a very calm tone, “Where is the red room?”

“Sir, we don’t…”

BOOM!

The old man’s son fell on top of him; his son’s brains were comingled on the wall with his father's.

Detective Kouassi grabbed a boy of fifteen, pointed the gun at the boy’s head, and asked, “Where is the red room?”

The boy's grandmother stood up before the young boy could answer and shouted, “Stop!”

Kouassi lowered the gun when she said, “It’s this way.”

The old woman took the detectives to the back of the house, revealing a false wall hidden behind a large wooden armoire. Inside, there were over a dozen wooden crates with air holes drilled in the sides.

The wooden crates were carried into the living room and examined. Posted on the sides of the boxes were fraudulent Cites permits that were used to ship Chimpanzees to countries around the world.

When the boxes were opened, each contained a baby chimpanzee wearing a dirty diaper with dozens of fruit slices surrounding it. They would be shipped within the crate for days, trapped, scared, and traumatized. The baby Chimps started crying when they saw a human face, holding up their arms, wanting to be held and comforted.

The police officers allowed news and television crews to document the successful breaking up of the largest ring of wildlife traffickers. The arrest of both male and female criminals, the taking of the children to child services, and the heroic rescue of more than a dozen baby Chimps.

After Detective Kouassi and his squad were through giving interviews to the press, he, his detectives, and the six uniformed police surrounded me and my team and announced that we were under arrest, being wanted members of the international Le Gang de la Clé de Singe.

I softly spoke into my mic to Sassoon, “Code Black. Over.”

“Copy that. Over.” Sassoon replied.

Bellator and Cowboy were standing next to each other on the other side of the room; I was over near the boxes when the police pulled their guns.

Bellator, Cowboy, and I immediately pointed our weapons at Detective Kouasi and his squad. It seemed that we were in a bit of a standoff when, at that moment, the two unidentified plain-clothes men announced themselves as Inspector Schneider and Inspector Ferrari from Interpol.

“Don’t be foolish; put your weapons down; no one wants this to end badly.”

Bellator looked at me and said, “Ice?”

Before I could respond, Cowboy gave out a yell, “Yippee ki yay, motherfuckers!” and started shooting, which set off a firefight that rivals the gunfight at the OK Corral.

After the shooting was over, Detectives Kone, Ouattara, and Okeke were shot dead, and two uniformed officers were killed along with Inspector Ferrari from Interpol.

Bellator and Cowboy were each fatally wounded as well. Detective Kouassi and I received multiple gunshot wounds and were rushed to Polyclinique Sainte Anne-Marie Hospital (PISAM), where we spent months recuperating.

PISAM – August 19th

While still in the hospital, I was interviewed by what seemed to be hundreds of times by Interpol, the FBI, AMERIPOL, EUROPOL, CLACIP, EUROGENDFOR, CIA, and a dozen or more local police forces from all over the world.

But, like any good soldier, all I would ever tell them was my name, Iceman. Even after they identified me by my fingerprints as Robert Lester, I would only respond to Iceman.

While handcuffed to my bed late one night, Detective Kouassi, who was being released the next day, stopped by.

"Know this: before you are taken away from me and my jurisdiction, I will have you for interrogation, and believe me, you will suffer mightily.

"You will wish that you had died in that gunfight. We shall see if you truly are an Iceman." Kouassi said, smiling.

PISAM – August 29th

I was due to be released from the hospital that afternoon. I remained in the custody of the local police for eight days of interviews at the Maison d'Arrêt et de Correction d'Abidjan by my old friend, Detective Kouassi.

Let it be known to the readers of these chronicles that from here forth, the entries are being written by me, Odin, the first officer to Red Team Leader, the Iceman.

I acquired this diary soon after Sassoon had retrieved the "red bags" from Bellator, Cowboy, and the Iceman's hotel rooms on the night of May 6th.

As was protocol, Sassoon contacted Headquarters and was given instructions to aid in his escape. He met a local contact who brought him to a safe house, where he stayed for ten days until it was deemed safe to move.

We finally met up together and had Bellator, Cowboy, and Iceman's red bags turned over to HQ. Upon opening Iceman's red bag, it was discovered that he was keeping a diary and had asked that in the case of his capture or death, I would finish chronicling his diary until his demise or imprisonment.

We have contacts within the prison, so I am able to continue his story...

PISAM – 29th

The Iceman was paraded in front of members of the world's new media; only Detective Kouassi took questions.

"Detective, can you tell us where you are taking the prisoner?"

"He will be held in Maison d'Arrêt et de Correction d'Abidjan for the next ten days for a series of interviews before being turned over to Interpol."

"Is it true that he is a leader in Le Gang de la Clé de Singe and is responsible for the deaths of dozens of poachers who've been robbing our country of its natural wildlife resources?"

"This man, Robert Lester, aka the Iceman, is a cold-blooded killer and is wanted in over forty countries. No more questions."

They threw him into the back of a black Mercedes AMG S 63 sedan with blacked-out windows and sped away. He was taken to the House of Arrest and Correction of Abidjan, where he was fingerprinted, had his prison mug shots, given a full body cavity search, deloused, and issued a prisoner's uniform.

Ice was placed in a solitary confinement cell for his "own protection." The cell had a metal bed, no mattress, no pillow, no windows, a metal toilet and sink, and overhead lights that stayed on 24/7.

Maison d'Arrêt et de Correction d'Abidjan – August 30th

His cell door opened, and the Iceman was escorted down the hall to the "interrogation room," where Detective Kouassi and two other men were waiting.

"Mr. Lester, it's so good to see you. You're looking well. I'm afraid that won't last," Kouassi said.

The Iceman said nothing. He was expecting a good old-fashioned beatdown but realized that Interpol would want him at some point, so whatever Kouassi had in store couldn't leave any visible marks.

"Today, you're going to spend the day at the beach," Kouassi said, smiling.

The two men grabbed him, tied his hands behind his back, and walked him into a room with a utility sink and a long wooden plank leaning against a metal construction horse.

So, it was to be waterboarding. The Iceman had experienced waterboarding during his training in the SEALS. Although it was scary and extremely unpleasant and could be terrifying at times, he found that if he could keep his cool and focus and get himself into a Zen-like state, he could survive.

As the two men strapped him to the board, he looked at Kouassi and asked, "Why?"

"You probably don't remember, as you've killed so many, but two years ago, you and your friends killed my brother."

"Your brother was a poacher?"

"He was just a boy, seventeen. He got caught up with a bad group looking to make some easy money."

"This isn't going to bring him back."

"Maybe not, but just as my family has suffered, so will you."

He nodded to the two men, who leaned him back approximately 20 degrees on the board, placed a cloth over the Iceman's eyes, nose, and mouth, and poured water on his head.

They waterboarded him eighteen times that day, twenty times the next day, and twenty times the day after that, asking the same questions: *What are the names of your accomplishes? What are the names of your superiors? Where are your headquarters located? What are the names of all of your local contacts around the world?*

According to our sources, they never broke him. They tried other methods of "enhanced" interrogation techniques, sleep deprivation, having him stand naked in front of several air-conditioned units running at full blast, forcing him to squat with his arms extended for hours at a time, and finally locking him bent over inside the "Syrian Box" for two days and nights. The box left no room to move at all.

On the ninth day, they let him alone. He was allowed to stay in his cell to rest. He was cleaned up with a shower and shave and was fed a decent meal.

Our man on the inside was only able to speak with the Iceman for a brief time, but it was just enough time for him to give him a message that was conveyed to the team and me.

Maison d'Arrêt et de Correction d'Abidjan – August 8th

Detective Kouassi wanted to show off his prize to the world's media one more time before handing the notorious leader of Le Gang de la Clé de Singe, Robert Lester, aka the Iceman, over to Interpol.

He brought the Iceman out in handcuffs and shackles, dressed in his prison uniform of day-glow orange. Ice's face was drawn and ashen. He had lost at least fifteen pounds and looked like a man who had given up the ghost. Yet there was defiance in his eyes.

Detective Kouassi stood in front of the Iceman, surrounded by armed uniformed police.

There was a scrum of about sixty reporters and TV film crews vying for position. Venus, Lu Wei, and I were in front of the crowd, acting as a film crew.

Iceman spotted us in the crowd and smiled. I looked over my left shoulder at the Pentecostal Church steeple behind me, then back to Ice. He gave me a slight nod of acknowledgment.

He momentarily looked up into the sky, took a deep breath, and then glanced over to the steeple. He saw two tiny flashes of light nanoseconds before the bullets fired by Sue B and Fu Hao struck Detective Kouassi and him in the head, killing both of them instantly.

That was the message that the Iceman had relayed to us from prison. He preferred death to a life of incarceration.

So ends the Iceman chronicles. But the war against eco-terrorism and trophy hunting continues. Whenever one of our comrades falls, ten more will take their place.

Like so many before him, those who die in the struggle yet remain anonymous to the world shall always be remembered and will never be forgotten in the hearts of Le Gang de la Clé de Singe.

THE END

the revolution continues in
Fury of the Beast

M. Ward Leon – the Author

M. Ward Leon is a former advertising creative director who started his career at Doyle Dane Bernbach, New York, during the Madmen era. While at DDB, his writing on the Volkswagen Rabbit campaign won him inclusion in the Smithsonian Institution Advertising Archives. His writing recently earned him two Emmy Awards for Public Service advertising.

He is a California State University Los Angeles graduate and an Art Center College of Design alumnus.

Other books by M. Ward Leon: *Blood of the Beast* • *Revenge of the Beast* • *The Strange and Curious Cases of Roscoe Brown, Detective NYPD* • *Ambush at Fig Tree Gulch* • *Ishmael. My Life After Moby Dick* • *City of Angeles Trilogy*